Forever Konrad

A Vampire's Vampire

Forever Konrad

A Vampire's Vampire

Martin Goodman

FOREVER KONRAD:
A Vampire's Vampire

Published in October 2017 by PS Publishing Ltd. by arrangement with the author.

FIRST EDITION

ISBN
978-1-786361-84-4
978-1-786361-83-7 (signed edition)

Design & Layout by Jaharisam
Printed and bound in England by T. J. International

PS PUBLISHING LTD
Grosvenor House, 1 New road
Hornsea, Hu18 1PG, England

editor@pspublishing.co.uk
www.pspublishing.co.uk

For Soshin

The Ferry Baby

1

IN A HOUSE ON THE EDGE of the East Yorkshire Wolds a woman was liquidising carrots. Above the counter a TV showed a baby and she could not look away. The liquidiser ground on, the carrot chewed up, the palm of her hand pressed over its feeding tube as though to silence it. The baby was on its back, its arms stretched out rather than tucked against its body as you would expect in a newborn. Its fingers were quivering though it was asleep.

And then it woke up.

The eyes snapped open and stared at her.

The *BBC Look North* segment continued. There was an interview with the captain of the P&O ferry where the baby had been found, and another with a woman passenger who had witnessed the baby's discovery. The woman reporter looked up from the cot, and spoke in the hushed voice fitting for hospital rooms. 'The question remains . . . Who could leave such a darling on the deck of a midwinter ferry at night? Just look at him. If only he could talk.'

But he could. That was the overpowering thing about this baby. Susan sensed it at once. Those eyes could talk. They were dark yet shiny. I'm strong, they said. I come from a place of beauty and pain. I bring the secrets of survival.

When the dentist came back from evening surgery he found no carrot soup to warm him. No dinner simmered on the hob. His wife was in the small back room they used as an office. Her face looked spectral in the glow from the computer screen.

'Look,' Susan said.

The image was of a baby.

'Don't those eyes just speak to you, Richard?'

They were big dark eyes, healthy enough he supposed. He didn't know much about babies. They were all gums to him.

'He's cute.'

'Cute?' That was so not the right word. 'He's alert. Bright. Sparky. Intelligent.'

'Whose is he?' He presumed some friend of hers from college had sent the picture round.

'Ours.' She felt the shock of her husband's silence, and turned from the screen to look at him. 'OK. You're tired, Richard, you're just back from work, I'm ahead of you here, but stay with me. It's important.'

Susan had run out to buy three copies of the *Hull Daily Mail*. One copy was already sealed away in a plastic bag, for the family archives. Pages from the others were laid across the desk, so she could stare at the pictures and take in the story. A headline told how the baby was abandoned on the ferry from Zeebrugge.

'It's in Hull!' she squeaked, as she pointed at a picture of the Royal Infirmary. They could get from their home in Cherry Burton to the hospital in twenty minutes if the traffic was kind. The baby was practically on her doorstep. In one news clip a witness spoke of a mother and a teenage boy falling over the ship's rails and into the sea, but the manifest showed no such passengers. It was a mystery.

'He recognised me.' Susan read the confusion in her husband's face. 'I know it makes no sense but it's true. I was making dinner, thinking whatever I was thinking, and looked up. *Look North* was on. And then this baby's face filled the screen and stared out. He knows who I am, Richard. That's what he told me. You and I made our decision, we're already on the fostering register, and this is why. We don't have to wait for bureaucracy to catch up. Our baby's ready. I'm to be his mother. I'm to take care of him.'

A sheaf of papers was already stacked by the printer. On top of the pile was the letter from the clinic. They regretted that she would never be able to have a child of her own. She noticed where he was looking.

'Isn't it funny? That letter felt like the worst news in the world when it arrived. Now I see what a blessing it is. It frees us, Richard. This baby needs us, and we're ready for him. We have a home. I'm getting together all the evidence we might need. Birth certificates, financial statements, mortgage records, the lot. We'll foster first of course but they'll want somebody who is prepared to adopt. We've got a big house. You're a dentist. You've got your own well-established practice. We're local. The village school is terrific. We tick every box, I'm sure of it.'

He listened a while. One of her home-made pizzas was in the freezer. He slid it into the oven, poured himself a whisky, and then returned to the back office. The pile of papers was now thicker. She spoke to him like he'd never left the room.

'They'll want to interview us both I'm sure but I can handle things on my own in the morning. I'll be at the council offices first thing and demand to meet with the head of social services. It's best to be there in person. I'm sure the switchboards will be jammed with people offering our baby a home. Can you be free at lunchtime if I need you?'

He sipped his whisky. She looked up at him when she got no answer.

'You are with me on this aren't you?'

'Perhaps we should talk it through.'

'Oh talk, Richard. We talk all the time. Sometimes you just have to do.'

She turned back to the screen where her baby looked out at her. And then the sense of what she was doing hit her. Her face crumpled. She gulped for air, her system swamped by emotions before the tears started flowing. She took the guidance of his hand to stand up and hold herself against him. His left hand held her while his right hand stroked her head. 'Pizza,' he thought, as the smell of baking reached back to him. 'That's what she needs. Some food.'

Susan hugged tight to the warmth of his body. They were young and in love and so ripe for this. Chris, that was their boy's name. In honour of

Christmas, and St Christopher who carried little babies across the water. Susan already had some baby clothes. She stockpiled them as presents to give away but now there was no need to. Sometimes the world seems so screwed and then it turns out so perfect. It was almost too much to bear.

Nurses called the little thing 'the doctor'. They picked him up because babies need holding but then he looked them in the eyes. It was fun at first, this game of thinking that a baby could pay them such attention. The trouble is, a nurse can't give way to emotions. Nurses see too much. Meet the patient's physical needs and move on, that was the key. This baby though, he conjured feelings from you. After just a few seconds of staring into his eyes, images popped up that you thought you had blocked. You saw the gaping wounds in a young girl's head. You watched a surgeon slice a knife into a baby's chest. You paused, somewhat stunned, as a mother pulled an ear out of a tumbler of ice and showed you where to fit it to her son's head.

The memory needs to dim images such as those. At work a nurse needs a clinical eye to stay efficient. Being upset serves no purpose at all. Yet one look from this baby brought up a nurse's repressed memories like they were a trailer for a horror flick.

Nurses turned this foundling around so he looked away from them. That was more comfortable.

He seemed content enough. Some babies simply don't need much physical contact. He grew restless on his back, kicking and squalling, but when they bunched up the pillows and propped him at an angle he grew calm. He needed to watch, apparently. Some portraits have eyes that seem to follow you round a room. This baby was like that. It was nonsense of course, babies don't focus at distance, but whenever a nurse glanced his way there were those black eyes. Watching.

Hence his nickname. The doctor. He sat there with his detached professional air, his eyes doing the round of the whole ward.

His blood pressure was so low they had to keep him under observation. Panic set in at times, his heart rate so slow that he seemed to be failing, but attaching him to a monitor showed a consistent record. When lights were dimmed for the nightshift his heartbeat went into near shutdown mode. It was as though he was hibernating. Perhaps that was what saved him in the winter's chill of the ferry's deck, doctors speculated. Such a child was likely to need close medical supervision for life, but at least he had a life.

2

THE NURSING STAFF PREPARED for the baby's release. A woman came forward. She and her husband were registered for foster care but beyond that he was a dentist. That medical background was welcome. Physiologically the baby was as though new-born but perhaps malnourishment was a factor. In behavioural terms he showed advanced traits. There was evidence of hand-eye co-ordination, for example. 'Oh he's special alright,' the woman said, and smiled.

Media interest waned with the New Year. The baby had been a Christmas story. The woman was accompanied by a social worker when she came to pick up the baby, since her husband was caught up in an emergency root canal operation.

Three nurses bunched together by the entrance to watch the baby leave. Their mouths curved into the shapes of smiles but in truth they were holding their breaths. They watched till the lift doors closed and sealed the baby from view and then they all breathed in at once; so deeply it was audible.

'Thank God for that,' one said, and though no-one had ever given clear voice to the effect the baby had on their minds, they all now laughed with relief.

Her husband called her Susan but her real name was Mum and after nine months the name came. Da-da-da arrived first of course, and even Richard wasn't fooled, but at least the baby was exploring its own mouth and that impressed him. It wasn't 'he recognises me' or 'oh look I'm his first word' but 'he's getting real control of that tongue of his, press release and press release against his palate while opening his throat and vocalising. Now isn't that something!' In learning to utilise his mouth, Chris was becoming the proper son of a dentist.

Then one day, after sitting on the floor and studying his hands the way he did, flexing one tiny finger at a time, he lifted his head and looked her in the eyes. 'Mum?' he said.

She heard her name for the first time, and she heard the question mark too. Is this the word? That's your identity isn't it? We have the kind of relationship where me and only me gets to call you Mum? They were the questions that fierce little brain of his was asking.

'Yes darling yes yes yes Mum mum mum mum mum,' she affirmed and whisked him off the floor to hug him close as tears welled in her eyes.

Susan had never for one moment believed her baby was autistic.

'High-level autism?' Richard once wondered.

'You mean like Sir Isaac Newton?' They had read an opinion that Newton suffered from Asperger's syndrome. 'Well, genius like Newton's yes, I could grant you that, but Newton was a loner. Chris has true empathy. When he's quiet he's not just quiet, he's reading your mind.'

Richard nodded. There was that about the mite. He had feared real disruption to his routine, but the baby seldom cried through the night and when he got back from surgery to have Chris plonked on his lap while Susan prepared the dinner there was strange comfort in it. Susan did her best to be interested in Richard's work, she asked about the hygienist's mother's health and recalled the names of patients with on-going cosmetic treatments, but a dentist lives in a lonely world. He talks his own language which comes out as code that his assistant claims she understands but all she can do is transfer the code to dental records. Even at conferences with other dentists the most exciting conversations are about technical advances in equipment. There's no language that captures the full adventure of dentistry. For Richard it was speleological, the lone charting of unexplored cave systems. At first there were the warm gusts as the mouth opened, and then he shone light into the darkness and zoomed in close. The teeth were stalagmites and stalactites and he the adventurer chasing roots through the cave floor of the gums.

That's fanciful. Language doesn't do it justice. But back from surgery with this baby on his lap, black eyes staring up at him, he felt no need to chatter. Images from the day startled him with their Technicolor clarity, the pinks and the greys and the whites and yellows and blacks and reds. Mouths are war zones and his job was really a professional clean-up operation, siphoning off the debris with streams of saliva and plugging and sealing the wounds, but the baby's attention soothed him somehow. He learned to slow down this visual playback of each operation, so as gums bled his job wasn't to stem the flow as quickly as possible but to watch. It was beautiful, this carmine stream across white enamel. It was so precious, this gift of his patients; that they should let him cut them.

The baby chuckled. The sound startled Richard each time yet made him smile, and he shifted his reveries forward from recall of one of the day's dental operations to the next. These shared experiences helped strengthen the notion that this baby was his son. At some deep level, the dentist felt himself understood.

And now, for Susan, came this spoken word from the baby's mouth. 'Mum?' Just nine months old and already the boy was speaking. His first word was so strong and clear and articulate.

Thinking she could put her English degree to some good use, she had taken a correspondence course in proofreading. A publisher employed her freelance and she was excited for a while. It would be her first independent income since babysitting. Then they sent her medical textbooks. She would have cried if staring into the tiny print hadn't dried her eyes. The work needed such close attention.

And just as the first parcel of proofs had come through, Chris became mobile. It was just slight shifts on his bottom first of all. He seemed still enough, but then suddenly she found he had reversed halfway across the carpet.

Reverse suited him for a few days. She thought of babies as foragers, finding new things on the ground to put in their mouths, but Chris's exploration was different. He was taking measure of the room and training himself in perspective. Those eyes of his stayed fixed on one point as his heels pressed into the carpet and kicked him backwards. Things that were close became further away. Size became relative to distance. When his back bumped against a wall or furniture he simply turned around and repeated the experiment in the opposite direction. Back and forth, he kept himself amused in this way till she was free to play with him again.

She could cope with that. But once he turned around and started to crawl she had to watch him all the time. He lost the capacity for reverse in certain situations. By flattening himself he worked his way under the sofa, and became stuck there. Again and again. OK, babies do such things, but surely they squeak in protest once trapped? They have vocal cords and their own inbuilt alert systems. You watch them as closely as you can, but in emergencies—that one time you let your attention slip—they can always scream.

Not Chris.

Susan finished scouring a page of index and looked up. Her baby was gone. The door from the living room was open. God how stupid, she had to be more careful. At least the gate at the bottom of the stairs was closed, she had that right. She ran past it and into the kitchen. He wasn't there. The cupboard under the stairs? Already she knew her logic was failing. The cupboard was closed, the handle much too high for him to reach, but still she opened it and looked inside. The downstairs toilet? The dining room? The fridge? He always seemed fascinated by the fridge, its smells perhaps, the colours and shapes inside, the blast of cold air and the bright light. You could open the fridge without touching the handle, just curl your tiny hands under the door and tug it open. The salad drawer would pull out easily and then you could crawl into the empty space it left behind. The door would shut and close you in. That would muffle all cries, and the cold and the dark and the shock would take your breath away.

The salad drawer wasn't on the kitchen floor but even so she pulled open the fridge door fully expecting to find her baby inside and at the bottom, his eyes staring out at her from a blue face.

The drawer was in place, filled with lettuce and spinach. The sight of it brought her to her senses. Think, Susan, think. This is your baby. You know him. What would he do?

It wasn't reading his mind. She never claimed that power for herself. She could read his expression, his looks, his tones, his gestures, but she could not reach into some hidden place and read his mind. She sensed his mind though, reaching out for her. Calm yourself, Mother, it said: not in those grown-up words but she interpreted it in the way she knew how. I'm fine. This is difficult but I can handle it.

The moment she steadied herself, she knew. She shut the fridge door and walked to the sofa. Bending down, looking underneath, she saw his knitted white bootees. He was still. The bottom of the sofa pressed his head against the carpet.

What to do? Lift the sofa towards its back and crush his head? Hoist it high from under an armrest and hope he has the sense to break free before your arms give in and the sofa crashes back down? Maybe crawl underneath yourself, from the side, taking the sofa's weight on your back as you move closer? The damn side wall was too close.

She took hold of his feet and pulled. Babies were pliable. Stretching was good for them. His nose raked against the carpet and then he was free.

'Stupid stupid boy,' she said, as he blinked at the sudden shift from darkness into light. She held him close but knew she had to put him down again at some point. It was time to clear the table of her books and tidy the room for the evening.

'Sit there,' she said to Chris. How long was she gone, putting the books away in the study? A minute at most. And there he was when she got back, his head already under the sofa, shuffling.

'No bloody way,' she said, and hurried across the room. She grabbed at his feet to yank him back. This time he did cry. She pulled too hard. The drag along the carpet burnt his left cheek red.

'You watch him,' she told Richard that evening, and left to wash the spinach and prepare dinner. Richard was in an armchair when she returned, a glass of whisky to hand. Her baby was gone.

'I told you to watch him!' Susan said, then fell to her knees to confirm her suspicions. There was Chris, lodged beneath the sofa once again.

'He's safe enough,' Richard said. 'I'll stay here. Put the dinner on trays. We'll eat from our laps. He'll cry out if he needs us.'

This was crazy. Susan fried some chicken, adding salad and chickpeas with a drizzled readymade dressing. It would have to do. She sat on the other armchair, ate quickly, and then waited.

Chris's feet appeared, the legs moving from side to side. Then his bottom. He paused, tried to lift his head, but it was too soon. He wriggled some more.

'See,' Richard said proudly when Chris emerged and sat himself up. 'He put himself in a difficult situation and worked his own way out. That's what boys do.'

What nonsense, Susan thought. You don't pull an iron off the ironing board and then work out how to mend the hole in your skull. You don't drink bleach and then resolve a new lining for your stomach. Babies have to be watched every moment of every day and there was only her to do it. Sometimes a baby could be too clever by half.

3

RICHARD READ A BOOK on child psychology. Playpens, he said, were like golliwogs. They belonged to an earlier era. You mustn't hamper a baby's need to explore its full surroundings. Well what about a mother's needs? The auction house in Driffield came up with a playpen in real beech that Susan got for ten pounds. It clashed with the teak of the living room, but it wouldn't be for long.

'It's for your own good,' Susan explained to Chris as she hoisted him over the railing and lowered him to the red leatherette mat. He looked up at her as she let go. That's right Chris, she apologised in her mind. I've just lied to you. I'm doing this for my own good. I need a break.

Chris wasn't one for cuddly toys but she threw in a few of her favourites, the lop-eared bunny and the baby tiger and the teddy from her own childhood with its ears chewed off. You don't get cuddly toys in prison, and bright building blocks with letters on them. This wasn't a prison, really it wasn't. He'd be fine.

He crawled around the perimeter first of all, while she watched. This preference to watch him rather than look into those cursed medical texts was something she would have to get over. Round and around he went, like a caged animal. Well at least he was safe. He couldn't hurt himself. She was there in the room, marking up her manuscript.

His hands reached round the bars, clenching hold, reaching higher. He was standing. Her little boy was standing for the first time. Susan longed to hug him, to pluck her baby into the air in triumph, to run for the phone and call Richard. But she kept to her own task, poring over her text. Up down, he went, up and down, exercising those leg muscles. She pulled him out for a break but he didn't need the company. He merely held on to the bars from the other side and went up and down again.

That was Day One. 'It's not a prison,' Susan explained to Richard that night. 'It's an exercise pen.'

Day Two brought a development. Chris managed to stand up while holding on to a bar with just one hand. That left a hand free. He used it to grab one of the bunny's ears. It took four goes to get the coordination right and then in one fluid movement he stood and flung the bunny from the pen. Tiger and Teddy followed. Now for the bricks. They were too bulky to hold in one hand. He sat, picked up a brick with both hands, and threw it to the edge of the pen. The whole operation was highly strategic. His crawl around the perimeter became a simple tour of duty. The bricks fit between the railings. He pushed each of them out. The pen was clear of clutter.

Day Three was a Wednesday. Susan was coming to think of this as Chris's first week of work. The day started with an hour's exercise, first using the two-hand grip on the bars and then holding on with just one. This freed him to turn his body slightly so as to experiment kicking with his feet.

Susan heard the thump of his landing and looked up to see her baby rolling on the leatherette mat. What had he done? She cursed herself for not watching but then she had to lose herself in these books at some point.

Chris pulled himself back upright, took a grip of the bars to stand up, and raised a foot. This new art he was developing required good timing. There was no use his starting to walk without letting go of the rail first. She watched him fall twice more, seeking to walk before he could let go. There was no frustration. A new logic simply clicked into place. He freed his hands from the rail without moving. For several minutes he simply stood. Then he lowered himself to the mat and turned around. With his back pressed against a rail for support, he slid himself back upright. And then he walked.

After two steps he fell. Susan stopped herself shouting out for the joy of it, witnessing her little baby's first steps in the world. She stayed quiet so she could watch what he did next, but something else stifled the joy. The systematic nature of his progress made her uneasy. His intelligence was eerie.

He managed three steps on the second attempt, and again on the third and fourth. Sometimes simply persisting is not the best way. Change is necessary. The baby decided this now. He lifted a corner of the red leatherette mat and tugged to pull it all the way up, although his own weight on the mat then stopped that from working. Instead he pulled a corner as high as he could and let himself fall sideways onto the scrap of hardboard floor this revealed. His body stopped the mat falling back in place to lie flat.

He worked his way underneath it and lay still for some time. Susan kept no pretence of working on her books. Her instinct was to hurry in and help, to lift off the mat and pluck her baby into her arms, but instead she was more calculating. She fetched the small video camera from the shelf in the study and sat waiting.

The mat stayed still. The baby seemed to find comfort beneath its dark covering. When the leatherette started to move she turned the camera on.

Chris sat up and pushed with his hands. An edge of the mat rose higher than his head and then fell to fold back on itself. A stretch of hardboard floor was now clear from one side of the pen to the other.

He pushed himself backward till his back rested against a rail. His legs flexed and he was standing. And then he was walking. Two steps, three steps, four five six. His fingers curled around the rails on the opposite side and held on. He had done it. It was only the mat that had been stopping him. Give him a solid surface and he could walk.

Chris was asleep when Richard got home. Susan kept the video for later. It was evidence for a tale that was otherwise hard to believe. When she checked on him after dinner she found him lying in his cot, eyes open. He raised his arms when he saw her, ready to be lifted free.

'I told you we had something to show you,' she told Richard.

She lowered Chris to the carpet, dangling him like a puppet so his feet could seem to dance on the floor.

'Very clever,' Richard said, with the sort of singsong voice used for idiots. 'You're dancing, Chris. Dancie dancie dancie.'

In fact Susan was just exercising Chris's leg muscles. She felt them flex and then straighten. He was ready. She lowered his arms to his sides. She took her hands away. He was standing.

Richard turned silent. He was holding his breath.

'Come,' Susan said.

She knelt on the floor about four paces away, and held out her arms. 'Come to Mummy.'

Chris started walking. One step, two steps.

And then he paused. Momentum wasn't everything. Standing still was an equal art.

'Well done Chris. Come on. Come to Mummy.'

This was hard. She was in the way. Progress required the ability to change direction while in motion. He needed a new technique.

He kept his head still but Susan saw the fast flicker of movements in his eyes, the black pupils shifting side to side in the whites. She was yet to learn the look. He was calculating.

Chris lifted his right leg. Standing on one leg was not yet in his repertoire so the next moves were rapid. One, two, three steps and he achieved an angle that took him beyond the scope of his mother's outstretched arms. He scampered a curved line that seemed, to Richard, in one breathless moment of hope, to show the boy was choosing his father, but Chris swerved to avoid the hand that reached out for him. Both parents watched as their baby completed a circuit of the room and vanished through the open door.

They followed him through to the kitchen. The Quarry tiles suited him. The leather soles to his bootees stopped him slipping and the hard surface gave him traction. His circles of the kitchen grew wider. Richard and Susan had never hunted before but the skills were instinctive. Susan shifted round the edge of the room one way and Richard the other. Susan stepped forward. Chris managed to swerve and avoid her and so ran straight into Richard's arms.

The baby's legs ran against the air. This was whole-body running, the baby's torso turning against Richard's chest and the tiny elbows ramming into his ribs. Richard worked his hold so as to cradle the child and smother the jabs and the kicks. He carried him back to the living room and sat on the sofa while Susan switched off the lights. Darkness often quieted the baby.

'Is he still?' she asked. Her own heart was racing. She reached her hand to touch the baby's chest and then took his tiny wrist to feel for his pulse. It was fast, but only for him. Such was his quickness she felt he should have the ticking heartbeat of a bird but his blood pressure was low. She wondered how fast herons' hearts beat. He had that utter stillness of a heron, the intentness, and then that stab of action so rapid she often missed it.

'Should we call a doctor?' The frenzy of his running, that squirming body on her husband's arms, were not normal.

'He's sleeping.' Dentists like to find doctors irrelevant when possible. 'It's been an exciting day. He's exhausted himself, that's all.'

'He doesn't know how to stop,' Susan said. She moved in closer and Richard raised an arm so as to hold her close to him. The room was warm but both parents shivered.

Some mothers are too defensive of their babies. There's no point socialising them if you're going to be overprotective. That's what Susan told the organiser of the local Tumble Tots group.

'This is all about play,' the organiser responded. 'Your Chris takes it all so seriously.'

'He's studying balance.'

'That's what the other children are doing. Your Chris has balance already. He even has poise. The other children are frightened of him. They go flat on the floor when he's around. If anyone stands, they know he'll push them over.'

'He just wants to play. To roll around with the other youngsters like cubs do. Fox cubs and lion cubs and tiger cubs.'

'But he bites.'

'They're not bites, they're nibbles. With his milk teeth. What's wrong with those children? He's not drawn blood yet.'

'I'm sorry Susan. If I let Chris come back he'll be on his own. The other mothers are determined. Chris goes or they go. They just don't feel safe when he's around.'

Susan took Chris's hand and mother and child left the village hall to walk the streets of Cherry Burton. She punched in the code to their security gate, waited for it to click shut behind her, and then let Chris go so he could hare off into the garden. It was just her and the boy once again. He had been expelled from his first educational institution at the age of one.

4

OTHER KIDS YOU COULD KEEP busy tearing out pages of an Argos catalogue. Their Chris grew still when set down in front of the galley proofs of an illustrated medical dictionary. Mother and child sat on the floor in front of the pages.

He stabbed a finger at a picture.

'Thorax,' she pronounced.

He just stared at her. Fair enough. She didn't really know what it meant either. She had always made do with the word 'chest'. She read her proofing text for meaning rather than typesetting errors, and then spread her hands across his body, from his neck down to his stomach. 'Thorax.'

He pressed his tongue against his teeth to prepare himself. 'Thorax,' he said.

He pointed at another picture. At a guess she might have said it was a seedpod. 'Thoracic cavity,' she read aloud.

He waited. This wasn't a game of turning letters into sounds. He needed to know.

'They've taken the lungs and heart out of the picture just so you can see things clearly,' she explained. 'Think of this as the home inside your body for the lungs, the heart and blood vessels.'

He knew 'lungs', 'heart' and 'blood vessels' for she had a good sense of those things herself. Now he gave voice to this new term. 'Thoracic cavity.'

She was pleased. When he said a word it meant he had understood it because she had understood it and she could move on. It involved a lot of study but she didn't mind. Chris was patient. He sat still. Sometimes she tried to bluff, giving an answer before she had made sense of the question. He looked at her then and stayed quiet. He could read the level of her knowledge through her eyes. That's what babies do, stare into their mother's eyes for learning.

Chris leaned forward to turn the page. His fingers were not yet supple so he pulled over a wad of pages that led him deep into the text, but he did so carefully. His attention focussed on aligning the top page with those below it, and then he studied what was revealed.

'The human head,' he said, in a brisk voice that showed recognition. It was funny how he kept using the word human, as though he were coming to know an alien species. It was always 'human ear', 'human neck'. She tried to joke him out of it, bouncing him on her knee and calling him her human baby, but he simply cocked his head and looked at her till she felt stupid and stopped.

Indeed he had turned to a picture of a human head. The illustration showed a man's head, as was typical in medical textbooks; the male anatomy was standard, female anatomy depicted only as a variant on the norm. This man's neck was thick, his head turned sideways and tilted so the Adam's apple was prominent on the right. The head was a pencil drawing, but pink, yellow and blue watercolour paints had been used to highlight what looked like a root system that was drawn across it.

Other colours marked the adjoining text, small blotches of orange and brown. They were tiny fingerprints. Chris had recently discovered Smarties. He picked food out of his mouth when eating, so as to get a visual of the latest taste. These fingerprints came from the Smarties' orange sugar coating and the chocolate insides. Susan might be weak on human anatomy but she was expert on such clues. She checked Chris's hands. They were clean. He had been studying this page before. Now he had turned straight to it.

He ran his finger up the pink trunk that rose out of the collarbone and into the skull. The jugular vein, she wondered? This was way out of her known territory. While Chris was absorbed in the picture she read the caption.

He looked up at her with those enquiring black eyes.

'That's the brachiocephalic artery,' she declared. 'The human brachiocephalic artery,' she amended, to pretend to some expertise and to humour him. 'It's like a tree, isn't it? It carries blood between the thorax and the brain. Look at all these little branches? That's how the blood flows.'

'Blood,' he repeated. It was good he was intelligent but his learning process really was very demanding. Why couldn't he be like other children, happy to learn to distinguish between fingers and toes while she named and tugged and wriggled them? So much of what he wanted to know was hidden from view.

'Neck,' she said, running a finger across the picture and then her hand along her own. She stroked his neck next. 'Human neck.'

'Neck,' he said, touching his own. 'Human neck,' reaching up to stroke hers.

She hooked a finger as though reaching in through the mouth of the pencil drawing and down into the man's body. 'Throat.'

She next said 'Neck,' running fingers along the outside of her own, and then 'Throat,' her voice strained as she jabbed fingers toward it.

Chris stood up. His face mooned large as he leaned forward to peer close. My God, she thought, he's like Richard after all, he's a dentist. The thought stopped her closing her mouth in time. You don't shut your mouth when a dentist examines you.

Her tongue was in the way. She had offered a view down her throat and now this tongue arched upward to block it. His hand was small enough to reach right between her teeth. In it went. His fingers found the surface of the tongue and pressed down hard. Teeth cut into it from below. She gagged and yelped at the same time, a helpless spluttering, her hands locked for support against the carpet so she couldn't even push him away without falling, his hand forcing her head to crash to the floor. Instinct took over, it was son or her, but this wasn't just son it was a force out to kill her. She jerked her head forward. It was a headbutt, not that she knew she was capable of such things, but she headbutted her baby son. His head was small and low and so it was the bridge of her nose that rammed into his forehead.

'Kiss it better.' That's what she said when her baby hurt himself. 'Let Mummy kiss it better.' He never seemed to understand and always pulled himself away from the contact, but he had been paying attention after all.

'Kiss it better,' she heard him say.

She saw the mark of her attack on his forehead. He didn't seem hurt though. He looked at her with round-eyed fascination.

'Kiss it better,' he repeated, and moved in close to inspect her nose.

It's true, her nose was painful. Her baby cared that she had hurt herself. He pursed his lips and placed a kiss on the dip below her nose, just as she had shown him when he was in pain, and then pulled himself away and smiled.

'Better,' he said.

He smiled at her, his lips bright red and blood trickling down to his chin. Then he moved in close again.

She felt his tongue this time, licking around her upper lip and then lapping inside her nostrils. He paused to swallow and then his mouth was touching hers and his tongue played across her tongue. It was all so tiny, that tongue of his, like a slug spasming on electric charges. It wasn't a kiss, it was nothing obscene, in fact it was soothing. She had bit her tongue and now his tongue was reaching into the wound left by her teeth. She tasted his tongue even as he tasted her blood. It was metallic somehow, like water drank from pewter.

This wasn't acceptable, of course it wasn't. Her hands took charge and reached his shoulders, set to push him back. But even as she moved so did he. She felt his gums and his teeth form a ring around her tongue and he sucked.

She swooned. She would tell Richard that she fainted and leave out most of the details, but swooned was the right word. Some hot rush zipped down her spine while simultaneously packing her brain. Her mental image was of a roseate whiteout, and then she was senseless.

She woke on the carpet where she lay on her side. A series of unlikely questions looked for answers before she opened her eyes. The first was 'What am I?' She was human, a woman, who went by the name of Susan. Next up was, 'Where am I?' She was at home on the floor of her living room.

She had had a bloody nose. Oh my God, the carpet! She sat up to inspect it. Wheeled round to her hands and knees and crawled about to make sure of the evidence. It was true. Not a single drop of blood stained the beige woollen weave. She stood and moved to the gold-framed mirror on the wall. Her hair was dishevelled and her nose was pink and inflamed, but there were none of the blood smears she expected.

She looked at her watch and then checked it again. Her mind was still in a fug but as she struggled back through the events of the day she was able to calculate that she had lost consciousness for three and a half hours. It was that long since she had headbutted her baby boy. Where was he?

'Chris?'

She swallowed the call so it was little more than a muted yelp. Panic was part of it, her vocal cords frozen as she processed the fears of all that might have happened to her baby without her there to tend him.

Squeezed alongside that was some fear for herself. It came back to her now. He had reached his hand inside her throat, ramming her tongue against her teeth. To protect herself she had hit out. He was just a baby, she was a grown woman, yet she attacked him to protect herself. A mother is meant to lay her life on the line for her children. What had come over her?

And then the blood. That look of wonder on the tiny boy's face as her blood turned his lips rosy red. And then the sudden fury of his kisses, like having her face surrounded by a cloud of moths, that's what it felt like, damp-winged moths, that rose-bud mouth of his fluttering and touching everywhere. It wasn't normal. It wasn't natural.

'Chris.'

She spoke louder now and set herself to run around the house. He liked cupboards. She had often found him curled into their dark corners. Or under the beds was another favourite. Susan was running now, sweeping clothes along the rail in her wardrobe to let in the light that might find him, dropping to her knees to bring the floor to eye-level, up and down the stairs till every angle was looked into.

The garden? It seemed unlikely because all the outside doors were closed but then Chris was a tidy little boy and put things back the way he found them. She ran out through the kitchen door.

'Chris!'

A quick movement caught her. It came from the shadows beside the pond. Chris was sat in the shade of the willow tree, his legs crossed in front of him. She went running across the lawn to pick him up, calling his name, but he didn't look her way. He was focused on some empty space in front of him. There, one more of those sharp movements that had made her notice him. Before it was his right hand. Now it was the left, darting out into the air, snatching. Thumb and finger had hold of something. Another movement, too swift to see, and he had flicked the thumb with his finger to send something into his mouth.

'Show Mummy,' Susan said.

She knelt before him and placed fingers onto his chin to pull his jaw down. He opened his mouth quite willingly and stuck out his tongue. A mosquito was squashed there, black against the pink but with a little pool of carmine red around it.

'No Chris, no,' she said, and wiped the tongue clean with her finger. 'It's not good. That's a dirty thing to do. These things are parasites.'

He looked at her, a blank look of incomprehension.

He was right. She needed to be more accurate if he was ever going to learn from her.

'Mosquitoes aren't parasites,' she admitted. 'They're vectors for disease. The parasites ride inside of them. They get transferred into your bloodstream when the mosquitoes bite you.'

But of course there were no mosquito parasites active in Cherry Burton.

His look showed her that her words were still linked to ignorance. She had no real teachings on the issue to offer to her baby.

'Come along Chris. We'll go and read about it in a book,' she said.

Chris smiled and let her take his tiny hand in hers and lead him back to the house.

The Birth Story

5

IT WAS A PLACE OF GREAT HEAT; a barren hill and walls of baked mud. It might have been Egypt. It was one of those nights in one of those countries of sand and starburst skies. Small walled compounds of whitewashed buildings were set among the entrances to underground tombs. Dogs barked when they sensed him, gums drawn back over their teeth, but they cowered and grew silent as he drew nearer. The Ancient made no noise of his own.

He scaled a wall and dropped down into a courtyard. No lamps lit the rooms. All were sleeping. He leapt up to a small, high window, held on to its bars and looked through. Inside the bedroom three young women lay on separate beds. They shared the same features; straight nose, slight flare to the nostrils, high cheekbones, long neck. All were naked so it was simple to study them. They were clearly sisters, each separated in growth by about a year. The two youngest lay on their sides with their bodies curled. Sabaa lay on her back, her body glistening though there was nothing but starlight outside.

The Ancient's outer form ghosted from his body and through the bars. He guided this projection toward the door, where it reached up to the wooden bolt with just enough strength to ease it back. The projection passed through the still-closed door. It knew its task. It walked along a corridor to the front door, used the last of its energy to pull back its bolt, and then evaporated.

The Ancient dropped from the barred window to the courtyard. The main door to the house swung back as he pushed it. The bedroom door opened without a creak.

The Ancient could have fed. That was his intention: to sup lightly from each sister. In the morning they would wake, somewhat sore, and perhaps scratch their itches and look for bedbugs, each with some dream of dark contentment closed inside them. But this one, the oldest of the three and already a full woman, lay with eyes wide open and stared at him.

That Sabaa saw him was no threat; even a novice can curl around a human mind and numb it. Somehow, though, the gloss in this young woman's eyes stalled his approach. She showed no shock. The pupils did not dilate.

She saw into him. That was the truth of it. Sabaa wasn't about to scream. The Ancient wasn't some tall dark stranger invading her bedroom. She saw beyond all that. For her it was like peering through a patch of night sky in search of a galaxy. She glimpsed behind his eyes. The glimpse showed her the weight of his darkness and that darkness can shine. A whorl of energy arced around him like the giant tube of an ocean wave. What Sabaa saw seemed like a cavern though its roof was beyond sight and there was no floor. The cavern was all history and the Ancient roamed within it at will.

Sabaa gasped at this point, catching breath, for though she had seen the structure of time she could not comprehend it. Humans pass from living into death and do not see what she had seen. The Ancient touched her mind, not to numb her but to still her.

Who was she?

He traced a hand across Sabaa's forehead. She was a woman who ran between dunes, her feet spitting sand into a storm that hid the trail behind her. Where she ran none would follow. She raced into the sea and arched her arms and kicked her feet for seawater was her element and she surged right through it. When she stood still it was to challenge the sun, ramping the fire within to match the heat that burnt through the sky. What he saw was unreal but true, so he drew back to see how human culture had worked to limit and define her.

He saw a woman veiled in black. Her running was a will of imagination.

The window of this room looked out onto an inner courtyard and this was her permitted world. She was to be married when the men returned from war.

As the Ancient's hand pressed on Sabaa's forehead, he kissed the salted sweat from her neck. She reached up and meshed the fingers of her hand inside his hair, pulling his head back to face her. Look, she said, though voicelessly. She led his vision to a spot above her and from there they both looked down.

'You are lush, firm, rounded and beautiful,' he offered from that part of his mind she could read.

This was true, and any man returning from the war would think the same.

'And you, my love, are tired,' Sabaa said.

He heard her say my love and knew it was true. Sabaa spoke from a love that was as old as himself. How so?

'My heart,' she said, for it is so. Love does reside in the heart. Her love for him pulsed out with her heartbeats. Sabaa studied his eyes. 'Your tiredness has gone,' she said.

'Yes.' The Ancient laughed. A tremor of youth surprised him. He was so old. How did she do it? How could she conjure a sense of being young?

'You have been missing me,' she said. 'It's alright now.'

Her slender fingers wiped at his cheeks.

'We will have a child,' she said.

She watched his eyes again as she spoke. Their focus scattered.

'So you're afraid? You feel young and you feel afraid. Isn't that good?'

And the Ancient laughed again.

'This is it,' he said. 'I am it. I don't have children.'

Pain seared his eyeballs like the nails of fingers scratched across them. 'Look again,' Sabaa said. 'Look deep. Can I have children?'

She watched the focus gather in his eyes. It was true. He recognised it. Sabaa had the power to give birth and she would not lose it. He could take her but he could not take that. The Ancient must leave her that.

It was a contract. The Ancient took Sabaa. He pressed slowly, so she could feel the moment of teeth puncturing her skin. It was exquisite, her nerves jolting messages to her brain as her feet kicked and her body went into spasms. She had never been more fully in her body. But Sabaa was her blood too. As her blood poured across his tongue and down his throat she wanted to stay with her body yet follow the flow. She could not do both. She went with the blood.

He sucked at the wound till her pulse stopped. His hand tugged at her jaw and his mouth met hers, his cold lips on her cool ones. Small convulsions of his stomach brought her blood back through his throat, her old warmth pouring from him and back to her. We are our blood. The same blood joined them.

'See,' the Ancient said, and though her eyes were closed she saw. She watched as his hand moved up to her face and pressed fingers on her eyelids. She was looking through his eyes.

'See,' he said, and pushed open her eyelids. She looked out to see him watching her.

He picked her up like she was a child, her legs draped over the crook of his arm, her head tucked against his shoulder. He walked her out through the house and drew back the bolts of the courtyard gate. Above them were stars. The night was warm and still, yet as he moved the air rushed past her.

'Am I alive?' Sabaa asked.

'Now,' he said. 'Now, for the first time. Yes you are.'

There was no hurry. The Ancient trained her. Decades passed into centuries. They lived in houses mostly, humble places across the mainland of Europe. As neighbours aged but they did not it became time for them to move on. They left the house empty and waited till all who knew them had died, and then they could move back in. This was their seventh such cycle in their house in Bruges.

The Ancient returned from the hunt one night to find Sabaa in company. A baby boy, pink and naked, bounced on her lap. It was skinned of its clothes which lay on the floor by her feet. Its face was contorted and it wailed but she did not still it. She simply smiled and held it out as he came in.

'It's ours,' she said. 'Take it.'

The baby squirmed in his hands. The Ancient smelt the milk on its breath.

'I could have taken it myself, but I've been waiting. I want you to take it. Then it's ours.'

It would be theirs for all time. This kicking, screaming bundle would be theirs forever and forever helpless.

That was nonsense of course. It takes strength to achieve the transition, to keep a body going once it's died, but such was her plan. He almost did it just to teach her, biting through the chest and into the heart to tear the creature apart. He held the baby in front of his face and stared at it. Its crying stilled and its pale blue eyes looked back unblinking.

'Let me hold him for you,' Sabaa said, and tilted the body onto its back with its head nestled in the palm of her right hand. The Ancient looked at her and saw the black gloss of her eyes and the soft smile on her cheeks.

'Take it back.' He handed the baby over. 'Back where you found it. This is not the way. We'll make our own.'

He sculpted her. Such it seemed. There was nothing in Sabaa from which a foetus could grow. The Ancient took express trains to new feeding grounds. He did not discriminate. He fed off the young and the old, the foul and the radiant, led by opportunity and not attraction. The final blood was the menstrual flow from three girls. He returned to his wife still touched with the shock of sexual excitement, and with the blood he needed for his penis to engorge.

Gestation was of the normal duration. The daily foraging to feed this growing life can be tracked through coroners' reports over a nine month period, most often in Paris but also in cities across Europe within a day's return journey by train from Bruges. No donor survived but each was abandoned with heart still beating. None were cheated of final death. The Ancient licked the blood from their skin as each heart beat its last and he stayed for their passing. These people died so his unborn child could live.

Their blood would add to the cells of a new being. He smiled at the wonder of it.

The couple's life became carnal in that they shed their clothes and lay together, his stomach pressed against hers, locked in a period of animal life. Their lips were fastened tight in a kiss of feeding, akin to that passing of blood when a human is taken and with something of that erotic charge. The blood from his stomach disgorged to fill his mouth and he fed it to her slowly, drop by drop in the rhythm of a pulse till he was emptied and she was full.

And Sabaa's belly swelled. In this way he was a sculptor, bringing her the blood from which this living form could grow. Her body stayed thin as her belly grew round and its skin ever more taut. They lay side by side as she pressed against him and took strength from his mouth.

The day the foetus kicked he felt the footprint in his body and broke free. The blood he was feeding her splattered their faces and sheets and gusted back down his throat to choke him. First he coughed and then both bodies lay, hands held, shaking with laughter.

6

SABAA STAYED INDOORS. Pregnancy smacked too much of the human condition.

Their neighbours in Bruges would feel the right to care for her if they knew. They would bring gifts as an excuse to enter the house. Once there, they would note how their breath gusted as clouds in the winter chill of the room. Wasn't she cold? Why did her breath not cloud the room? Where was the kitchen range and the electricity? Why was there just a bare table and two wooden chairs? What were those stains on the floor, and what was that smell?

Sabaa stayed hidden, but they could not control the birth. She roared. He could not ask her to be quiet. Her roaring was not for pain, for pain is merely a passing phenomenon. The sounds she made were the tremors of an opening that would have killed her could she die, a full-throated shuddering of her entire system. The bats in the attic above their room shook out of hibernation and fluttered, dazed, into the dusk. Her mouth strained wide and locked open, tongue quivering, neck strained, back arched. She pushed and convulsed as the baby's head emerged.

The Ancient knelt naked between Sabaa's legs but did not touch her and made no sound. She needed no consolation and it was pointless to encourage the inevitable. His job was to watch and in some way to magnetise. He was the past from which this baby arose and the future into which it was being born.

He waited till the shoulders were revealed, bunched and slippery, and then reached out to pull the child forward. It was a boy. They always knew that much. Time springs surprises but the Ancient can lock in certain facts when he focusses.

He slid the creature up its mother's belly to rest it on her chest. It was limp. The feet seemed stuck together and trailed slime and blood across her skin. Sabaa picked it up to stare at it. One hand cupped its head for support, and she shook it a little. The Ancient took the feet in one of his hands and lifted them high. The baby's arms hung useless and the tiny fingers were without a twitch. The curve of its spine pressed into his hand as he slapped at its back. The mouth opened and a mewl came out.

The creature's brain held flashes of red, blue, orange and yellow. There was nothing else to read there. The Ancient was surprised. Such destiny as this creature had should have come with a higher charge.

He chewed at the umbilical cord. It was tough. He opened his mouth wide and clamped down fast to cut it clean. That was it. The child was severed. It was on its own. Sabaa licked the blood from her baby. The Ancient watched, and then worked his tongue to clean the flesh of his wife's body. And then they lay still.

They were a family, complete in a moment of exhaustion.

It lasted moments. Sabaa felt the baby tremble against her breasts and raised the tiny thing so as to study him. His eyes, licked clean, opened with no focus. His body was shifting from white to pale blue.

'He's dying,' Sabaa thought and it was clear. They had stoked her body to a temperature that could maintain a human foetus, but a freezing room on a Belgian winter's night left the baby tugging icy breaths into its lungs. Her own skin was chilling down and the Ancient's touch was as cold as ever.

'Fire,' Sabaa said.

The Ancient thought it was a word she had beamed his way but he saw the baby flinch and knew the word had been yelled into the room.

'Fire!' she shouted again.

It was a command for him to bring her baby heat.

He heard and he understood. He also knew, instantly, that others would hear and misunderstand. These houses were held together by ancient oak beams that ran through one wall into the next. Fire in one would see them all smoking. A call to emergency services would see firemen pitching axe heads into their front door.

He pressed a hand over Sabaa's mouth to still her. The neighbour to one side, a lone old woman, was inquisitive. He cast himself through their dividing wall, nothing visual to shock her, just the power to listen. Yes, she was on the phone. 'Fire,' she said. 'There's been an awful yelling, yelling like murder, and now a woman's screaming fire. Send police. Send a fire brigade. Send ambulances.'

The house on the other side was empty. The young couple who lived there had gone to the wife's parents for Christmas. 'I'll open next door,' he said. 'Take the baby down. There's electricity there. We can make heat.'

The Ancient lay still as his projection rose from him and passed through the connecting wall. He sent it down the stairs to the entrance hall. A small half-moon walnut table stood beside the door. A spare mortise key lay among loose change in the table's slim drawer – he had earlier picked up such information with a simple scan of the neighbour's mind. His projection took out the key, unlocked the door, slipped the Yale lock off its latch, and then moved through to the kitchen. The hob of the stove was gas but the oven was electric. It took more energy than he could muster to heave open its door, but he set the temperature gauge to 200 and pressed the button to start it heating. The Ancient had no further need of his projection. It had nothing to bring back to him. He let it evaporate.

He dressed and fetched sweat pants and a loose top from the end of the room for his partner. 'Here.' He set them down on the bed and took the baby from where it lay against her chest. Its blue was more uniform now, its breath coming in gasps, its whole body trembling.

Sabaa stood, made sure of her balance, and dressed as directed. Birthing was tough, but her body could recover as well in motion as in repose.

'Go next door,' he told her. 'The front door's open. The oven's on. I couldn't open it, I hadn't the strength, but do so. Hold the baby to the heat. Not too direct, don't cook it, but what seems hot to you will be warm to it. What burns you is too much. Go.'

'I can make warmth. Find me food and I'll make warmth.'

'I will. But go next door. The neighbour's called the police. They must not find you.'

He saw Sabaa's eyes dilate and caught the quick shudder of her head. An image flashed from her mind to his. The neighbour lay on her staircase, her throat bared, her feet kicking. This is what she wanted him to do.

'No,' he said.

'Yes. That woman next door, I hate her.'

'We need her. She called the police and the fire brigade. She must answer the door when they come. Now go. Go to that oven. Sit there. I'll be with you.'

Sabaa paused, but as she grabbed the baby from him he saw she would do as he said. She pulled her top over her baby's head and held him against her body as she hurried down the steps.

They had used a mattress for the birth. Babies are vulnerable things. It seemed good for it to land on softness so fresh from the womb. They had not thought of rubber sheeting – or any sheeting. The mattress was sodden with blood. The mess of discharged tissue and the length of umbilical cord spoke of birth rather than of murder, but neither the true nor the false tale was one he wanted to have told. He picked up the gore and flung it under the bed, back by the wall where rats might find it. The underneath of the mattress was stained dark when he turned it over but at least the blood was not wet.

The bed was ready for show. If people searched the house now the problem was not with what they might find. It was with what they would not. A few clothes hung in the wardrobe. The couple did not bother with underwear and had no need for the warmth of different layers, so the drawers of the dresser were empty. Apart from the bed there were no other signs of habitation here at the top of the stairs.

Among the rooms on the two floors below, nothing was obviously a bedroom, a kitchen or a bathroom. All were bare but for a ground floor room that held a table and two chairs. A white plastic cloth covered the table, which they licked clean whenever they had chewed on butcher-bought meat. There was no running water, no glassware, no knives, no crockery, no comforts, for they had no need of such things. For people this house was clearly uninhabitable. They would ask questions.

And the smell? Elements of Sabaa's physiology were brought back into function after an age of morbidity. She needed them to give birth. Soon after conception heads turned in the streets as she passed, people finding her odour to be foul. Before winter struck to kill them off, flies had battered against the windows of her room, swarming toward the stink of death as she worked to produce a life. He was inured to it, but the room must be rank with the smell of that birth.

He pulled back the shutters, pushed open the window to let in the blast of winter air, and then moved to the fireplace.

There had been no fire in centuries. Old newspaper had been stuffed into the chimneybreast. He supposed he had done it himself but could not remember why or when. He pulled bundles of it clear. The newspaper had no pictures, just broad sheets of small-sized print in columns. Soot and an age of birdshit and bat droppings dropped down as he pulled the last wads of paper free. He let it fall on him, hitting his shoulders and sticking to his hair. The chimney was still blocked above that. His hands curled around the softness of feather, and took hold of something round which collapsed as he pressed it with his hands. He pulled out handfuls of collapsed skeleton, feathers still attached to the fragile bones, a pigeon stripped of its organs and flesh by a parade of ants.

This was no use. He bunched up a fist and rammed it higher. More mess cascaded down. Bones, fur, feathers all mixed inside the soot, but here was a pigeon still fresh enough to rot. And here was a dead bat. Did they stink? He didn't know but presumed so. These creatures should do.

Knuckles smashed against the front door. There were shouts in the street. Red and blue lights pulsed through the open window to reflect on the bedroom ceiling. Stay silent and it was clear they would hammer the door down.

'I'm coming,' he yelled, and stamped his feet to make noise as he hurried downstairs.

He freed one hand to haul open the front door. Two police officers stood at the head of a group that clustered in the street.

'We've reports of a fire,' one of them said. The sight of the man who answered the door left the other one stupefied.

'If only,' the Ancient said, and laughed. 'Light a fire in there and the whole place would be ablaze. Every fireplace is blocked. I'm clearing them. Hence this.'

His left hand held up the legs of the blackened, decomposing pigeon, clutched alongside a stretched wing of the dead bat.

'Sorry,' he said, and chucked the corpses behind him. His appearance had shocked them, he could see that, but it had done its job. They had evidence for an alternative story to the one that had been phoned in. He watched the sense of it register on their faces. 'That's no way to greet people at the door, I know. I'm just so cold in here and thought I would get a fire going while I checked the place out. I've inherited it. This is my first visit. I'm still in shock, to be honest, at the state of the place. You say there's been a fire?'

'A report phoned in.'

The Ancient stepped forward of his door and looked to his right. His neighbour caught his eye and retreated back into her house.

'From next door?'

'I'm not at liberty to say, sir,' the officer said.

'My attorney told me about the neighbour. Poor thing. She's quite delusional apparently. He made one cursory inspection visit and already she was banging on the door, warning him to get away while he was still safe. Here I am on my first visit and already she's called the police. Honestly, the place is trouble enough without the neighbours causing problems. There's no electricity and not even any water. It might be simplest for me to offload the place to a developer and be shot of it.'

'You're visiting from where, sir?'

'Nijmegen. And I must say I'm shocked that the authorities in Bruges allow a medieval townhouse to be in such a state. It would never happen at home. Still, the façade's intact and the structure's basically sound.'

'We've had reports of shouting.'

'That was me, probably. My apologies if my language turned a bit rich. Wouldn't you shout if the shit of centuries had just fallen on your head? It was so dark I didn't know what was happening. And now the whole room's covered in soot. It could easily have looked like smoke as it burst through the window. A cloud of soot that looks like smoke and smells like fire, and me screaming God knows what, I can see where people got the idea of calling the fire brigade. You must want to come in and inspect the place now you're here. I'm glad of the company to be honest. This place is spooking me out.'

The Ancient stood back so the officer could peer inside.

'I don't think we need bother, sir.' The officer was backing away. 'I think you've cleared up the misunderstanding. If you don't mind a recommendation, get some professionals in to look over the place. And start by having those chimneys properly swept.'

'I will officer, I will.' He stooped to pick up the dead pigeon and the bat. 'I've now got a room full of these things. Any idea how to dispose of them?'

'As I say sir, call in the relevant professionals.'

7

THE ANCIENT SHUT THE DOOR and cast an aural projection into his neighbour's house. The fire officers knocked on her door and settled down on her sofa. She gave her name and began her report.

There had been lots of yelling, she said. She thought the voice was a woman's but it could have been a young man's. It made no sense to her, but then the couple who lived next door were foreigners, gypsies most like, you could never tell who they might bring home. There were cries of pain, and the crashes and bangs of struggle. It was a relief they had answered her calls this time, that was for sure. With so many murders, all those young people found dead, a woman's suspicions should be treated with respect. She didn't know what they were doing, but the comings and goings in the middle of the night were not the way of respectable people. The nightmares she had had since they moved in, you'd never believe them.

Yes, she knew the place was uninhabitable, so how come the couple always looked so clean and smart? Their skin was dark but it wasn't dirty, you could see that much. Now that's a mystery worth solving. No water, no electricity, yet a couple emerge from the place like it's a regular home.

Could the noise have been of a man unblocking chimneys? She thought about it. She had her own chimneys swept every six months. It never entailed any noises like that. No, she feared murder when she called the police, and the more she thought about it the more she was sure that was what she had heard. She wished to report a murder.

The Ancient heard an officer close his notebook, preparing to leave. He stopped listening and opened the front door. The police car was still parked outside but the other emergency services had left. He shut the door behind him and moved in through the door to his left.

Sabaa sat on the kitchen floor, her arms stretched out in front of her, turning the baby in front of the open oven door as though it were on a rotisserie. The baby was silent, the palest pink now appearing through the white of its skin. A vein bulged and pulsed on the side of its head.

At other times Sabaa might have laughed at the sight of him, all smeared in soot, but this baby had changed her. 'You're a mess,' she said.

'The police came to the door,' he explained. 'I had to speak with them. I blacked up with soot. I don't want them to recognise me when I am washed.'

'We need food.'

'Soon.'

This house had a doorbell. It rang.

'That's the police,' he said. 'Tell them about that woman on the far side. She's called Birgit. Tell them about the lies she tells and the fantasies she cooks up.'

He walked upstairs to the bathroom. The young couple had left the central heating set to 15 degrees so the pipes would not freeze. The heat was dry and oppressive. The shower pumped out water hot enough to scald. He turned it to cold, dropped his soiled clothes onto the floor, and climbed in.

He seldom showered and never washed his hair, but then he never got it this dirty. He expected to visit Birgit. He meant to leave no clues for forensics to trace back to the soot-stained man next door.

He listened to the conversation at the front door as the water ran down his body. Sabaa had taken the baby with her. It was good thinking. She could not stand and chat for long with a naked baby exposed to the chill December air. She apologised, said as much, she was about to put the baby in the bath. Just twenty minutes into the role and she was already playing the young harassed mother to perfection. No, the house next door was abandoned. Had that mad Birgit been spreading her nonsense stories again? Somebody should take her away and lock her up.

The officer thanked her and left. The Ancient stepped from the shower. The cold water on his skin cooled him as he walked wet through to the couple's bedroom. Jeans were too coarse against his skin so he ignored them and chose linen trousers from a summer suit instead. A drawer gave him a simple maroon T-shirt, and a pair of tan loafers in the bottom of the wardrobe fit him well enough.

Back in the bathroom he stood beside the shower and leaned so that the palms of his hands lay flat against the wall and supported his weight. As he kept still, his projection moved on through the wall and stepped out onto the first landing in their own Bruges home. It continued, crossing the house to pass through the opposite wall.

The timing was lucky, but it was perfect. The coffee and the excitement had left their neighbour desperate for the toilet. The stairs were a pain, given her lumbago, but she found herself hurrying up them more fluidly than in years. She was just shy of the top step, the bathroom door open at the end of the corridor, when suddenly her way was blocked. This man came through the wall. She knew he did. It cannot happen but she saw it, first a tan loafer and then a dark trouser leg, and then the whole man stepped through.

There. She was right. She recognised him at once. She always knew he was a strange one and here was proof enough if anyone needed it. He had just walked through her wall and now faced her on the top of the stairs.

She needn't have fallen. In fact this apparition was so insubstantial she might have walked through him. She was surprised of course and did stumble. She couldn't say he pushed her, for though his hands jutted out she felt no touch of flesh, just a sudden jolt of air that sent her reeling. Her cry was short, perhaps of triumph as much as shock because those police hadn't believed and now she was proved so right.

The break was clean; her neck snapped the first time her head hit the white painted wood on the edge of the crimson carpet runner on the stairs. She stayed with her body as it tumbled down to the pretty lily-patterned tiles that marked the hallway, but somehow she was already separate. She would phone her friend. She would report this to the police. They would have to believe her now. And yet while this made all the sense in the world it made no sense at all. Now where was she? All was dark and she was tumbling still.

The Ancient let his projection fade and walked down to the kitchen. His partner stood by the door. No-one's senses were more acute than hers. She had leapt to her feet at the moment of death.

'Birgit,' he confirmed. 'That neighbour. Now she'll be quiet. I'll feed off her while she's still warm and bring her blood back.'

'I'll feed myself. You fetch food.' Without looking at him, Sabaa took the baby out into the street and closed the door behind her.

The creature was helpless. It would be years before it could hunt on its own. Their son's lips were quivering to be fed and they had nothing to give. Sabaa could not lactate. And so the Ancient must take money and search out baby formula sealed in a tin. Then he must buy a feeding bottle. Could he sense the right temperature for the milk? Perhaps. Pits in the skin around his nose were well attuned to human body heat. Still, he should probably buy a thermometer as well.

They would have to find a home where they could keep it warm. Whatever kept the baby warm would cause it to sweat. Whatever it ate it would shit out. This constant soiling would need cleaning. It would need clothes. It would need and need and need. This baby would harness their life to its needs.

The Ancient was not prone to obligations. He needed a new strategy.

8

SNOW WAS FALLING. A cold wind sheeted the paving with ice. The Ancient took the incline up to the high street, where cars and vans ploughed the slush of the gritted street. This winter evening was garish with neon. White lights like captive stars were strung in orb webs of wire across the streets. Humans gripped shopping bags and pushed against each other on narrow footways. Such was Christmas.

The wet of the snow dampened his shirt so that it clung to his skin in transparent patches. People stared, this madman dressed for summer in the winter's chill. He didn't belong, of course he didn't belong, but no-one was meant to see it. The baby's needs had drawn him out of the safety zone.

She was back before the oven when he returned to the house, sitting cross-legged with her naked back held straight. The lights were on full-blast. He worked the dimmer switch and watched the light splay softer shadows from the ripple of her spine. Sabaa was holding the baby close. He walked around so as to see them.

She was feeding him. The creature had its eyes closed, its mouth suckling her right breast. The baby's mouth avoided the dark aureole though. It was sucking lower on the breast. Liquid spilled red from the corners of its mouth. Sabaa had slit her breast and was suckling it with blood. Her eyes were closed, her mouth smiling.

The Ancient mixed the baby formula according to the instructions, and warmed it in a saucepan on the hob.

'In case he's still hungry,' he said, closing her hand around the bottle.

Sabaa opened her eyes and the look of them quaked him somehow, this open and unmitigated stare of a mother. It was an elemental power the equal of his own.

A metal wastebin stood on the floor beside the sink. That would do. He had kicked off the loafers on entering the house. They were sodden and gave no grip. Bare feet were better. Few would be out to stare at him in this quarter of Bruges. He need not go far.

Winter had frozen the canals to make his job easy. Each muscle in the Ancient's legs flexed to maintain his balance as he trod down the icy stone steps. This was what he needed, the alertness of every fibre of his being. The ice of the canal stuck to his bare skin but his feet were tough; he ripped them clear each time and hurried on. He aimed for a ledge that ran just above the waterline below one of the stone bridges. For centuries this had worked well as a runway, and it was working so now. He saw the shadows fleeting along it as he approached.

Four. He needed four. One two three four. He struck faster than he could count. He raised the lid of the wastebin only once and then slammed it shut with all four rats caught inside. He had turned to begin his return trip before they even started to scrabble their claws against the bin's stainless steel walls. He needed to let them loose before they tore into each other's throats.

Shaking the bin a few times kept them stunned. The whole expedition took less than two minutes. Birgit's door was unlocked. He let himself in and looked down. She lay at the bottom of the stairs in the posture in which she had fallen, head tilted on its broken neck, one arm against the wall and the other pinned behind her back. Her legs in their thick winter tights still lay on the stairs, her feet curiously crossed at the ankle. The cause of death should be obvious to any who found her. Yet this was not so.

He should have come and fed off this woman's warm blood as he planned. Best was when the heart pulsed blood to an opened vein. After that, tidy eating required techniques. Instead, Sabaa had incised a deep cut in the woman's neck and then thrust her mouth into the opening. She needed to feed in order to suckle her baby in the best way she could. She did not care for the consequences.

So he had guessed right. Sabaa sensed her baby's hunger and grew careless. She ripped out a neighbour's throat with her teeth. That was no way to lead a quiet life.

He raised the lid of the waste bin and tipped the ball of rats onto the ground. They ranged in a line to face him, their sharp teeth bared, but when he did not move their noses twitched. They turned in one wave of movement to the corpse. One rat charged over the grey curls of Birgit's hair and across her face, two ran round one side and one the other, and soon the wound in her neck was widening. The woman's head twitched as snouts pressed in and pulled at her inner flesh.

The evidence would be clear. A coroner would confirm accidental death: the woman fell down the stairs, broke her neck, and rats subsequently consumed her corpse. The Ancient had built a storyline to dampen suspicion.

Until Sabaa felt the drive to feed her baby again.

How do you pull a mother from her child?

'He didn't want your food,' Sabaa said. 'He wanted mine.'

She nodded to the bottle beside her on the floor. It was still full. The baby lay asleep in her arms.

'Aren't you the beautiful one.' She touched the baby nose-to-nose and then drew back to gaze at it once more. 'We have to name you, don't we? What name would you like? Ezekiel?'

Sabaa turned to the Ancient. 'Does he look like an Ezekiel to you?'

He couldn't do this, even to humour her. He wouldn't pin this child to a name.

'Here, you hold him.' Sabaa stood and placed the baby in his arms. 'I'll fetch his clothes.'

'He has clothes?'

'The woman in this house went broody. She's filled a whole drawer with baby clothes. There are diapers too, in a box under the stairs. She plans to get pregnant over the holiday. That will be nice. Ezekiel will have a friend to play with.'

The baby's head was too big for its body. The neck clearly gave it no support at all. A goat, a lion, almost any creature would touch ground from the womb and rise shaky to its feet. The human model was so puny, so dependent. Yet this baby had already demonstrated the power to mould its mother to its needs.

She took the baby back from him and cradled it in her arms. 'You must hold it like you love it,' she said, and carried it upstairs. He followed her to the main bedroom. She lay the baby down in the middle of the double bed and pulled open the bottom drawer of the dresser.

'See?' The drawer was stacked with tiny clothing. Sabaa sifted through it with her fingers. 'We've enough for a week at least. There's nothing really warm but then we don't need to go out yet. You'll have to buy a stroller. We don't want an outward facing one. A baby needs to keep eye contact with its mother when they're out walking. It aids development.'

'Who's been telling you all this?'

'Rebecca. The woman who lives here. She buys all the latest childrearing books, look.' A pile of bedside reading was topped by *More than just a Copy: Giving Babies a Say in their Lives*.

'When did you come to know Rebecca?'

'I scanned the house. It's a good home isn't it? I like the décor. Soft washed greys on the walls, stripped wood floors, hints of pink in the soft furnishings but nothing too frilly. And this is a fine bed. Soft enough for the baby and big enough for him to sleep between us.'

'And this Rebecca saw you?'

'Hardly. I was just a projection. It was like she imagined me. I placed an image in her mind first. Then I let her see me by degrees. By the time we really met I was a comfort not a shock. I guess I faded like a dream once I withdrew, but people learn from dreams. Her husband doesn't want children yet. He thinks they both need to earn and save for a few years first. One look at Ezekiel and he'll change his mind. What man wouldn't want to father a boy like this?'

Sabaa had been ghosting, inhabiting a human life and running it as her own. It wasn't worth challenging her with it, but it was clear. While he had been out gathering the blood she needed, she had fed her way into the young neighbour's mind. Even now, as she was chattering away and sorting among the new baby clothes, a part of her mind was locked into Rebecca's.

Her wonder at this new baby, the fun of choosing his clothes, left her unguarded. He located that part of her mind easily. The neural links to the visualisation were bright. Even as she dressed her baby in the couple's bedroom, she was in another room and looking out through Rebecca's eyes. And she was no passive witness of the scene. She was its driving force with all her senses engaged.

Sabaa was inside Rebecca's head and looking out through her eyes. The Ancient looked too. Across the room sat Rebecca's parents, each in a padded armchair. The mother was quite trim in a wool skirt and satin blouse, rather smothered by the cushions, while the father's belly swelled and his bald head glowed in the overhead light. Christmas tree lights were strung through a plastic tree behind them and a bottle of champagne stood in a winecooler on the coffee table.

Rebecca sat on the red plush sofa, her young husband by her side. She undid the buttons of his white cotton shirt and slid her hands inside to cross his skin and move up to his chest. Her fingernails caught in his chest hairs and moved on through. As the Ancient watched the scene through the portal of his partner, he felt the warmth of the young man's flesh come through the palm of Rebecca's hand. The young man was sweating.

'Sure,' Rebecca said, and the parents' eyes widened for the voice that came through was much deeper and huskier than her usual one. It drawled somewhat. 'You want grandchildren? Do you think we don't? So why waste time just sitting here?'

Christmas is so much more special when children are around—that's all the mother had said. That wasn't too pushy, was it? That wasn't offensive? Now why was their sweet little daughter, voice gone guttural, sticking her tongue down her young man's mouth in front of their eyes?

Not now, the young husband was thinking, but what the hell they were her parents. They bored him witless. If this was what she wanted. His mouth responded. His tongue was wet and hot as it probed her mouth. His dick pulsed beneath the tight jeans and grew thick in the clasp of her hand.

'Look, here's my baby, a baby boy, isn't he beautiful?' and an image of the newborn settled into Rebecca's mind. Sabaa was using her child to enflame Rebecca with a desire for a baby of her own.

The Ancient went unnoticed. The red heat of sex blinded the room. Rebecca was now consumed by Sabaa so he entered through the young man's mind instead.

The human sexual act was part of a cycle. You fuck, you conceive, you're born, you grow, you're dead, you rot. Every moment of existence carries all other moments in it. The human frame seems solid when young with all its power and speed, but it's no more durable than a thrusting stream. Cells are born and cells die, birth and death are constant. As humans age they grow more still and melt into the ground. That's all he did with this young man; he slowed him down. Stop a human moving in this senseless progression from moment to moment and you have a living death, like a stream that floods a field and has no way forward but down through the mud.

At first there was the smell. Humans carry all the chemicals for putrefaction within them so for the Ancient that was no strain, just a simple remix as the young man's bodily system collapsed. Rebecca's hand did the stirring. Even as her fingers slid over the sweat on her husband's chest Rebecca felt them drop deep inside, pressing round his bones. His lips turned cold as his face collapsed beneath the press of her mouth.

Sabaa's presence drove Rebecca toward sex, with a momentum she could not withstand. She needed to make a child. All she could do was keep up her drive toward sex. With the Ancient in charge of the chemistry of her husband's body, she was making love to a carcase. It was more than she could bear.

Rebecca' fingernails clawed into her husband's arm. The Ancient boosted his transmission. And Rebecca blacked out.

For the parents the change was instant. Their daughter pawed their son-in-law and then yelped and collapsed.

The Ancient stayed with the scene and looked out through the young man's eyes for a moment. The mother directed the father to the phone, to call an ambulance. A mess fouled the cushions of the sofa, but otherwise the scene before them was outwardly sweet. Unconsciousness looked like sleep, and a young woman lay in her young man's arms. The hospital would examine Rebecca's brain for tumours and find none. The couple's nightmares would be absorbed and their young lives resume.

The Ancient returned his full attention to the bedroom of their house.

9

THE ANCIENT LOOKED AROUND the bedroom and did some accounting of their new life. Blood from Sabaa's cut breast had stained her sweatshirt. They would have to clean it, to stuff it into the washing machine in the kitchen and find some detergent. Those baby clothes too. They could bathe this baby, dry it, wrap it up in new outfits, wait for it to puke or piss or shit and then pile those into the wash too. Or work through that box of diapers under the stairs, chuck them into the garbage, and buy in more boxes somehow.

They could keep this house intolerably warm and leave the baby naked, roll some sheet into a box for a nest, but then it would foul that nest. Though still in its first minutes of life the baby was enmeshed in the human condition. Its skin was already flaking into dust.

'Two days,' he said. 'You have him for two days.'

Sabaa heard him, the news registered as a slight jolt in her head, but she did not look his way. Her face was pointed at the baby but her eyes were focussed so wide she saw only a grey haze. A rose light had shone intense around her head but now it was fading. The current of Rebecca's energy supply had been switched off. Its residue was escaping.

Mother and baby would have to form a different bond. This wasn't his business. The Ancient withdrew.

He walked out of one door and in through the next, climbing the stairs to the open window at the top of the house. Rats were already working at the afterbirth beneath the bed. They grew silent a while at the tread of his weight across the floorboards, and then resumed as he grew still. Snowflakes blew in through the window and touched his skin. The cold cleansed him.

Sabaa needed something she did not have and he could not give her. She had melded with Rebecca and he never noticed. Now he had cut her from that source. Sabaa would react. She would find another female to link to. He waited for one to pass.

Few walked the street outside. He waited nine minutes before the first couple came along. Each wore black woollen coats with hoods pulled over their heads. They linked arms for balance and kept close to the walls of the houses, taking small steps in the virgin snowfall, their conversation broken by laughter each time their feet slipped. They were young, a man and a woman, in their early twenties.

They passed below his window and by the next-door house their conversation stopped. The woman let out a squeal. The young man's arms broke her fall but he couldn't support her and they both crumpled to the snow. He bent over her face, shouted at her, reached for his phone and answered questions even as he looked about for the name of the street and a number on a door. Then he was kneeling, hood tossed back to reveal his black knitted cap. He placed one hand on top of the other on the young woman's chest and thumped down, kissed her, and then pressed down on her chest again.

She coughed. She was breathing. He turned her on her side so her tongue would not block her throat. She was in good hands.

A blue light flashed from the end of the street as an ambulance worked through the slush toward them. The Ancient drew back from the window. He waited for the excitement to pass, for the young woman to be lifted onto the stretcher and placed in the back of the ambulance, for the doors to close. The whole emergency was carried away from the street. Then he walked downstairs and out through the snow, back into the neighbour's house.

The baby was awake, kicking its legs and paddling its arms on the mattress. Sabaa was standing, looking down at it, her arms by her side. 'Now what?' she said.

'You let her go?'

'That woman outside? She was useless. There wasn't a maternal instinct in her body. She had nothing to give.' Sabaa nodded at the baby. 'Pathetic, isn't it?'

'It's a baby. Do you still want to call him Ezekiel?'

She studied the Ancient's face, for some gesture that might make sense of nonsense.

'That's the name you gave him.'

'What does he need a name for?' Sabaa considered a moment. 'Rebecca must have named it. She did the things I couldn't do. Named it. Loved it. She could intuit its needs and supply them. I carried it to term. My breasts never swelled. My nipples have the sensitivity of shoe leather. I was a vehicle not a woman. You've got your baby now. I'm done with it. Leave me be.'

Her eyes watered. She let the tears wet her cheeks and watched for his response. She saw shock. Was there repulsion? Probably.

'Don't worry,' she said. 'Tears are just a by-product. You revive parts of a human organism and other parts flare up in response. So wow, I have tear ducts. They'll dry. They'll shut down. I'm entering full system closure. I'm going next door to lie down. Do what you want with the creature.'

Sabaa made the speech but didn't leave.

'Why tears?' he asked. 'We don't do tears. We don't do sad.'

'We don't do sad?' She wiped both hands down her face then slapped them onto the Ancient's cheeks. 'Take these. Tears from my face onto yours. You see how it feels.'

The tears cooled the Ancient's skin for a moment. That felt fine.

'They're not your tears,' he explained. 'They're Rebecca's. You took in her emotions. They're discharging themselves.'

'You see that so clearly, do you? So where were you this time last year? Rebecca and I have been bonded for all these months and you never knew. You never bothered to notice. You were out there, getting off on the father-son thing, hunting blood as though that's all we needed. Now, when we need it most, you cut Rebecca and me apart. So what have we got? A helpless baby human on a bed. Strip me of Rebecca's feelings and what do I do? I'm on my own. I look down at this creature and do you know what I see? I see a snack.'

'Lie down. Lie down here.'

'It's too hot.'

'Trust me.' The words were a command. She lay flat on the floor.

He picked the baby off the bed and held it inches from his face. Behind its dark eyes, inside the cavity of its skull, he located a sea of blue.

He reached his mind toward Sabaa. Her consciousness was black yet fired with storm flashes. He held the baby above her so its breath puffed against her face. Sabaa's fire charged toward it and its legs kicked and its arms flailed. The baby's blue became the white of vast cloud made pregnant with its mother's electricity.

He laid it on her body and brought her hands up to cross over the baby's chest, holding it in place. Both mother and baby were still.

'Rest. Both of you, rest,' he said. 'You gave your baby your energy. It pumps from the baby's heart. See how it presses into his toes. He's your baby. You can know him. He can know you.'

Both lay still, but he watched and saw the baby's toes twitch. And he saw Sabaa's fingers quiver tiny strokes across its naked skin.

10

SABAA DIDN'T BOTHER with the small print. The wording on the side of the tin came in six languages, all of which she spoke to some degree but none of which she could read. She knew the heat of human blood so tested the temperature of the baby formula with her tongue. It felt about right. She spat the powdery residue onto the floor.

The smell of the rubber teat made her nauseous, but she had nothing in her to throw up. The baby too pulled a face and turned his head away, but he sucked when she pressed the teat into his open mouth.

Sabaa hadn't clothed him. Somehow the whole dressing-up-baby game snapped clean away when the link with Rebecca was broken. Naked was better.

She bunched up a bath towel on the kitchen table, laid a sheet on top of that, and that's where the baby spent much of its time. It slept mostly, but sometimes it startled her. Sabaa was by the washing machine perhaps, staring through the thick glass window as the laundry churned, when she felt herself being watched. It wasn't obvious. The baby couldn't turn its head. It simply lay on its back with its eyes open. It had her in its peripheral vision though. She was being tracked.

Rebecca had told her about the blur of a newborn baby's gaze, and the flailing reach of its soft blue eyes. Not her boy. His eyes were dark and shiny. There was no use making the creature walk. She had tried, holding it under its arms and twisting it from side to side in a parody of male swagger. She pushed it forward, its legs dangling so its feet brushed the floorboards. It was funny for a while and then made her angry. The legs were floppy with no sinew. They crumpled as she released the baby's weight on top of them. This was no son of hers.

But those eyes.

They would not be so different on a man, so dark and large and deep as they watched her.

Sabaa could identify with such eyes.

His skin was never white. She wouldn't say brown either but then the colour of human skin was no issue to her, it was what ran beneath. His skin had the hue of health, some pigment bronzing it. And the lips were darker still, not truly pink but she could see the blood quite flush inside them. She had never bitten a human on the lip. Looking at this tight bud of her son's mouth she wondered why. Her feeding had always been functional. Perhaps she could take more pleasure in it.

Once, as the teat popped from the baby's mouth, Sabaa reached in a finger and ran it across the slippery warmth of his gums. Then she took his right hand and placed it inside her mouth, running those filaments of his fingers across the range of her teeth. Babies had destiny. They wouldn't always be feeble. Her son needed to know what was coming to him.

The baby cried once. Sabaa presumed he was testing his voice, discovering its scope, but when she checked in on his mind she found panic. His fists bunched, his legs kicked, his head turned and her baby squawled. It was the cry of a trapped beast. The mind knew immense power, it had infinite potential, yet it was stuck in an incapable body.

Sabaa picked him up and probed his mind with hers until his screwed-up eyes relaxed and he could look back at her. She let their minds merge. See, she told him. Your mind can travel even while your body grows. Everything is yours.

Even as Sabaa held him a stream of piss arced out of his tiny penis and splashed against her chin. Her eyes flared wide in amazement, and then she laughed. She had laughed before, she was sure of that, some gusty blast of triumph in some distant year, but this was different. The voice was a light soprano, starting high and then chuckling down the scale. Only as its silence collected in the space of her heart did she realise the laugh was hers. It was a human laugh, some genetic throwback to her previous condition.

She let the baby's urine dry on her face and in the fabric of her sweatshirt and sat down on a kitchen chair, the baby supported on her lap with his head pressed against her stomach. She took some time to think about laughter. It was a spasm of joy that shook her. Perhaps she had laughed in this way once, with her sisters. That time held no memories for her.

Near the beginning she had asked permission to go back and collect her sisters. With just two bites the three of them could be together again. It would be fun to have their company. They would be her first true takes.

The Ancient let her go. The sisters were easy to find, as though the scan of her mind had always located them as distant specks. Each lived near an oasis but in separate towns. Sabaa found each in a darkened room within a low complex of such rooms. Their minds held an absence where she had once been.

Investigating further, she saw their minds were largely composed of absence. Each had children who had become adults and left them. Those spans of their children's lives survived as memories. The children themselves were vanished fragments which lived on constant replay in these women's heads. This fragment was a daughter skipping as she sang. This other was a boy struggling to hold a live fish in his hands. This one was a different girl, eyes blinking dark out of a face covered in flour. And this was a boy, peeling back the skin of a dead rabbit to peer inside its corpse. All these children were now adults with children of their own, who had already grown beyond the memories that clustered in the sisters' minds.

Sabaa pulled back to look at their bodies. One was plump and the other thin, but neither were the lithe young girls that were her sisters. Their hair was bunched and grey and their skin was old.

She left without biting either of them.

We chose each other and you stepped out of time, the Ancient explained to Sabaa when she returned alone. You have stayed young because what count as years for them are just a moment for you. Your sisters were locked into memories. They filled with all that had vanished and let it consume them. You know only immediacy. Live inside the moment and it does not stretch.

And so Sabaa had learned. The past takes form as memories and feeds upon the living.

Her sisters' bodies were long since burned. Their flesh rose as smoke and flaked into ashes and their bones were smashed to join the desert's sands. Sabaa sat with a baby pressed against her skin and remembered them.

Sabaa did not notice the blast of cold air as the Ancient stepped from the street and into the house. He stood and watched as the baby pooled liquid shit onto her lap. The shit's smell contained traces of the blood Sabaa still fed it at times from small cuts to her breasts. A slight frown creased her brow. It would stay there. Ageing happens in tiny increments whenever memories take hold, and compound as decades pass.

He picked the sleeping baby from her soiled lap and took it to the sink. The cold water from the faucet made it wake with a gasp. The sound of its startled breath snapped its mother back from memory and into the present.

A light flashed on the front of the washing machine. The Ancient pressed a button to set the load drying.

'Take off your clothes and put them in here.' He nodded at the sink.

Sabaa did as told. He pressed the baby, still dripping, into her hands.

'Now bring him to the bedroom. You can dress him as we talk.'

The baby clothes were still on the bed, all now rolled together. She lay the baby down.

'Come shower,' he told her.

Sabaa obeyed. Such obedience would not last. He set the shower to cool. The water hit her body and took her shape as rivulets over her skin. He listened to it as he worked through the clothes in Rebecca's wardrobe. He pulled a black blouse from what seemed like her business section, and found some dark jeans. They would do.

A dark purple hooded cloak hung in the closet under the stairs. It matched his own black one. He would wrap it around her before they went out. Sabaa didn't need its warmth but she could fold it around the baby. It was best to hide the baby if possible. And it was wise to appear affected by the cold. He wanted to attract no notice at all.

Sabaa dripped a trail of water across the bare wood floor and onto the carpet. He handed her the clothes. She shoved her feet down through the legs of the jeans and yanked up the waistline. He heard a tear in the cotton as she thrust her arms through the sleeves of the blouse. The shower had done its job in shaking her out of her reflections.

'So we're moving,' Sabaa said. She did not bother to read his mind. Her focus was on the baby. She had her own plans. 'Heading south. We'll find somewhere warm for the baby. It's the only way. East through Turkey and then into Syria? I think so.'

She began to wrap the baby rather than dress him. The little thing would need all his clothes. The layers would keep the baby warm on the journey. The outfits were mostly one-piece. His arms sometimes went through sleeves and sometimes leggings. No matter, a limb is a limb and they were all so puny and useless. The baby kept his head still, dark eyes open and watching her, as the layers made him ever more ball-like. Two hoods ended up roughly in position so she pulled them over his head. He was done. They were ready.

'We'll take the train,' she said. 'And then a boat. He'll do better on a boat.'

Sabaa took some pink trainers with Velcro fasteners out from under the bed and slid her bare feet into them. That was it. She didn't ask about the baby's food, its bottles, its diapers. The logic was simply one of flight.

That made it easier. The Ancient wasn't deceiving her. His plan was apparent in his mind if she cared to discover it there.

'What a strange power the baby has,' she said. 'He can't walk, talk, sit, grab, hunt, or feed. His mind is an ocean, so deep I can lose myself there but it's utterly without form. His eyes watch me but without intent, he's just sucking in all he sees. And yet look at us. We're on constant watch, guessing at his needs and trying to serve them. He dictates our lives. We serve him like we have never served anything else. It is such a strange power he has.'

The Ancient took the baby from her while she fitted on the dark purple cloak, and then passed it back. It's what they call love, he could have told her. You are rational and love is irrational. Love is parasitical in that way. It feeds on an unwitting host.

He kept silent though. For now it was better that Sabaa did not understand.

11

THE ANCIENT SCOOPED up the last of the coins from the walnut table in the hall, and they left the house. They walked too fast, like shadows raked along the sides of walls by carlights, but no-one paid them particular notice. The few who were braving the street kept their eyes on their feet, watching for ice, mindful of slipping.

Drivers sat in the dim interior light of their buses outside the rail station. The doors were closed, the engines churned, the drivers were keeping warm. A train had just arrived from Brussels. People dragged their luggage out from the station and into the snow. They headed for the bus that would ferry them to the port.

The Ancient was following a different route. He led his family across the station hall. Its lights were garish. The place was full rather than busy, people hanging out, unwilling to step beyond its warmth.

Two ticket counters were open, each with long lines. The Ancient chose not to follow the normal technique and blank out the conductor's mind. It took energy to blank a person's mind and he needed to retain every scrap of strength. He pumped his coins into a ticket machine. Tickets in hand, they headed straight for the tunnel that led beneath the platforms.

The lights in the tunnel were muted. Some platforms were bright on top of the stairs but he ignored those. Those platforms were for express trains and he did not need an express. Their train was a local one. A teenage girl peered through the murk of one window, but otherwise the train looked to have been abandoned in a siding. They climbed into an empty carriage and settled down on an old plastic-covered bench.

Sabaa held her baby close beneath the cloak, folded so the big eyes in that tiny face could look up at her. Its warmth worked through all of its layers of clothing to touch her skin. The baby was still, of course it was, it was wrapped too tightly to squirm or kick, but its face too was calm. Sabaa fed it the idea of warmth. Even as the train rattled and shuddered its way through the snow she passed her son a vision of sky burnt soft by sunlight, of baked mud walls that radiated heat at night. They were memories of a girlhood she had once known. Soon her baby would be in a place as warm as that. She would throw away its clothes and her little human would grow free.

The conductor would recall them for a speculative piece in the local newspaper. A young couple with a baby, foreign he'd say, they had that drawn-in air about them. You get those types especially near ports, full of secrets held in different tongues. At least they had tickets. Be civil, do your job and move on, that's what he does when folk don't want to talk. They'd been arguing, that's what he'd guess. There was something dark and brooding about them. It's tough being young with a kid, that's all he knew. Nothing prepares you for it.

The train ride was short. Zeebrugge was the end of the line. They stepped out into fog and walked back along the short platform and then jumped down onto the tracks. The snow had stopped and the rails were a black line through the white. The Ancient took the lead and Sabaa walked two steps behind.

A line branched right. They followed its tracks past the platforms of small commuter stations while up above them streetlights smudged orange haze into the fog. Traffic roared, a rush of trucks so heavy that the ground shivered. Diesel exhaust smeared the air around them and beyond that was the weight of sea.

Humans saw the sea as blue but then they lived life in the shallows. For Sabaa the sea was black and no black was darker for none was deeper. Sabaa felt kinship with sea the way humans do with death. She kept it at a distance but now it was either side of her. The rail tracks they followed were for freight and lay between containers stacked like canyon walls. Steel cranes arched overhead. The sea was to both sides and ahead as well.

The tracks stopped at buffers and they walked on till the sharp edge of a concrete spur was visible in front of their feet. A ship was passing, something of a ghostship in the fog but bright with lights. Was this their ship, coming to collect them and take them south? Sabaa touched the Ancient's mind. It seemed so.

Sabaa smelt her baby. Its lips were losing colour, turning blue, and out of them piped tiny steams of breath. The Ancient took the folds of her cloak and pressed them back, and then took the baby into his hands. Sabaa should have guessed. She would curse herself for not guessing. He held the baby and turned to face the sea, but as he did so he stepped back. He stepped back but stayed where he was.

There were two Ancients and the small one beside her was the projection. He was the image of himself yet only half the size, more like the measure of a twelve year-old boy. His hands were also smaller, their fingers still long and slender but their capacity was less.

This was all wrong. Projections emerge from the body. That's the way Sabaa knew the world to be. In this case the body had retreated to leave the projection behind. The Ancient with his full size stood behind her, his eyes open yet blank, his hands loose by his sides. This shrunken projection of the Ancient held her baby.

If he let it slip it would bounce off the concrete and tumble into the sea. How was it possible? A projection could carry an object with the weight of a key and steer it into a lock, but not a baby. This was a crazy game. Her baby was in danger.

Sabaa reached forward to grab the baby. In the same instant, it was gone. The Ancient stood as a full-sized statue behind her. His projection streamed as energy across the blackness of water. It carried the baby with it.

The jaw of Sabaa's face dropped and froze into position, her mouth open. She left her body to stand on the dockside and projected out across the darkness in pursuit.

The arc of her baby's flight brought it to the lit steel flank of the ship. Just a breath away from impact it paused, the flight arrested. The baby did not spin but turned slowly. Hands materialised around it and this boy-sized form of the Ancient took shape. The tiny Ancient's feet were on the deck, his arms raised.

Sabaa stretched out her hands to take the baby. Her fingers reached through the layers of the baby's clothing toward its flesh and kept on reaching, scrabbling toward its heart, feeling nothing. She had no substance. Her projection was too rushed, it contained no more than the idea of her physical self.

And yet she ached. The ache was in her body bereft on shore, staring out toward this passage of the ship, longing for the touch and warmth of her baby's skin. Here on the deck as a projection she could only watch and know herself to be apart.

The Ancient lowered the baby to the deck, and lodged the bundle next to the ship's steel wall. That kept it from slipping over the iced timbers as the ship rolled. All she could do was kneel and reach forward her hands. Sabaa ghosted some memory of touch across the baby's cheeks. She stroked the baby's forehead and looked into its eyes.

The baby saw her, there was that at least. His black eyes glowed as he looked up at her. Then she saw how the skin of his face was paling to grey as his lips took on the colour of mould. The glow in his eyes was his life receding. The frozen night air was killing him, the sea wind biting at the last of his warmth. The baby stayed calm but soon all would be blackness with no light left to him at all.

The Ancient folded his hand around the handle of the door that opened from the deck into the ship. He was set to turn it and pull. He felt the shape of the metal, he had kept enough substance for that, she could tell, but he was too weak. He had shrivelled to this ridiculous boy-size and spent all his energy in stealing her baby away from her. And now the baby would die. They might just as well have tossed it into the sea.

Sabaa couldn't port the baby through the steel hulk and into the warm interior. It was human and therefore stubborn that way; it couldn't just de-atomise and shift from material form. Here they were, two projections standing on the deck of a ship while the heft of their physical bodies were stranded on shore. Even as the Ancient flexed non-existent muscles and tugged the heavy steel door to break the seal the winds pressed around it, Sabaa's projection passed through him.

The metal of the door from the deck was thick. As she took shape on its far side she saw she had arrived nowhere. Sabaa was closed into an empty box, the door from the deck now behind her but a further door to the ship's interior still ahead.

She pressed her head through its metal first, kneeling so her appearance would be below eye level. The glare of lights dazed her vision but she caught some chambered darkness away to her right. Legs were passing, people walking, slow and kind of aimless. Sabaa streamed between them. The chambered space held slot machines, lights flashing on their screens, but no-one was playing. She took shape, flipped the hood over her head, and ran forward out of the chamber's shadows and into the broad bright passageway.

'My baby!' she yelled.

A woman passing by looked at her then hurried away. Sabaa entered the woman's mind and saw herself, hands flailing, mouth open but with no words coming out. She had no vocal powers. She had to yell from where her body stood on shore, that she could do, and let that voice resonate through her energy field here on board.

The figure on shore, staring out toward the ship, opened her mouth and let a scream rip out above the seas.

'My baby!'

People saw Sabaa now. Everybody saw her. They looked at her and flinched. She was a horror show. What language had she used? She wasn't sure, but what she registered in people's minds was some guttural slashes of consonants coming out from her throat and wrapped around a long keening wail.

A man stood closest to the door; middle-aged, pale-skinned, made tubby by a quilted anorak of bright blue. A rough black woollen cap was pulled down over his ears. He had taken a cigarette out of a packet, put it in his mouth, and was sliding his hands back into gloves. Smoking was not allowed indoors. He was preparing to step out into the cold and light up. He would have to do.

'Help my baby. Open the door,' she said in English.

He stared at her. Sabaa frightened him. Soon he would walk away.

She switched languages and tried Flemish. She spoke more softly.

'Alsjeblieft, help mijn baby. Doe de deur open.'

Somehow the order got through. He was set to open the door in any case. If that's all this wild woman wanted he'd do it.

He pulled. Even for him it took real effort. He freed both hands to take a grip. Sabaa followed him through into the boxed area, crowding the space behind him to urge him forward but keeping some of her form inside the thick steel door to leave him room. He mustn't be forced to touch her and find she wasn't there.

He heaved himself at the door. It opened. He pushed through, working to keep his balance as his feet slid on the ice outside. He held the door open as best he could and looked back for her but she was gone.

She was through. That's what he saw next, the same woman bent over a white bundle on the ground. She had a boy with her, a teenager, her son maybe, dressed in black like she was. Both backed away as he watched them. They didn't jump, they must have jumped but that's not what he saw he swears it. They backed toward the railings of the ship and passed through them. That's what he saw.

He tried for the railings, to see where they had gone, but slipped. The ice was that bad. He reached forward to break his fall, and moved his left hand at the last moment so as not to crush the white bundle. It wasn't too bad. He didn't hurt himself, just bruised his knees, that's all. His head was close to the baby's. So tiny he was. He looked like a corpse, one of those ancient things they pull out of graves on the History Channel, but the eyes weren't cavities as he first thought, just dark. And the baby's mouth opened. The cry was thin but it pierced him. He picked the baby up, held him tight in one arm, and hauled himself upright by holding on to the handle of the door.

Soon he was inside, holding the baby out in front of him, shouting and shouting till folk paid him attention. He wasn't a hero, he wouldn't say that, he did what any man would. An officer came, well someone with gold cord sewn onto the shoulders of his dark blue jacket at least, and so at last he let go. The officer hurried off, carrying the baby toward the nurse. He's glad the wee thing survived. It's a miracle, they say, but that's Christmas for you. It's a good time for babies and miracles.

12

THE SHIP CHURNED into the distance. Sabaa appeared to be watching its lights recede. Her eyes were open and unblinking. The Ancient passed a hand before her face. She did not register it. Her eyes were blank. She stood on the very edge of the concrete pier, her arms held out above the sea. Her mind was as blank as her eyes. Sabaa was gone.

The Ancient touched a finger to the skin of her cheeks and rubbed through the salt that was crusting there. Her absence was total.

Daylight would come, the fog would lift, and men would find Sabaa here, a statue of flesh reaching out across the waves. They would take her for an image of a wife reaching for the spirit of the man she loved, one who had died chasing fish through storms. Her photograph would fill the front pages of newspapers. Coroners would then slice in and dig down to the reality of what they took to be a corpse.

It could not be.

He tilted Sabaa so that her heels dragged along the ground and then eased her upright again. The body had no give in it at all. He pressed Sabaa's eyelids closed and ran his hands around her head, along her spine, and down through her limbs. Her neural network was still receptive. He could not enter her and give her normal bodily function but he could ease the rigidity away.

Some slack came into Sabaa's fingers. Her spine curved. Her arms loosened. The muscles lost their tension but had no grip. Her legs would not hold tight around his waist. He lodged his right shoulder below her breasts and reached backward to snatch her left leg from the ground and wheel her round. Her body looped around his neck. Sinews cracked but gravity did its job and folded her in place.

And so the Ancient walked.

If Sabaa's projection was still on the ship then this body round his neck was all that was left of her. The rest was as scattered as death.

It was best not to think. His mind stayed fed into the neural network of her body, and he walked. The darkness of night and the enclosure of fog meant there was no need to hide. He made his way back along the rails and then mounted the bank to walk along the roadside. Cars and trucks were few, their lights lowered as they edged past him. The pathway became metal for a while, he was on a bridge across some water, the fog thicker still, and then the roadway continued.

Finally the roads diverged. The highway sped on toward the Netherlands while he took the narrow way that sloped down to the sea. He passed a white lighthouse that stood on the promenade in front of a cliff wall of seaside apartments. He sat on a low stone wall and eased Sabaa's body around his neck till he held it in his arms.

Behind him waves were breaking on the shore. Ahead of him was the small white tower. He waited for the sun to rise and smear away the darkness. The top of the tower, the green dome of its roof and its lighthouse lamps, was still indistinct in the fog but he saw her shape. She was there, her projection's hands curled tight around the railing and her head lifted to look beyond him and toward the sea.

Come, he let out, no words but a hum of invitation.

Sabaa stayed still. She would not come to him. He was not what she wanted.

He sensed what she was doing. Her projection on the lighthouse rim followed the passage of the ship that carried her child. Her dimension was broad. Somehow she spanned the entire North Sea, read the currents, rode the winds. She willed the ship to be safe.

Here, he sent out as thought, and stroked the belly of the body on his lap.

He came from here. Our baby was born of this flesh. This body and our boy's body are the same.

Sabaa's hands released the railings and she stepped back. She was gone.

He waited. The steel door at the base stayed closed as she emerged through it. She walked up the ramp to the level of the promenade and crossed to stand before him. Still she was looking out toward the sea, but even as she stood there she dissolved.

The process was gradual, reluctant. The toes of her physical body sprang wide inside her shoes and muscles contracted to make her knees jerk, but while the legs of the projection atomised from view, from the waist up it still hovered.

Her backside had been as firm as stone but now the weight of her sank into pliant flesh on his lap. Her shoulder moved against the cup of his hand. All that floated in front of him now was the projection's face, its chin vanishing, the cheekbones whisked away, till there were just the beacons of her eyes, staring.

Her head rested against his arm. He looked down. Slight movements juddered behind the eyelids, and then they opened. Her look was wide as though he was not there, he was something to see through, a block on a horizon, and then the pupils contracted.

Sabaa was back.

'He's landed,' she said.

The Ancient brought a hand to his face and wiped away a tear. That was novel. He had been staring, unblinking, till this moment. His eyes were dry yet still they watered. She had come back. He had not known that she would.

He waited, and then guided her to sit up and stand. Taking her hand in his he began to walk, leading her in short steps.

The covering of snow up on the sand was thin and crisped to ice. Their footsteps crunched. A fence of thin wooden stakes strung together by wire blocked off the dunes, apart from one passageway through to the sea. It was just broad enough for them to walk side by side. Ice broke for their feet to sink ankle deep into the water of puddles. The path wound around bends but always ahead was the sound of the sea.

And then they were through. The path opened out onto beach. The sand was free of tufted grass and the fence was behind them. Daylight had come but the fog was still close. He tracked the shoreline through sound, following the rhythm of collapsing waves as he led Sabaa across the strand.

The sea was only steps away before they could see it. They did not pause. He led her on till the water rose above their shins and then reached their knees. That would do. The retreating waves sucked the ground from beneath them. When the soles of their feet were left to rest on miniature islands, they shifted sideways for level ground. Otherwise they stood still.

Sabaa's hand in his tightened, gripped hard a moment, and then relaxed.

'You've found him?'

She nodded, her head rocking and rocking, her eyes fixed.

'Good.' The sea pushing and pulling at their legs was to shock her back into physical existence as much as anything. Her baby had gone. Sabaa felt no need for the power of touch. She had to get it back. 'This water doesn't divide us. You understand that? Our boy is earthed now. He's in England. The sea is no division. It's a conductor. It connects us to him.'

In the beginning, when the Ancient had first taken her, Sabaa went as wild as this. She ranged so far then, her body abandoned for the thrill of being freed from it, like she did not know her body was the most precious thing on Earth. He had trained her. Her body was no longer temporary. It was no longer dispensable. She must love it as much as he did.

The Ancient reached his free hand up to her face and drew the nail of his middle finger across her skin. It did not cut. Sabaa needed her blood, but he pressed hard enough to score a blue line across her cheek. He let go her hand and curled his fingers through her tresses, gripping and pulling the hair back from her scalp. He pressed his mouth to hers, their teeth clashing before he gnawed her lower lip.

And then he pulled back his head.

'You felt that?' he said. 'You feel the sea?'

'My baby.'

'He's there.' He raised an arm to point across the waves. 'We're here.' He gripped hold of her shoulders and pressed through the muscle toward her bones.

'I can't touch him.'

'So? What's time to you? You birthed him. You fed him. You held him. Now let him grow. He's there for whenever. You're here.'

He released Sabaa's shoulders and clamped her face in his hands.

'You went away.' The Ancient spoke slowly, the words separate, so she would hear his voice and not the sea. 'You're back. This is us. This is it.'

And then he left her. She must return to him of her own free will.

The wind chilled the absence his hands had left on her cheeks. Sabaa turned to face her baby across the sea.

The baby was gone. Waves raced at her out of fog.

She turned back to the land.

The Narrator's Tale

13

I WAS BORN A HUMAN in the city of Görlitz in 1656, in a country since known as Germany. I became what you would call a provincial journalist, penning pieces for the local gazette. As such, I wrote about parents who murdered their children; men who set fire to their neighbours' homes; limbless heroes of distant wars whose families died of starvation; brawls on riverboats which left corpses floating in their wake.

One day I attended the aftermath of a particularly gruesome exhumation. A couple in their late twenties kept bearing children but could think of no way to feed them, so they fed them to themselves. The neighbourhood wives had their suspicions when the woman screamed in childbirth and her husband called on no help. Time and again she had brought a baby to term, yet the neighbours saw no children. Women borrowed spades and dug the garden. They uncovered the skeletal remains of six newborns. They entered the house. It smelled of pork. The body of a baby simmered in a pot on a fire built from wood scraps. The women beat the young couple with their spades till they were senseless and then they torched the house.

I stood within reach of the heat of flames and listened in as men gathered round and made sense of what their wives had done. I took notes. Men banked in front of me, the flames above their heads. Their wives were decent women, they said. They had done right. A man snatched my notebook from my hand and flung it toward the fire, its pages flapping. This is a sad accident, they told me. A chimney caught fire and a couple died. The same thing as could happen to your parents in their home, young Konrad, for we know where they live. That is what you will write. That is the story we expect to read in your newspaper. Now go. There is no other story for the likes of you here.

As I walked away, a man walked beside me. It was night, but I felt I was walking in his shadow. It was winter, but he emitted an extra chill. I did not look at him directly, because I believed he came from the townsfolk and so carried a sense of threat.

'You are shaking,' he said. 'I will buy you a drink.'

His voice was deep and resonated in my spine. He laid a hand lightly on my shoulder. I wore a thick woollen coat but felt the impression of each of his fingers.

The Inn was crowded. Four men sat around a small table in an alcove. They were drinking and arguing about horses. My new companion paused in the doorway and looked their way. They did not look back at him but simply rose mid-conversation and carried their tankards to the bar. We sat where they had left. A bar girl brought a snifter of brandy and set it in the centre of the table. Her hand stayed on the base of the glass, and then she slid it across the table toward me. She left us.

He saw that I noticed how people did as he wanted without his asking.

'Do you play chess?' he asked me.

'I used to.'

'Humans are as chess pieces. Each is programmed with possible moves of a very limited kind. They repeat their moves in a workable chaos. Their brains are largely vacant. It is simple to impose a little strategy.'

'But those drinkers cleared the table without a threat. The bar girl brought a drink though you placed no order. It is as though they acted on some wordless command.'

'Wordless command,' he repeated. 'That's a fine phrase. You have a way with words. Tell me about your life.'

So I spoke. My brandy was finished and replenished before he made a comment.

'I asked you about your life and you told me about your trade,' he said.

‘That is my life.’ I was still overwrought with the tragedy of that day’s fire and slaughter. ‘I document the mundanities of human horror. That is what I do.’

‘How endless,’ he said.

Till then I had looked to the side while speaking, the way humans do when they work to recall horrors. Now I looked him in the eyes for the first time. All I recall was intense darkness. My next sensation was the cold of his palm pressed against my forehead. He had reached forward at my faint to stop my head crashing against the table.

‘You need clean air,’ he said. ‘And a change of perspective.’

His arm supported me and we walked from the Inn and out into the cold shock of the night.

‘We will meet again,’ he said. ‘Tomorrow at six, by the crossroads to the west of town.’

And he was gone.

We met, and we met again. I spoke about myself. It was something I had never done at extent. On the first night my story streamed from me in random episodes. On the second I tried to stitch it together with some meaning. By the third, my whole life seemed pointless.

‘You’re young,’ he counselled.

‘You’re pretty young yourself,’ I snapped back. ‘How old are you?’

‘Aah,’ he said, a sigh that was not loud but was of fathomless depth. We were walking side by side along a country lane with only stars above, but my vision changed so that in just three steps I walked across desert, across tundra, through savannah, at the centre of a large paved square, and along a mountain path whose incline made me stop. Now I was back on the country lane and my head was dizzy with darkness.

‘I pre-date time,’ he said.

Moments before I would have taken this as intellectual pretence. Now, while I could not understand it, I knew his statement was simply one of fact. The places I had seen as in a vision were scenes from his beginingless life. I began to question him. My era had no language with which to make sense of his responses. In more than a century from when we spoke Jean-Baptiste Lamarck would be ridiculed for positing a theory of heredity, and it would take fifty years more before Charles Darwin began scraping at the layers of human myth.

My companion grew silent in his talk. I felt some darkness wash incredulity from my brain, and then he spoke in terms that 21st century science is only just appreciating. He led me back through countless generations and traced my lineage through divergent forms of man, until I was settled in an early mode of primate consciousness. And then he brought me forward, and then paused. Along one track lay the stages of human evolution. Along a separate track I watched a being step out of kinship. At the far end of one track stood myself. At the far end of the other was my companion.

'So we are different species?' I asked.

For a human of that time, it was a profound question. For him, my speech was blank of meaning. He charged my brain with a fluorescent spinning image of a double helix. It shone, but taught me nothing that I could understand.

'We are cousins, you and I,' he said. 'What is present in me is latent in you.'

This was both true and it was a lie. He told me his name was Istvan. He told me many lies. He told me that if we were to meet one more time, he would lead me to the far side of being human and then beyond. While now he walked so fast I sometimes trotted to keep up, I would never need to hurry again. We would share an eternity.

If I cared to leave my world and enter his, I should meet him by the river.

My home river was the Neisse, a tributary of the Oder that courses through Görlitz. Istvan and I walked a riverside track. It was winter and there was snow and I shivered but I wore a fleece and was not cold. My heart beat so hard that it hurt my chest and when I breathed I gasped for I had forgotten to breathe and the inrush of cold air scalded my throat.

Istvan said nothing; he did not even look me in the eyes. I had shown up which meant he had already won me. He walked as though at a saunter, his limbs loose, yet he moved at such speed I sometimes ran to keep up, like a child, like a cat.

Blocks of ice flowed down that river, turning slow circles as they moved. I stopped as though to watch them. It was night but the sky had cleared and there was a moon. My eyes watered so the view was obscured but I smelt the air with an intensity I had not known before. The river was not just a wash of freshness for while it contained much that was living much was also decomposing at its bed. Gases welled up from deep mulch.

I wiped my eyes before they could freeze and looked toward the river by my feet. What seemed to be a large leaf floated there as a platform for snow, but I knew this was too far into winter for such fallen leaves. And besides, what had caught my attention was not this supposed leaf but the smell that rose beneath it. It was perfumed, almost sweet, but weighted by must.

I looked closer. The leaf was an ear, frozen as ice and afloat on the river's surface. Below it was the body of a fox. Any blood inside that fox would be frozen. Its guts were blocks of ice. Even so I could smell that it was rotting.

The air beside the river path was charred with woodsmoke. I separated it into the smells of burning beech, of resined spruce, of silver birch. At the far edge of town birch logs flamed in the fire of my family home. It was the smoke from these logs, the very ones I had helped to fell and chop and stack, that I smelt now. I knew this because tucked inside their scent was my father's aromatic tobacco and behind that my father's breath, and the steam from my mother's broth on the hob. The broth was well-water stuffed with barley, alongside onions and carrots and weighted down by the carcase of an old chicken.

I lifted my head and turned my nose toward my cottage. Istvan studied my stretched neck and then he spoke.

'Your mother's broth?' He smiled when I looked at him. 'It's what she cooks on a Tuesday. I smelt the broth on your breath as you slept that

Tuesday night. I was standing about here with a mind to leave town when I paused. You have such sweetness in you. That smell of you from across the town made me stay.'

I would not have believed that a breath could be detected across a town, but here I was, detecting such scents from home.

'You are entering a sensory world,' Istvan explained. 'Such power of smell is within your human capacity as you can see. It needed triggering, that's all.'

That was a lie. Humans have hallucinatory powers that can help them believe anything but they can't trace single molecules through air to a distant source. Istvan had linked my brainwaves to his receptors. That's fine. It was a kindness.

'I smell what I love before leaving it behind,' I said.

'Why so?'

'Years will pass and I will not age. That's what you tell me. I can never go home again.'

'You can go wherever you like. The world is not divided into home and not home. It is all home.'

'My parents will grow old and die. It would kill them to see me stay young. They can never know the truth.'

'Touch me,' Istvan said. 'Touch my face.'

Snowflakes fell on his cheeks but there was no heat there to melt them. They clung. I brushed them aside and felt their moisture on his skin but beneath them the skin was dry. His face had the look of a twenty year-old's, but its skin had hardened.

'Let your parents touch you,' he said. 'They will remember your baby skin. One touch of your face will be enough. They will know you have changed. Pity will stir their love. They will forgive you anything.'

He reached both hands to my face. His fingertips brushed wide from my forehead and down the sides to rest on my cheeks. The dryness of his touch meant nothing for its electricity passed through me. My heart speeded to the point of hurting, thumping inside my chest, and it was as though my blood vibrated for I trembled at every nerve.

'You have a particular beauty,' he said. 'It is untouched. You should walk the earth forever as you do now. That is a good thing.'

I took his words as love.

He was my first Ancient. He curdled my emotions. I don't wish to write about him. I don't want to write this preface. I don't care whether you humans read this book or not. It wasn't written for you.

I have been studying the 'vampire literature' of the last century. It is a farrago of nonsense that is seeded with occasional truths. As a human I was as fanciful as you. I asked Istvan to tell me of his superpowers. Could he fly?

'Can you?' he answered. 'I am not being facetious. What you might call my superpowers are extensions of powers you have. You can imagine yourself elsewhere. I can do the same, but project myself with such a force that some physical structure coheres. You can go fast or slow. I can summon extreme speed, though it expends energy.'

He told me such mundane truths. I imagined glories in them. His world was a reality. Mine was the fantasy. I did not want his powers. I wanted to lose myself in him.

I no longer cared to write about humans. I needed to write about him. And so I let him take me. That way I could write his true story from the inside.

He left me on the road outside the inn, for he needed to feed. What he promised to do for me required energy and restraint, so it was best that he dampened any physical hunger. I paid for an upstairs room. He commanded that no fire be lit, so I lay beneath the covers for warmth and I waited. When he entered the room I did not hear him. He pulled the covers from me and peeled away my shirt. I shivered. He reached for my shoulders. His hands on my skin were cold and yet I stopped shivering. His touch stilled me.

I looked into his eyes. I was in love, and felt sure I would see my love reflected there. I saw no such thing. My love for him was hungry. Nothing could satisfy it. His hunger for me was different. It was calculated. His eyes revealed the burn of some dark fire.

He turned my head and pressed it into the pillow. It was a relief. I needed his touch but not those eyes. His moistened finger iced a trail across my neck, and then turned to slice the same line with its nail. It left no pain. His tongue came next, its cold tip wet with my blood's warmth. It probed the wound and brushed past nerves, his tongue a sensor that mapped me from the thrills those nerves sent back. I lay still and yet I quaked. That is the best I can describe it.

He emptied me.

My head turned on its pillow. His mouth was gone from my neck. He moved above me. It was as a mirror for a while, his eyes the brown that mine had been in my reflection. He smiled. I wanted to smile back but my face could not respond. It was as though he wore my smile and I no longer had one of my own. He brought his mouth to mine. It was my first kiss. He wound his fingers through my hair to hold me still.

His eyes resumed their fire so all I saw as I stared into them was red. It was a flood of red that I heard as a breaking wave and his stomach muscles surged against my flesh. His body rucked and my mouth filled to gagging. It was my blood, disgorged from his throat into mine.

He pulled away and sealed my mouth with his hand.

'Swallow,' he said.

I did. The movement of my throat set my body convulsing. I wanted to be held, but not the way he held me. He kept one hand wrapped in my hair to pin my head to the pillow and pressed the other on my chest above my heart. He lifted that hand up and then hit its heel against my chest, blow after blow, beat beat beat.

'Breathe,' he snapped. 'Breathe, you fool.'

I tried. My tongue had turned limp and blocked my throat. He let go of my hair and thrust fingers in my mouth to pull my tongue clear. His hand beat down on my chest.

'Breathe!'

I did. A small, tight gasp.

'Again.'

I tried. It worked.

He brought his face close, his mouth above mine without touching.
'Again.'
My breath puffed into him. He blew it back.
'Again.'
I breathed out.
And breathed him in.
His breath was rich and sour and fungal and sweet. It was the taste of ice and mould and nectar. It spangled across my tongue and through my brain. He breathed, I breathed, we breathed as one. A point came and I did not see it happen but I breathed alone.
He was gone.
I thought he was gone.

The only logic for a human edition of this book is that it gives you material from which to make an informed choice should you find yourself in the same predicament as I when I was human.
That is flawed logic. Love bewitches. When you encounter an Ancient, no informed choice remains.

I have written many biographies of our kind. I include humans in my tales where possible, so that my books are not devoid of comedy and emotion. One thing I had never written is the tale of an Ancient. Istvan was my first and only Ancient, and he left me with no greater tale than I have given here.
Centuries passed. There were rumours of another Ancient. My community came calling for me. I wrote this account for them.
It has been edited for human consumption.

14

HE MASSAGED MY JAW to release it and pulled open my mouth. My lips were cracked from a century of disuse. 'You're tired, sir,' he murmured. 'You've lain here an age, but here's a story to bring you back. It's a love story sir, the kind you like. It's got rage in it and sex and death, all that stuff you do so well, but this one's different. It brings about a baby. The baby of an Ancient.'

He moistened around my gums first, and used a syringe to draw blood from a glass and spurt it against the insides of my cheeks. The blood dropped into the fissures and raced through them as though they were veins. And then he turned his attention to my tongue.

The blood landed on my tongue and scattered across its surface. My brain's response was instant. It took in texture first of all, a certain thick wetness and shifted to awareness of temperature. My surroundings were chilled and yet this blood was still warm. The donor must be somewhere in the building. I flashed through the constituent parts of the plasma. There were the nutrients, the ions, the cellular waste, and yes, the hormones. The blood was from a female. A healthy young female. My tongue quivered.

He poured direct from his glass. The sensation flooded me. My head jerked forward. The man was too clumsy to react. He clutched the glass against his chest, but the blood that near filled it surged like a wave from the crystal. It covered him.

'Your shirt,' I said. 'Give it to me.'

His fingers were clumsy as he stripped the shirt from his body. Some of the blood had coloured the grey of his skin. I pulled the cotton to my mouth and sucked at it.

'I'm sorry it spilt. That blood is good, sir? They tell me it's good. It's a donation from Melanie. She's the masseuse on your revival team. That taste is just a sample. She is keeping the rest at body temperature. She wants to feed it to you herself.'

'And you?' His hair straggled. His skin was old. His eyes were hidden in the shadows of a sharp nose. His lips were grey. 'What do you have to give?'

'Very little, sir. My blood is not for connoisseurs. My name is Viktor. I'm the librarian.'

'So they've sent you to take me off my shelf.'

'You could say so, sir.' He waited till I had sucked what blood I could from his shirt, and took it back from me. 'Now keep those eyelids closed. Your eyes are dry. They'll burn in this air. We'll carry you down on these boards, sir, to the resuscitation room. You'll need lubricating before you move. It's been years, more years than you know. I'm a fourth generation attendant, sir. They've let me read all of your works but I was losing hope of living to read more. I'll be back soon sir. Back soon.'

Porters came. I smelt the sweat of their fear. They carried me a short way and then hooks were inserted into the ends and sides of my boarded platform. I heard my first ever buzz of electricity. The boards swung as I was lowered. My platform settled. The heat of humans clustered around me.

Water flowed across my brow. It was warm. Small hands with lithe fingers massaged my scalp. My head was tilted back above a hand basin. A woman was washing my hair.

The water stopped. Hands rubbed a warmed towel into my scalp and then a comb pulled through the tangle of my locks. I tensed my neck and raised my head. The chair's back tilted with me to give support. I opened my eyes.

'You're young,' I said. Her hair was blonde and thick and cut to points about her ears. Her face was plump, her cheeks were pink, and her eyes were blue and startled. She was pleased to be young, and excited that I had noticed. How easy humans are to defraud. 'Your name?'

'Melanie, sir.'

'So young.'

Assistants did not used to be so young. They used to take them after they had turned through middle age, when they had nothing to preserve. Their time had come and gone. They did not want to be preserved at the age they had reached. We paid people enough money to help them prosper in a brief old age.

'If you're ready, sir.' Melanie pulled back her hands and dried them on a towel. Her top had short sleeves and her right arm was bound by a rubber tourniquet above the elbow. 'They tell me you'll be careful. That you'll just suck and not bite. That you don't need too much at first.'

Viktor stood beside her. He touched a scalpel to her skin. It was a fractional cut but I smelt the blood even before the first drop oozed above the flesh. My tongue was dry. It stuck to her skin but I ran it against the drop as more blood flowed. I clamped my broken lips to the heat of her arm and sucked.

Melanie swooned. Two colleagues collected her in their arms and pull-ed her away to a chair. Four others moved toward me, as though I were set to bound after Melanie and drain her of more. Perhaps I was. Who knows?

I pressed the soles of my feet to the vinyl and prepared to stand. I was back to do a job. Humans think writers stare from windows and that imagined worlds have value. That is their folly and it keeps them amused. It is not my way.

My bones and tendons clicked as I adjusted my frame, straightened my spine, pushed back my shoulders and swanned my neck.

'That's good, sir,' Viktor said. 'You've kept your shape. Your muscles haven't wasted at all.'

We live forever; these few knew this, yet still they expect us to share their decay.

'You tell me you have read my books, Viktor.' The fool blushed at the attention, my purring of his name. 'How was that permitted?'

'It's by special dispensation, sir. I maintain the library of true books. I've digitised them.' He threw this word at me that he knew I would not know. Images he was proud of flashed in his brain. I saw a book pressed flat and its pages strobed by light. Words transferred to a bright and flickering screen. They scrolled past with a speed even I could not have read had I not written them. 'You'll find the entire library in here, sir. I've prepared you a special collection.'

He stepped across to the boards from which they had moved my body. A metal tablet lay there, beside items of clothing.

'You've been gone a long while sir. You've skipped a whole century. We tried to call you back a number of times but you weren't interested till now. No matter. These books tell the story, and your kind who stayed through it can alert you to the details. This is an ebook, sir.' He pressed a button and the tablet shone dim light against his face. With just minutes in this world he had managed to bore me.

The youngest man there had moved to the far side of the boards. I watched him. He had Asiatic skin yet his hair was dyed blond. His shoes were soundless. His shirt had no collar and the neckline was like a woman's. A diamond stud glittered in his left ear, and a small square of jet was pinned to his lower lip. His waist was thin yet cinched with a broad black belt. He was set to introduce me to my clothing.

'These are jeans, sir.' He ran a delicate hand across blue fabric. 'Soft brushed blue denim, tapered. This, sir, we call a zip.' He gripped a metal tag and ran it along the runnel that enclosed the crotch.

Clothes are clothes. They set up a screen around me. I took off my old clothes, let them fall in dust to the floor, ignored a flimsy under garment and dressed myself in the jeans, its belt already looped, and a white shirt with pre-attached collar. On my emergence the young man smoothed the wrinkles in my shirt with and the palm of his hand rubbed across my chest. In return, I touched his neck. Blood suffused his face.

'That's mine?' I asked.

He held a jacket on a hanger and took the chance to move behind me and hold wide its sleeves.

'Armani,' he said as he guided it onto my shoulders. 'It's a high-end label. Raw silk blended with cotton for the perfect loose hang.'

His hands lingered just a moment on my shoulders. His touch was light but his pulse was fast and electrifying. And then he moved away to the last of his items assembled on a bench.

'And this sir, your watch. We've gone beyond pocket watches. In fact we've gone beyond watches, but a man of your class needs the show. I've chosen a Patek Philippe. Here, let me fix it on.'

There was something of the puppy about him, that flop of dyed hair brushed around his ears, the dark eyes looking hopeful. I let him hold my hand and turn it. He slipped the watch's gold bracelet across my wrist and pressed home the clasp. Enough. I pulled my hand away.

'And finally the socks and the shoes.' He picked one up and I snatched it from him. 'We do still use laces sir, but I chose these. They help define your contemporary image. They display the sleek athleticism of a powerbroker.'

Oh how they drivel when nervous. I was fond of this young man in some way but would like to have silenced him. Bending was hard for each sock but for the shoes I was already limber. So all this was fashion. At least it wasn't at the expense of comfort.

'Viktor?'

The man grinned. He thought this was his time to guide me through his tableted library. I had watched every movement of his fingers and seen the images spark in his mind. He had nothing left to show me.

'Are there none of my kind to meet me?'

'Indeed sir. But first we thought we would introduce you to this changed world.' He held up his tablet, not to pass it to me but to keep it back. 'This is more than an ebook, sir. It shows films. Moving images. It has the power to search all the information of the globe and return it to you. We've thought it through, sir. The world out there is all a rush. We've selected what we feel you need to know.'

I had been reading the pictures in people's minds. I paused to reach into that duller region where they devise words to fit their concepts and achievements. 'So you will teach me about genetic engineering and solar panels,' I said. 'The international aviation industry. The rendering of oil into plastic. Social networking supplanting friendships. Women empowered by contraception. The sudden vanishing of cities into atoms. A continent ravaged by Aids. Seas stripped of fish and lands of forests. You bring back your storyteller so you can tell him all these things?'

Viktor lowered his hand. I reached for the tablet and he passed it to me.

'You devise machines to reveal at a distance the powers you contain in yourselves,' I advised him. 'Downloading is nothing new. I have been accessing human minds and downloading information for centuries. Don't worry for me, Viktor. You think you devise the game but the game devises you. The rules are quite apparent. I shall play them well enough. You mentioned a birth. Keep me interested, Viktor. Show me to someone who can share with me some sense.'

I headed for the door and opened it. I had read the journey in Viktor's brain and knew my own way well enough. Light blasted through from the corridor outside. I slammed the door against it.

The young man stepped closer and pressed some spectacles over my nose and around my ears. My world went black. 'Shades,' he explained. 'We rehearsed for you so that we could do our resuscitation work in almost total darkness. This is a brighter world than you remember, sir. These shades will protect you.'

'Thank you,' I said. It's bruising to return to a world of obligation.

I let Viktor reopen the door, very gradually, and then lead the way.

15

I HAD LAIN DOWN in a complex of interlinked farm buildings in rural Bavaria. The location could not have changed, but everything else was altered. The corridor passed a window that looked into a small indoor swimming pool. Men and women lined the width of it in ranks, the shorter of them at the front where presumably it was more shallow. Their arms were raised from the water and they were rotating from their waists, left to right.

'What has this place become?' I asked. 'Do we farm our own supplies now?'

'Please, sir.' I had paused. Viktor was coaxing me onward. 'It's best not to stare.'

'But they are so huge.' How could I not stare? 'So round.'

'We are a state-registered health spa. Bureaucracy is intense, sir. The premises are inspected on a regular basis. It is fine for us to seal away our attics, but otherwise we need an official reason for existence. It is good for our clients to see you, sir. You are such a picture of health. But you can understand their discomfort at being observed, especially during aquarobics. This way, sir.'

Viktor had moved forward and stood beside a door marked 'Direktor'. His finger was poised near a button on a contraption fitted into the doorframe. He pressed as I stepped toward him. After a slight buzzing a trim light shone green and the door clicked open. Viktor pushed it wide, waited for me to walk through, and then closed me in.

The room was dark. I could see nothing.

'You may remove your shades.' The voice was deep yet on the verge of feminine. 'We have dimmed the room for you.'

I took off the spectacles and dropped them into my jacket pocket. Vision leached back, slowly.

'We have expertise, Konrad.' I could not have given my name if asked, it had been so long since I had use of it. That spoken 'Konrad', resonant in this dusky voice, was like having my life breathed back into me. It was the first return of some warmth to my system. 'You are back from a timeless zone. This is what we are doing; we are reintroducing you to time. We hold you while you adjust. You can see me now?'

I could. The voice did not fit her body. It came from somebody heftier. She was slight, with a slender neck and oval face, blonde hair shorn to her scalp, ears that stuck out like a lamb's. She had stood to greet me. She wore a grey buttoned shirt and loose grey trousers.

'Are you pretending to be a man?' I said.

She smiled, thin and quick, and turned to look at one of a bank of screens fixed to the wall behind a desk. 'You're alert, Konrad, so I won't patronise you. I looked in on your performance just now. You read much of the twenty-first century simply from glimpsing those human minds. You'll soon grow familiar with the nature of CCTV surveillance. Look at this screen top right. It shows the attic rooms where you have been at rest. Tell me what you notice.'

A view panned slowly across the top row of bunks, left to right, and then returned to show the lower row. Two other screens relayed similar scenes. Bodies were laid on them, mired in dust. Only one bed was empty of a body, presumably the one I had just vacated.

'Some of them I recognise, some I don't.'

'And?'

'You are clearly busy. When I came here I had a wide choice over where to lay myself down. Now there are no clear berths.'

'You are a rare opportunity. We have few returnees. You were struck by nothing else?'

I considered a while. 'A longing, perhaps, to resume my space up there. To lie down again and leave all this. My return feels like a mistake.'

'And if you did lie down again, you would be doing so exclusively among males. We have no resident females. I didn't expect you to notice that fact, but your disregard proves a point. These screens show the old world order; one that is male, tired and defunct. We don't segregate the sexes. We serve those who arrive. Males are bowing out. They grow weary like you. No, I am not pretending to be a man. I am a female assuming a natural position of power. You males retired from the scene. We females have chosen to be awake in this world where time operates, for our time has come.'

I had studied the screens while she spoke.

'Looking for someone?'

He wasn't there. 'Has anyone visited me?'

'Ah, so it's true.' She smiled. I was revealing too much. 'I have heard tell of your love story, but could not tell if it were true. You should write about it.'

'What good would that do?'

'Is love frailty or strength? You might teach us.'

'And you might answer my question. Did nobody visit?'

'Nobody? Not somebody?'

I do not care to be teased. She noticed the dilation of my eyes and retreated just in time.

'We have no news of Istvan, Konrad. He is part of your story, not part of our reality. We have looked for news of him, but we have found nothing. I'm sorry.' For this she was sombre, but she had the ability to flick between modes of discourse. She brightened on the instant and her voice moved up a register. 'But I can see we were right to call you. Your emotions are still in place. It seems what we have for you is indeed a love story.'

'And a birth.'

'So we understand.'

'Birthing is one of these new powers assumed by our females?'

'We have only rumours. We need the true story.'

I sighed. She looked at me, waiting for more.

'Perhaps this is one for a female to write. This no longer sounds like my world.'

'Maybe you're right,' she said. 'We need the best, but perhaps that's no longer you.'

She picked up a metal tablet from her desk and drummed her fingers across it. Other screens on the wall took light.

'Use your shades if you need to,' she said.

My eyes were adjusting. The light was bright but not painful. The pictures were of bodies slumped against brick walls or flat on stone walkways.

'We have access to police files.' Hence, I supposed, the coding on the images and the dates. 'These are all from the last ten days. All derelicts. All of them were young, both men and women and boys and girls too. The youngest was seventeen, the oldest twenty-four. You'll have noticed their faces.'

The eyes of the corpses were open, and their mouths fixed in what might have been smiles. Their clothes were pulled open about their necks, unbuttoned and sometimes torn.

The images changed to ones of animals.

'Some had dogs for company. These, you can see, were killed too.'

'All killed but none taken?'

'So it seems.'

'And there were no signs of blood on the scene?'

'Licked clean perhaps, and then washed. The police report no traces of saliva. The sheer numbers mean they are forced to investigate. All the deaths occurred within a 1500 metre radius of the Grand Place in Brussels. We track patterns of such deaths. The last occurred in Paris in 1996. Council members shadowed each other in the city as soon as the pattern was recognised. No aberrant greed was reported. They reported sightings of an Ancient. We have no further details. As you know, Ancients predate the Council and are under no obligation to register. Still, we have improved our surveillance techniques. We track all Ancients as we can. One relocated two weeks ago. To Brussels.'

'You have a name and location?'

'We have prepared a whole file.' She picked the folder off the desk to show to me.

'But this is death. You called me back to a story of birth.'

'Are the two ever far apart? The Ancient has a partner. She was once human. We accessed the name lodged in the meso-cortex of her brain. She is Sabaa. The Ancient and Sabaa have assumed tenancy of a vacant property in Bruges. They have established a local identity. The details go beyond the regular limits of politeness, acknowledging the neighbours and then moving on. She speaks of a son in England and tells stories of his achievements. They bought special meats from the butcher to celebrate his eighteenth birthday. It's a possible fantasy, but an eighteen year-old boy now would equate with conception in 1997. An Ancient was reported in Paris then, and this Ancient and his partner are in Brussels now. Derelicts die and a child is born. Is this what happened? Is there a link?'

'You've brought me back for this?'

'Back from where, Konrad? We fed you what stories we know. Are they true? You will tell us. You're the truth-teller. We have fed you many lines over the decades. You have responded to none till now. You are a writer of instinct. Your instinct is like you; it cannot die. Instinct brought you back.'

She pressed a button on her desk and the door clicked open. Viktor pushed his way through and shut it behind him, to protect me from the light.

'You have the car ready?' the Direktor asked. 'And the supplies?'

'Yes, ma'am.'

'Then it's best you go. Konrad will travel with you. He will take the time to decide. Provide him with nutrients along the way. He will need what energy he can muster.'

She handed me the file. 'Here you are, Konrad. It contains all we know. Do you have any questions?'

'A car?' I asked.

'Oh don't be naïve, Konrad. You can't skip a whole century then ask me to fill you in on the details. Work it out for yourself.'

Brussels

16

I SNACKED ON VENISON CARPACCIO, pressing the meat around my palate before sucking it down.

The car purred along. A glass screen separated the rear from the front. I could lower or raise it with the touch of a button. Outside beyond the tinted windows snowflakes streamed in headlights. The front was heated for Viktor while the rear seats were air-cooled for me. I could adjust my seat to lie flat if I wished, but chose to sit. We rushed from what Viktor informed me is now Germany into Belgium without stopping.

It was curious to be travelling at such speed. Humans have achieved superpowers through mechanical means since I was here last. Viktor hunched his body and gripped his wheel. I lowered my window and let snow fly in to chill my face.

I took a deep breath to allow the air to coat my lungs. And choked.

'Best wind your window up for a moment, sir.' Viktor spoke through an electronic speaker behind my head. 'The truck ahead is belching out diesel. These roadworks last a kilometre or so but I'll get past as soon as I can.'

The coughing felt good and my lungs were now burned with what he called diesel. When flush with the first bloom of immortality I tossed down poisons for the bravado of staying alive, and I acquired a refined taste for them. I stole my poisons from pharmacies, and now they float them in the air. Diesel particulates are cloying of course—for preference please give me poisons with more bite—but at least the century has come up with something different. I stuffed a wad of the raw venison into my mouth, sucked down the juices, and spat the residue onto the floor.

Viktor parked the car and slid down the screen. He stared at my face and then passed back a handkerchief made of paper. 'You might want to wipe your chin, sir,' he said.

I did as told. The handkerchief came away smeared with venison blood.

'The food was energising, sir?'

I burped in response. He had the grace to smile.

'May I take it that you are ready to commit to this project?'

I blinked at him.

'The story. This vampire baby story. You're ready to pursue it?'

'Oh that.' New stories bubble up as ideas and float merrily enough. Then you sense the work involved and the bubble bursts. True stories are so tediously hard to begin. 'I guess so.'

He ducked out of sight and then returned, passing across a package. 'Clothes, sir. A hooded coat and boots. A Scarf. Winter stuff.'

The coat was natural wool with a mustiness that was close to the smell of sheep. Boots were leather and thick soled. The scarf was black cashmere.

'You're costuming me as a prince of darkness,' I said. Not that I minded. Black suits me. Colours can leave me dizzy with distaste.

'We aim to keep you warm, sir. And discreet. Your skin is startlingly white still, hence the hood. The boots have a tread to keep you upright on ice. I had hoped to shadow you by car sir, but these conditions are lousy for vehicles and you'd be long gone while I was still skidding into parking places. You'd best get dressed. He could appear any moment.'

'He?'

Viktor nodded at a house across the way from where he had parked. It was a plain white bourgeois house of three storeys, part of a grand terrace. A window had been fixed into the steep tiled roof, illuminated by a dim light from inside. All other windows were shuttered.

'The Ancient. The house is vacant. Electricity's shut off. One of your kind inspected the room sir. That light comes from an oil lamp. We believe it is a plaything to attract moths. It keeps Sabaa amused while she's waiting. They've both been going out of an evening. She goes first. She's been out and come back. It's his turn now. Be ready, sir. I suggest clicking the car door open now so he won't hear you when he comes. You'll need to keep close by him, sir, in this snow.'

'I'll work from here,' I said.

'You have that reach?'

I glared at him.

'I'm not presuming, sir. I only know what your books have taught me. Beyond five hundred metres the control of projections grows wayward. Isn't that right? You'd want to be in full control when tracking an Ancient, I'd have thought.'

I began the contortions one needs to put on clothes and boots in the confines of a car.

'It will all come back to you sir. You've been dormant too long, that's all it is.'

Not dormant, you fool. Coiled. I dressed in the outer layers, tied the laces on the boots, and then pounced. The coat beat like a wing as I flapped it over the seats and followed. My thumbs pressed into Viktor's cheekbones as my fingers gripped his neck. 'You're condescending, Viktor.' I breathed the words as cold air against his face. 'That's my least favourite human trait.'

He tried to speak. The tip of his tongue stuck out from his mouth and trembled. I squeezed tighter and watched the veins bulge on the side of his neck. I'd had enough of his talking.

'Know your place, Viktor.' I slid his head down the car seat so his knees tucked in against his chest. 'Stay low. Stay out of sight. This car should look abandoned. He's coming.'

I understand Viktor filed a complaint about that evening. He believes he was mistreated.

What are we now, kestrels tethered to the human's gauntlet?

You must appreciate what I endured. The fool was spared.

I let go of Viktor's neck and climbed from the driver's side. The car door shut as the house door opened. Does Viktor really think I need his advice? I was tracking the Ancient even as Viktor muddied the air with his inane prattle. As the Ancient stood on the step and sniffed the air, I sniffed it too.

Warm-blooded creatures should not linger outdoors on nights as chill as this. Their smell hangs low and crawls along the streets. The pheromonal tracks of the Ancient's prey were strong.

This Ancient walked with a barrel-chested strut. In comparison I slunk. So did that make him better? I question the air of superiority these Ancients have, but let's consider his perspective.

He didn't see me. Why should he? I am like so many creatures he has turned. We bore him. He has lived through so many ages that events can only repeat themselves. Whatever might happen he has seen happen, so he lives in a world without consequences. It doesn't matter what he does, only that he does something.

He walked with purpose. I followed him through the European quarter and down the steps to the concrete entrance to the European Commission. The space was covered to give shelter from the snow if not the winds. A bottle of vodka lay alongside a man who was curled within a sleeping bag. A blanket was bunched on top of the bag, and a cardboard box flattened as a mattress beneath him. The Ancient bothered with no preambles. He placed his legs either side of the man and crouched.

The vagrant had instincts. He grabbed for his bottle and swung it. The Ancient caught the bunched fingers even as he stooped his head. The pressure of his bite kept the man's head still even as the feet kicked within the cocoon of their bag. The feed was casual, like a whisper of assistance, and as efficient as any I have witnessed. The Ancient drew back his head, wiped a handkerchief across his lips and then across the wound, and stood. He walked away without turning.

The vagrant's heart still pulsed. One beat, two, three and then it stopped. The Ancient had the best taste, the blood gushing with heartbeats into his throat. I was too slow. My bite was broad for I had to suck. The wound was far from clean.

I understand the mess I made forms part of another complaint. So what am I to do, run shy of my own gut instincts? You don't find the truth without mess.

I admit the feeding moment was a distraction. The Ancient was gone from sight when I looked up. Still, I had no choice. The Ancient had refuelled himself. You don't enter a duel and leave aside the weapons. I refuelled too.

My senses were heightened. I replayed the sound of his footsteps and heard the slight resonance of echo before it dimmed. He left no scent trail of course, we are hardly creatures of sweat, but the opposite was true. He cut a path through the cold city stink and this absence of smell still held traces.

I ran because the trail was fading but my direction was clear. He had gone underground.

A moving stairway, its steps made of grooved metal, sped my journey. A short bare corridor gave only one direction. A piebald dog was grubbing at a woollen bundle halfway along. The wool was a blanket and the bundle was a body. Its fist was still clenched around the dog's leash. The dog licked the face, its tongue rasping stubble, but to no effect. I checked for puncture wounds. They were clear. The Ancient hadn't waited for the pulse of blood to fill him this time, but bitten and sucked and run. I ran too.

The corridor ended in a chamber lined with ticket machines. Another body was slumped against a wall. I leaned over it. The vagrant's lips were burring in sleep.

Distant, and below me yet again, came a roar. A barrier was simple to vault. There were staircases to run down. I chose one. A train was pulling in alongside a track as I started down. Four people climbed on board. The Ancient was the most distant. He had undone his camel-hair coat so that it swung behind him as he moved. I stepped through an open door which sealed closed behind me and the train moved off.

I make guesses about the Ancients based on my own needs. Being accustomed to eternity you would think they would scorn this little buzz of mechanical speed thrusting passengers beneath a city's streets. Still, here he was, out for the ride. He had glutted on blood and was in a hurry.

Ancients don't break patterns nor do they act without clear logic. That much I accept. This pattern of gluttony and haste is not recorded in our true books. Its logic seems distorted because we view it through the veil of expectations. He was doing nothing we would expect. His purpose was radical. Fathom it and I would find a deeper truth than any we have known.

My own purpose was now clear. I was in pursuit of a story, and one that had eluded others. To tell it I would need the details.

The train made stops and some climbed aboard but none got off. When we approached Central Station everybody stood. They all had the same destination. From the anonymity of the cluster of people on the platform I watched the Ancient pass. It was safe to look. I would have stood out had I not stared at the Ancient. He drew everyone's attention.

You know his skin. I would call it Semitic; that dark olive hue, the skin of some pure-bred Persian or Babylonian perhaps. His hair is full, licked to a quiff and cut around his ears but plunging to sideburns that feather into stubble. There was my detail.

The stubble showed three days of human growth but how? I have not shaved in centuries and would not care to. He had changed his physiology to grow a beard. How and to what effect? Did taking on this aspect of the human condition mean assuming others? The stubble suggested aging if only by days. Debate persists about the ageing process. A current consensus suggests arresting it at eighteen. I would have guessed the Ancient as twenty-seven. He looked old enough to carry authority but kept some appeal of youth.

Where the humans around him were swaddled in layers of thickness his coat hung open. Beneath it a cotton shirt of no collar dipped its neckline towards his heart. The shirt expressed the musculature of his body, but it was the open skin of his neck and chest that won the real attention. Who could be so brazen against the cold? A snakeskin belt bound his waist, and its golden buckle was the head of a snake with fangs expressed. His jeans were cut to the shape of his legs and his shoes were snakeskin fashioned into pointed toes. They would not survive this one outing through snow. He had everyone's attention but it was not the attention he sought.

He had other prey.

17

PLASTIC SHIELDS GUARDED EXITS from the underground railway, but they opened on my approach to let me through. Beyond them the station was busy, but crowds parted like those shields as the Ancient walked through them.

Corridors here were broad and brightly lit. Vagrants sat and rattled cans in slots not occupied by stores, but the Ancient had had his fill. He exited the station and descended a hill. His shoes were absurd upon the ice, they could have given no traction, but he stepped with the confidence of bare feet on sand. I could keep close in the crowds. Snowflakes coated his hair white without melting. He brought up his hand to wipe them away.

Humans know these narrow streets as medieval relics. Even I from centuries ago remember them as old. When an Ancient wanders into the Gothic splendour of the *Grand Place* though, does he remember when it was a meadow or a swamp? He walked with absolute conviction of direction. I sniffed the air but found only a confusion of smells.

The street opened out into the square and still he didn't hesitate. The Grand Place was filled with a crowd who stared up at the façade of the town hall. Speakers broadcast songs about Christmas while a projection of reindeer pulled Santa's sleigh across the whole building. He had entered the scene of a sound and light display but he did not turn to see it. He kept up his pace, weaving a route around stationary people, and walked between the stalls of the Christmas market.

The stalls were brightly lit but he paid them no notice. He had spied his target now. His head found extra poise. He was on the scent.

I sniffed and found it too. I would never have known without his direction. The air was stiff with the animal smell of humans, their sweat and their farts and the tobacco and alcohol on their breath, the decay that's ripe in the elderly and the sugar burps of babies. Stifling odours that were layers of fried air from the cooking of waffles and potato fingers and sausages spitting fat. Inside this was the mingling of three thin clouds of cheap scent. And inside that was the blood of three girls just past the cusp of puberty.

They were young so Christmas was still essential. Each was decked in false furs, white dotted with large black spots with red ribbons tying capes around their collars and thick white tights beneath fur-hemmed skirts, everything white with large spots of black. Their minds were scattered with images from an animation film called *The 101 Dalmatians*. They were headed for a fancy dress party, and expected to be seen as three spotted puppies. One girl was tall and black-skinned, her hair gathered around her head like a halo formed from the night. Another was Asian, her hair thick on top and shaved close from a line with her tabs of ears, her head flicking around to notice faces in the crowd. The other was Caucasian, wispily tiny, her pale face dominated by a smile, her hair blonde and brushed to lie across her back.

I am told that even females of our kind are affected by the smell of menstrual blood. Young female humans with bonds so close that they harmonise their cycles can draw our kind through the streets. It's not pursuit. Our kind do not follow for the kill; they tend not to feed from grouped women in such instances. Power has somehow switched for a while, our kind simply caught in a tow of fascination. (I speak theoretically. I am mocked because I feel no such pull myself.)

The Asian girl noticed him first, her pert head turning above her thin shoulders. The Ancient paused and held her gaze. The crowd held itself clear for long enough so that the other two girls felt the heat of his attraction and turned his way.

The Ancient's coat had been open throughout his walk. The snow had wet his shirt so that his skin showed through. The Caucasian broke from her friends to step forward. She joked about the wetness and pulled off a glove and pressed her hand against his chest. Her hand jolted back at the cold of what she felt and the hardness, like reaching for flesh and touching bone. She laughed at the shock and a smile turned rigid on her face.

I expected the girls to walk away then, to turn and head off the *Grand Place* down one of the alleys, past the lights of restaurants until they were distant enough to feel safe. They would not be safe. But I was wrong. The Ancient spoke. The girls looked at each other, nodded, and followed him. It was as simple as that, like birds turning to roost when night sweeps in. They went where they were destined to go.

The bar overlooked the square and was packed with noise. The room inside was two storeys high, the upper level a broad gallery that looked down on the cavern of tables below. All chairs and stools were taken and the crowd, mostly men but with women pressed between them, stood in the spaces between. Yet even as the crowds had parted at the station, a way opened up inside. The Ancient slipped a word and some banknotes to a waiter who twisted a path to a broad oak staircase and led the girls and their young man upstairs.

I waited and climbed to the opposite gallery, and found a space in the shadows where I could stand and watch.

The waiter returned, his tray poised on the bridge of his stretched fingers, and placed four round glasses onto the table where the Ancient and the girls were settled. Each contained beer that was coloured red. From across the gallery I detected the flavouring of cherries. The Ancient placed his lips against the rim of his glass but did not drink. The girls spoke in turns. When one girl was talking the others drank, successions of sips. They told him of the party they were going to, and of the friends they would meet there. It was a private party but they could probably get him in. They would have to think up a name for his costume. Wasn't he almost chilled to death, out in the cold and wet to the skin?

He emptied his beer into their glasses and soon all the beer was gone. It was time for them all to move on. First they must go to the Ladies. They left their capes on their chairs as a promise that they would return.

The toilets were at this level. The one with a top hat and the letter H on the door was crowded but the women in this bar were fewer. An attendant took coins off the girls and they entered the Ladies on their own.

The Ancient allowed the door to close behind them and picked up their capes. He layered bank notes onto the coins in the attendant's plate. She understood and rose to stand guard outside the door once he stepped inside.

I waited. It did not take long. The Ancient emerged. His face was clean and his coat was buttoned. I needed to follow him, but I also needed to know. The attendant resumed her seat. I walked into the Ladies toilet, as though by mistake. The three girls had just stepped from their cubicles. They looked at me but did not take me in. Their eyes were glazed.

The smell of their blood charged the room. So the Ancient had fed, but had not bitten.

I pushed my way down the stairs and out through the Christmas crowds in the Square. This was a time for speed. I found an empty alley and slipped into overdrive.

18

VOYEURS FIND SEXUAL gratification in what they watch. You will accept I have no such motivation. My comfort zone sees me dormant, switched off from the ways of this world. The duty with which you have entrusted me is all that stirs me now. I watch so that you will know. I am the chronicler. That is all.

The grid of the streets of Brussels was still imprinted on my mind. A century changes details only. Snow reduced the traffic and left the sidewalks largely bare. I leaned my body forward to add momentum to my speed. I could not believe the underground train was quicker than I. I was back before he was. Surely.

Viktor sat upright, his knees jammed up against the steering wheel to form a work surface. Violet light shone from a screen to turn his face sepulchral. He was reading text which scrolled at the shift of his finger. This was the man whose job was to watch the front door. My face pressed against his window and even so I had to click my fingernails against the glass before he saw me. The man is pathetic.

I stepped back and removed the coat while he fumbled his way out of the car and opened the rear door. He took the coat from me and I climbed into the back and pulled off the boots and socks. Technically there's no extra difficulty in adding layers of clothing to projections, but I've never found that so. My aim is to receive impressions rather than make them. Clothes are a burden. I took off my jacket and pressed buttons that I thought would move my seat.

'You want it flat . . . sir?'

'Please, Viktor.' My voice was sharp but my language was polite. Despite what some say I can be conciliatory.

Viktor pressed commands into a panel and my seat lurched forward. I snatched up my bare feet to save them being crushed. My spine arced as my cushions reared and surged into a bed.

'You'll be sleeping, sir?'

'Working, Viktor. You can assure me, I presume, that the Ancient has not returned.'

'We are tracking him, sir. He entered the Metro. We have someone waiting on the platform for when his train arrives.'

'He's in a hurry. Why would he wait for a train?'

'They're quite frequent, sir. The wait isn't long.'

Men are such fools. They make us in their own image. An Ancient lives beyond time even more than I do. How could a wait be long or short? It is simply tolerable or not. I had seen the opportunities posed by the Metro system. Between trains the tunnels are empty. There is no need to wait.

'Meanwhile you have been observing the house?'

'We have him tracked, sir, don't you worry. His location is marked on a map on my screen.'

'Has the front door opened and closed, Viktor. That is all I need to know. The Ancient will wait for a train or he will not. He will let himself be seen or he will not. He came out of the house in substance. He will return as such. The door must open and close to let him in. That is what I need you to tell me. Has the door opened and closed?'

'I don't think so sir.'

'So this whole operation now relies on what you think?'

I let my scorn resound in my words.

What did I think? Three girls were now vacant-eyed and crying most likely, with arms thrown around each other in a toilet in an Inn in the Grand Place. They, like Viktor, had not the faintest idea what force they were encountering. Viktor had some surveillance officer waiting for the roar of an underground train arriving at the platform. The officer felt the wind perhaps but did not see the whirl of movement as the Ancient leapt from the tracks and passed behind his back. Such was my own intuitive guess. Viktor is an utter fool. Time is not on his side.

My projection rose even as my body lay still and spoke. It passed through the door of the car and its feet left no marks as they walked across the snow. I did turn to find Viktor watching me. I had allowed some friction to come between us. My body was still grumbling in its brain even as it rested on the back seat of the car. This was no use. I needed to be clear.

I bowed my body to Viktor, and then stood and watched and waited. He nodded his head to me. My brain niggled for a moment about the indignity of bowing to humans, and then let it go.

Good. I was clear to proceed.

Fully integrated into my projection, I turned back to the house and passed through its front door.

I was spied upon when I was human. No-one that I know of has been interested in me since. I believe this is standard for our kind. It is we who pass through walls and into bedrooms to spy on others. This was to my advantage. The Ancient and his female would not expect my intrusion.

Against me was the fact that they were experts in any tricks I might deploy. I needed to keep this act of surveillance as simple as possible.

I trod the stairs. Floating has never been my style. My projections are ambassadors for my body. I have them proceed through normal physical motion as much as possible, so that the brain in my actual body keeps a tight rein on their experiences. The simple process of moving one foot after another, of maintaining notional contact with the ground, steadies me. I pay a keener regard to my surroundings than if I succumbed to flashes of speed.

For now, I sniffed.

I ignored the layers of nostalgia that come with the scents of an old house and focussed on the present. The result was dizzying.

I sniffed, of course, for blood. That primal instinct is too strong to deny. There it was, streaming down the stairs from the upper layers of the house.

So be it, you would think. I am a balanced being, I moderate my appetites and blood need not excite me. At the heart of this smell, gusting toward me, was that peculiar excrescence of a vaginal blood surge.

This particular smell is not on record. This vaginal surge came from the blood of one of our kind. It was raised to near the temperature of human blood but was composed of the headiest layer of all blood types, the blood of ages. This was our kind, a female of our kind, primed to sexual arousal.

And I responded.

It triggered a quickening in me, some electric pulse of yearning in my brain. The smell, its heat, its sheer liveliness, stripped me from my senses.

I visit human mindscapes but find no attachment there. This, I swear, swung me back to that noxious mindset of my own time in a human state, that melting of a body by desire. I believed it was transcended, this trembling toward oblivion, but no. It's merely stifled. The whole procreative folly is seeded somewhere in our DNA.

Did my projection lose its form? I don't know. I was swirled out of sense for a while. I pulled back from smell. Sight returned. I was on the stairs of an unfamiliar house. And there was sound. I tuned in.

'Is that you?'

The call came from the top of the stairs. This was the voice of Sabaa. She couldn't have heard me. That was impossible, surely. I was soundless.

I stretched my hearing wider. Pushed it back through time. A door had opened and slammed closed. A heavy tread cracked in the timbers on the bottom steps. He was back. The Ancient was climbing the stairs.

I let myself run, still mimicking regular motion but four steps at a time. The door to their room was open but I dropped to the ground and crawled in the shape of a shadow as I passed it. Sabaa was watching the doorway. She must not see me.

The skirting boards were high. I reached my hands through them to the wooden floorboards beyond, pressed my head through the wall's wood and plaster and eased myself behind. This was their room. Ahead was their bed. I could slide beneath it but from there I could only hear. I needed to watch.

A large walnut wardrobe stood to my right. I slid through its side. It was roomy enough and the old wood was warped. The double doors were closed, but left a crack. I lowered myself upon a bed of old shoes and looked out.

Sabaa's hair was loose and long, with straight black tresses hooked behind her ears and touching her shoulders. The mattress was bare but she had a pillow wedged between herself and the oak headboard. She was reclining rather than sitting, as though she had sagged with the boredom of waiting. Her legs were parted and her knees bent to push her upright. She was naked.

Her skin was white and showed no sign of cuts or abrasions. She was adequately fleshed; though not rounded, her bones were not prominent and her muscles gave some definition. I took special note of her breasts. They were small but full, the veins showed their map and the nipples were dark and erect.

An oil lamp did glow on a side table, as was reported, but I saw no moths about it. Enough illumination filtered up from the street so I thought at first it was there for effect, the lamp's soft lighting some concession to romance. She looked toward the door as the Ancient came in.

'You found them?' she said. 'You're ready?'

They chose to speak rather than scan each other's minds. I can speculate as to why but prefer merely to record here. The Ancient walked toward her and came into my view. Beside their bed he leaned toward her. She turned her face to his, but both stopped short of a kiss. He opened his mouth and breathed at her. I saw the slight gust of steam from his breath so he had some heat in him. Her face wrinkled as though in disgust but as she pulled it back she smiled.

'You could have wiped your mouth,' she said. 'You're still sticky with them.' She ran her hands through the wetness of his hair and then used her fingers to wipe at his lips and his chin. 'How many were there?'

'Three.'

'All young?'

'As soft and silly as babies.'

She pulled open his mouth and pressed her nose against his teeth. 'Not babies,' she said. 'They were ripe.'

What she smelled had satisfied her. She pulled up her legs so as to kneel on the bed and cupped her hands around the globe of the lamp. He straightened and pulled off his camel coat. The coat in hand, he turned to the wardrobe where I was hiding.

I had not planned for this. Habits are engrained by centuries and it seemed the Ancient would hang his clothes properly even as he stripped. I reached back a leg, out through the rear of the wardrobe, breaking through the wall, setting my toes on the floor of the corridor. I needed to stay but mustn't be found. He looked my way and seemed to stare straight at me. I tensed myself to withdraw.

He took two steps toward me.

'Now,' Sabaa said. 'I'm ready.'

He draped his coat over the knob of the bedstead. Crossing his arms, he tugged the shirt up over his head. It ruffled his hair but he did not trouble to straighten it. He laid the shirt on a wooden chair and then prised the shoes from his feet and slid them under the bed. His feet were bare. He undid the gold snake buckle and let his belt hang loose, easing the jeans down across his thighs.

He was naked underneath. His penis was not shrivelled as one might expect in such cold, but nor was it in any way erect.

I noticed what I could.

His balls did not hang, they were still compact against his body. The penis was of reasonable length and seemed heavy. It was circumcised, fitting the Semitic roots suggested by his skin tone. His chest was hairless but the bush of hair at his groin was thick and dark.

He stepped from the jeans, laid them too on the chair, and turned from me. His hands were still by his sides. He made no attempts to arouse himself. She looked his way. Her inspection was brief.

'Good,' she said.

Would I say good, with my view from behind?

In human terms, yes. His back had the musculature that shimmers even in repose, his buttocks were tight, his thighs were broad. Most telling for me was his stance, the even distribution of weight on his feet. It is easy to disregard a body and sense it as a vehicle. Here he inhabited it in full consciousness, and harnessed the power inside of his skin. He was rendering himself animal.

'Here,' she said. 'Come.'

Sabaa's hands were now warmed. She turned from the lamp and opened her legs wide once again. He shifted to the mattress, knelt on it, and moved himself close. Still supported by the headboard she reached forward and curved her warmed hands around his penis. Her arms did not move, she was offering no friction, just this holding. They looked into each other's eyes.

'Aah,' she said, and smiled.

He laughed, just a snort of breath.

She pulled her hands back to the mattress and slid herself down so as to be flat. He pushed back his legs to lie straight above her. Neither stroked the other.

Her hands stayed by her sides as he reached to guide himself inside her. I saw no sign of lubricant. Entry seemed stiff for a moment but he pushed with his buttocks and was in.

His hands pressed on her shoulders. It was a quick rutting. I would say thirteen thrusts, perhaps seventeen, who knows, I was watching but not counting. He roared so loud I am told my body in the car juddered at the sound.

I lost my own senses for a while and became a dark presence in the wardrobe. Then I was back, almost instantly back.

He withdrew from her and kneeled once again. His back tensed as he leaned forward. He bent his head and pressed his face into her vagina. Was it a kiss? I don't know and cannot even guess.

'There,' he said and stroked his hands down her sides.

She was trembling. His touch was easing her.

She stayed silent. I was tempted to enter her mind but held back. He turned to the side and lay down beside her, linking his left hand with her right. I did check, raising my head just enough to peer over the bedstead. He was slightly tumescent still, but it faded as I watched.

'It's taken?' he asked. He had been scanning her, I can see that now. He was checking. Her hand flexed in his and he squeezed back. 'Now be still. Rest.'

'We'll keep this one?' she asked, turning her head to his. 'I will give birth to it and we will keep it with us? We won't abandon this one?'

'Somehow,' he told her, and squeezed her hand again.

Sabaa relaxed, settling her head back on the pillow, and closed her eyes. What was she thinking? It seemed right to know. I slipped inside her mind.

I expected peace, but the emotional register was different. Its tone was of grief and loss and longing. The image was hazy, a sweep of fog, but I focussed and it became clear. This was no lack of clarity but real fog sweeping a landscape. I was inside a memory. She stood on a shore and stared out to sea. Something was out there, something she loved.

The memory snapped to blank. Sabaa was back in the present. From inside her mind I was staring at the wardrobe. I flashed back into seeing. The Ancient sat upright in the bed. He looked straight at me. He too had been in her mind and found me watching.

He was slow, still rooted in the animal and therefore locked consciously within his skin. His projection rose, as naked as him. I watched a moment, curious, fascinated, and then reached my leg back into the corridor.

As he moved forward I withdrew.

19

RECUMBENT IN THE BACK of Viktor's car I could have jarred myself awake. My projection would have evaporated. All that I had witnessed would have scattered. My projection carried the details. I needed to round the journey and bring it home.

I ran it down the stairs and it barely touched the ground. It landed and darted at each of the narrow turns.

With humans there are no chase scenes. Walk through walls and they will not follow. The Ancient knew no such limits. Did I think his projection would come charging after me, his naked figure leaping down the stairs, set to pounce if I moved too slowly? Such is fantasy. I am a writer of truth not fantasy. Projections do not grapple and fight.

Yet I ran.

On the final stretch of staircase I sped down the steps. The door was ahead. Walk through it and I would be clear. I knew no better.

It passed me from behind. I slowed but not because it held me, more because it contained me. All freedom to move stayed mine, but I had nowhere left to go. The door had gone. All surroundings had gone. In my vision was a colour, nothing but a colour, the colour of olive-toned flesh.

I knew before I could understand. The Ancient's projections were not like mine. My projections took my shape and size and looked like me. His knew no such restrictions. It inflated to fill the house, and to find me out.

The colour grew denser like particles fusing. He was focussing and condensing form. I moved one leg and then another. My run was now a walking shuffle. Stay steady and I could carry all that I had witnessed back with me. The Ancient was now a miasma of flesh. He was a thickening cloud and I would walk through it. Keep moving I told myself, keep moving. My body lay in a car outside. It was a natural attractor. I must go steady and lock onto that. Step by step I moved forward.

The miasma dimmed. Flakes of white drifted through its edge. I was outside. It was snowing. The car waited across the road.

I ran, through the metal of the door and into my body.

'Drive, Viktor, drive!'

I swear he was asleep. His body jerked as I sat up and yelled in the seat behind him. He had kept the engine purring for its heat and so was quick to react. The wheels skidded for purchase on the icy surface. He steered into the road and stopped.

A figure stood ahead of us. The Ancient, naked, his right hand held out, a finger pointing.

'Drive, Viktor, drive!'

'But sir . . . '

'Watch the snow, you fool, can't you see? Does it catch in his hair? Of course not. He's a projection. It passes through him. Drive, Viktor, drive. Drive through him.'

He turned to look behind and considered reversing.

'Forward!'

The wheels skidded, the car lurched. The Ancient was smashed into a daze of cloud and then we were through. The road was clear of all but the snowstorm.

I yelped.

Viktor could not know, he could not see, he merely drove. The Ancient had driven his projection into my skull.

'Scum,' he said.

My visual was of his mouth moving. I saw nothing else, felt only the pain he drilled into my mind, and I heard his words.

'You daytrip into our minds and steal our memories? You get off on that, you find it fun? Let me strip that memory back, scum, with every other relic of your existence. I'll blank your brain and leave you gaga. But first, scum, come back. Heave this sick body of yours up the stairs. We'll talk.'

And he was gone.

'Where to, sir?' Viktor asked.

I opened my mouth but had no words. I left the fool to drive.

We parked. It seems Viktor is unable to drive and think. He turned on the tablet computer that is a substitute for his brain. A search engine had scanned European newspapers for news items of eighteen years before.

'Read it to me, Viktor.'

'Seven babies are listed as abandoned that week,' he began, and droned on through details scattered through the cities of Europe. I left a residual part of my brain to scan his mouthings for relevance.

'That one,' I snapped. It was obvious the moment I heard it. 'I need full background details and everything known about the kid since.'

It took him twenty minutes. A further two minutes told him of a store that was open and available to print out what he had found. A woman's voice spoke directions from a device on the dashboard, and we crossed Brussels and back in a further fifty minutes.

It was before dawn. I slid three vials of blood from the car's supplies into my jacket pocket. The sheaf of newly printed papers when loosely rolled fit within the inside pocket of my overcoat.

I crossed the street. Snow crunched beneath my shoes. I didn't knock on their door. I was expected. The doorknob was topped with snow. I closed my hand around it and turned and the door opened. Stairs creaked under my feet.

20

THEY HAD DRESSED; the Ancient in his clothes from the night before, Sabaa in a red tartan shirt worn over jeans. Her hair was hooked and pinned behind her ears. Both sat on wooden chairs at the far side of a round table. A third chair was set to face them.

'I'm Konrad . . . ' I tried.

'We know who you are,' the Ancient interrupted. 'You're Fool-for-Love.'

It was a cheap jibe. Still, if we were going to use personal knowledge against each other I had come well-armed.

I pulled the vials from my inside pocket. 'Do you have glasses?'

Sabaa checked for assurance. The Ancient nodded. A range of glasses stood on a shelf near the window. She brought across three, each mired in dust, and I poured.

The Ancient sniffed. This was good blood, Viktor had assured me, none of your plasma. The Ancient sipped and she and I followed.

He gulped, somewhat noisily. I watched the Adam's apple flex in his throat. It was a distraction and it fooled me. He turned to face the female. She seemed to be holding a smile in her cheekbones, and then pursed her lips as though ready to kiss.

Sabaa had not swallowed and I had not noticed. The blood spurted from her mouth with such force it stung my eyes.

I was blinded. As I wiped my hands across my face, she screamed at me in a stream of language I did not recognise.

'As she spits out your blood she will spit out your flesh, but that will not help her rip the taint of your presence from her mind,' the Ancient translated. 'You slid over her bed and raped her memories. Now you will pay.'

I licked my fingers clean and, with my hands now moist, wiped my face again. Her mouth dripped blood but she was not so fastidious. Spittle from her invective splashed my cheeks. Her eyes were dark. Her breath smelt blacker still, with the stench of her leathered guts churning.

'You spit on me,' I informed her, 'and you spit on the Council. I am their representative.'

Her mouth screamed louder and faster, close to my face so I saw nothing else, and then she pulled back. She was giving herself room. Her hand moved so fast I did not see it. It imprinted itself on my left cheek, the hand so small and the slap so fierce.

I managed to keep to my seat.

'The Council has legitimate concerns.' I kept my voice calm. My job was to observe her anger. 'The spate of recent deaths threatens the feeding pattern of all of us. We survive on discretion. Were you a Council member we would have asked you to report on your actions. You have always refused to join.'

'*Always*,' the Ancient said, as calm as an observer himself. 'You use that term like you have a hold on time. I saw you come and I will see you go. You are not part of my always. You are a blip.'

'Other Ancients have joined.' It was not quite true. I reflected, and saw no value in the lie. 'Well, they've affiliated. One once attended a meeting. As the direct take of an Ancient I was not required to join, but chose to do so.'

'An Ancient is your term, not mine. An Ancient is anything older than you. That's how you see it. It is juvenile.'

'Then teach us better. Join us.'

'And accept your rules? What will you do when I break them? Punish me? Of course not. You have no such powers. You're like children who throw pebbles at the sea for making their feet wet.'

'You speak of children,' I said. 'Then so will I. I speak of Christopher.'

They both went still at the name. I don't think they recognised it but they sensed my intent.

'He goes by Chris. He's your son. You will admit the very existence of an Ancient's child is cause for Council concern. We knew nothing of this potential for breeding.'

The Ancient's hand had moved without my noticing and settled on the back of Sabaa's head. His touch stilled her. He spoke.

'And so your Council sent a voyeur to spy on us. What have you learned, Fool-for love? Nothing.'

'We know about your son.'

'You have data. You have a photograph. Your human driver found these for you on a cursory trawl of the Internet. I have been in his mind. At least he has bothered to assemble the data on our boy into a simple-minded story. Your mind is otherwise. It is a sewer. Nothing inside it is clean. You loved and lost. That is your entire story. You use it to taint everything you see. You watched us naked. The scene is on replay inside your head. It is one of many scenes. You fill yourself with others' lives and yet your life stays empty. Now you have a picture of our boy. It's curled up in your inside pocket, with sheets of facts about him. You think that gives you power, that you have found our son and we have lost him. You have come to do a trade. Good looking, is he?'

I blink.

'Be honest, Fool-for-love. You're still pinned to human desire. It's what makes such a fool of you.'

He withdrew his hand from Sabaa's head. I was right. He had been holding her in check. She moved fast, but not to strike me. She grabbed the papers from my pocket and stared at the photo of her son.

The photo came from a social sharing website called Facebook, Viktor had explained to me. It lacked what he termed megapixels so the quality of the enlargement was poor. He forwarded it to digital technicians for enhancement. The resultant image was quite crisp.

Chris was in evening dress. From the photo tag on the website I knew this was the leaving ball at a High School he had once attended. The photo was taken some hours in. The boy to his left wore one of those prim little bowties that come on a piece of elastic. Chris had bothered to tie his own but now it hung loose and the top two buttons of his shirt were open. His neck was taut, his head leaning forward while his arms were linked around the shoulders of the boy to his left and a girl to his right, her dress of red sequins as tight and close as skin. His hair was thick and dark, the fringe waxed into spikes. His mouth was open as though to shout. His eyes were red.

'So that's our boy,' Sabaa said. 'He's beautiful.'

How old was Sabaa? She is no Ancient, but while we have her human name we have no record of her turning. In looks she was perhaps two years older than her son.

'I thought he would be taller,' Sabaa said.

'He was malnourished,' I said. 'I understand he's lucky to be alive after the way he was abandoned.'

'He's still growing.' The Ancient was not arguing with me. He spoke as though I was not there. 'This photograph was taken some months ago. He's taller now.'

Sabaa was not listening. I spoke in order to goad her. It had worked.

'He was not malnourished.' She knew the word but spat it out as something distasteful. 'He was strong.'

'He had the body of a baby two days old. Scrawny at that, something that had come sickly out of the womb. But his eyes were dark not baby blue. That meant he was months old.'

'Ha! You think you know things? You know nothing. He was born with black eyes. And they focussed. When I wiped the eyes clean and he opened them he saw me. He recognised me. He was two days old when we left him, but he will never forget his mother. Isn't that so?'

She looked at the Ancient. He held her gaze a while then turned to me. 'Go. Leave us.'

'A cigarette saved a baby's life,' I resumed. 'That was one headline. A man came out on deck for a smoke. The deck was icy and snow was blowing across it. He was pushing the door to go back inside but the door was heavy. It stuck for a moment. And in that moment some movement caught his eye. Two figures in black, he said. They climbed onto the railings and jumped. He moved to look, but could barely keep to his feet as he tried to cross the deck. Then he saw a bundle on the ground, wrapped in purple cloth. It was moving. He picked it up and it grew still. Eyes stared out at him, your baby's eyes. He pulled the cloth back and touched his fingers to the baby's cheeks. The skin was cold.'

'You! You sneak into our room. You bring us this picture.' Sabaa held the photo of her son flat, spit into its face, crumpled it up and threw it at me. It hit my chin and fell to my lap. I put it back into my pocket. 'We want nothing from you. You know nothing. Get out.'

'It seems you can fuck and spawn,' I tried. 'That's clever. But it's animal. You were never a mother. You left your baby to die.'

The Ancient held up his right hand. In truth he was right. I was overstepping my role. It is fine to goad people in interview, but only once flattery is exhausted.

'Fool-for-love speaks,' he said, 'and he expects us to respect his judgment.' He reached his hand forward and stroked my cheek. 'You are so young, Konrad. You don't know yourself and yet you seek to know others. Tell me what it is you need to know.'

He kept his hand on my cheek. His face was close. In the black of his eyes I lost my hold on speech. Words were there, they evanesced for my attention and then burst. I could not harness any logic.

'You poor thing,' he said, and pulled his hand away.

I had said nothing, but was left sitting in that blank space that follows confession, when all the power of maintaining an outer lie is spent and you are open and blank and vulnerable.

My mind came back and I found them talking. When she calls him a name it is some combination of a guttural click, vocalised breath and telepathy which I cannot transcribe.

I asked them their names directly. She clicked her fingers by her forehead, and he arched an eyebrow as though disappointed that I should interrupt them with something so naïve.

'What names do you put in documents, such as your passport and your residence card?' I persisted.

'This conversation is absurd. You expect us to comply with human records. What species are you? Why not have us sniff each other's arses like dogs? It's about as relevant.'

'But everybody has a name.' I turned to Sabaa. 'As a human, they gave you an Arabic name to be like the wind. My Council who know nothing have found that out. Your people called you Sabaa. If you had a dog, I am sure it also had a name. Even dogs have names.'

The Ancient stared at me. He was right to do so. I was being stupid.

'You're the writer. Make up whatever lies you want. Turn us into your dogs. Give us names.'

'So I will call your wife Sabaa. And you, what does your wife call you?'

The Ancient grouped his fingers by his lips and then flicked them toward me. 'Wife!' He threw me the word. 'Again and again, these words of human reference. You, little writer, need a break from language.'

In demonstration, my vision opened as though my eyes were unglued and then it promptly went spinning unfocussed around a room that was not the one I was in. He had returned me to the moment of my human birth and all its chaos. It is as though memories are seeded and he can reach through time and break the capsule so that what is past floods the present. I believe I cried, a gasp of first breath, and then I was back. It was a sharp lesson. I said no more.

'Fool-for-love was taken too young.' He had turned from me to report to the female. 'He was birthed but forgets it. He can kill without dying. He crouches in the wardrobe to watch us mate and learns nothing but shame. You frighten him, Schätzschen.' And so he did have a name for her. I presume it is a pet name for 'my little treasure', drawn from *mein Schatz*. 'Have pity. Teach him just a little.'

Sabaa opened her mouth. Our kind taste life and it is sweet. Something in her had curdled. This process of birthing steamed in her guts. The gust behind her words made me wince.

'Nothing will teach him,' she said. 'I will tell him of my boy. Let the story consume him.'

21

SABAA AND THE ANCIENT told me this tale of how they met. They spoke of the birth of their child, and how they abandoned him on the deck of a boat. They spoke to me of standing on a winter beach. They stared out at sea toward the life their boy would live in England.

A biographer knows the right time to leave. Questions are exhausted and some clarity of understanding has been achieved.

That's in normal circumstances. I blinked at the attic room. In my head I was still on that Zeebrugge beach on that winter day of eighteen years ago.

'So you have what you need?' the Ancient said. They both stood up, as though I was dismissed. 'You remember our pact? We have told you his story as far as we know it. Now you leave him alone.'

Pact? What pact?

I asked myself the question and the memory came. It was as clear as he said. I was a biographer in search of a story. So long as they told me all they knew I would leave it there. The Ancient made the terms very clear. I would write up my tale and allow their boy to live his life without further interference from my kind. The boy was human. Outside of the account of his birth, his life was outside my remit.

We shook hands.

Did we? It seemed a curiously conventional thing to do. And would I not remember the touch of his hand?

As I looked for the memory of a handshake, it came. His thumb hooked with mine. I felt the firmness of his grip, his left hand came in to hold my arm a moment and we looked into each other's eyes. I nodded, gave my assent, and he let go.

The memory was too complete. The Ancient saw me look for a memory, and supplied it.

'There was no such pact,' I said.

Sabaa had returned the glasses to the shelf and was looking around. I knew what she was about. They were vacating. She picked up both their chairs and set them back beside the window, positioning their legs in the holes they had left in the dust when first moved. Everything would be left in place as though they had never been there. She came and stood before me. She needed my chair.

I needed to sit.

'We agreed nothing.' I have never sleepwalked, but that was close to my experience now. You inhabit one world and then wake to find you are somewhere else entirely. There is no connection. 'You're planting memories in my head.'

'Of course.' He stared at me. 'You're a biographer. That's what you need us to do.'

'I want real memories. Not false ones.'

The Ancient drew back his chair and placed it to sit opposite me. My hands were resting on my lap. He picked them up and held them.

'Those memories were real. It was good that you had us share them. We had never done so. Now we each know the full story of our boy; what we tried for, what we hoped for, what we did. Thank you.'

He squeezed light pressure into my hands and coaxed me to look up at him. I did so and I smiled, just a slight fond twinge of a smile. I confess that here. I am too easily charmed. He smiled in response and as I recall it while writing I smile again. I took pleasure in his seduction even as I calculated its effects. My smiles are as innocent as a baby's even as my mind trips in to analytical mode. Those smiles were our only form of agreement. We shook hands. In acting as I did I would betray no pact.

'You're good at your art.' He squeezed my hands and let them go. 'I see why you have been given your role of telling the true stories of our kind.'

It was 'our kind' now, not 'your kind'. I noted the switch. Flattery is one of the keenest tools of my trade. I know when it is being used against me even as I enjoy it.

'We had no story till you came. Just fractured memories. As we spoke with you, you pieced those memories into a whole.'

Did they speak with me? I wasn't sure.

And even as I wondered the memories came in. I watched Sabaa's face as she told me her tales. The Ancient had abandoned his memories of the time on board ship along with his projection. Sabaa had abandoned her body so as to keep with her projection and nurse those memories. She had never told him what happened. As she spoke she glanced his way, checking on his responses to this new information. Otherwise she looked to her left, staring into some near distance as respondents do in recall of tender moments, her eyes smarting with tears. She wiped these tears away with the back of her hand.

It was very touching. I should write such details into my account somehow. Sabaa stood now, her impatience with the whole scenario close to anger. Her hands were on her hips but they were not resting; their fingers clawed into her flesh. She looked up into the corner of the room, her chin thrust high, desperate for this whole charade to be over and all of us on our way.

Who would have thought that such a creature could have opened her heart to me in the way she had?

It was impossible. Those eyes never cried. Sabaa loathed me. She would give me no confidences. My memories of her telling me her most tender secrets were simply implants.

As the suspicion settled, a challenge to it arose in my mind. Of course Sabaa loathed me. It's natural to resent the person who conjures secrets from you. Subjects always come to hate their biographers.

I shook my head hard. Shaking didn't clear it. Holding the back of the chair for support I stood up.

'You're good,' I said. 'Did we talk at all? Am I even here now? You've been reading every doubt that arises in my head and feeding me some visual image in response. You and I never touched till you took my hands just now, yet I remembered the pressure of your handshake. The whole story of your baby's birth and its early days is clear in my head. There are no gaps to fill. It is lucid and coherent. How did you do that? Was any of it real? Was it a tale you told or did you have me do all the work? Did you feed me snippets and leave my imagination to invent connections as my narrative line required them? What do you want of me?'

Sabaa looked at me then. She clicked her fingers in the air. The sharp sound was my extinction. She was done with me. A few words of her unknown language gave the Ancient some instruction. He did not bother to translate.

'We want that you leave our boy alone,' he said instead. 'You write about your kind. This is nothing to do with you. Our boy is eighteen. Next year he will be nineteen. In eighty years or so he will be dead. Let him be.'

'He carries your genes. He is the son of an Ancient. That is coded into him. Surely that's of interest? How does such a genetic code play out in a human life? I would like to meet such an eighteen year-old. The story of such a young man would be extraordinary.'

'You will do wrong, Fool-for-love.' The Ancient's tone had changed. We were no longer in dialogue. They were dismissing me. Sabaa blew out the light in the globe lamp as he spoke on. 'Have them send someone else to investigate our boy if they must. You are far too partial. Biographers belong on the sidelines. You yearn to be included in the story. And just look at yourself. Look where your emotions have led you. You're tragic, Fool-for-love.'

I wonder still how I might have responded. As the Ancient's words landed, someone knocked on the bedroom door. The door was open, but a hand had reached in to knock on it even so. I turned and saw Viktor.

'Sir,' he said. I believe he was addressing me, but as he rose from his low bow his eyes took in all three of us. His face was lit by spectral light from below. He had brought his tablet computer up from the car. 'Excuse this interruption. My news is urgent I'm afraid.'

Viktor held the tablet out in front of him and shuffled forward, his eyes focussed on the floorboards. When he reached level with me, he paused. I looked into the light of the screen.

'It's the morning newspaper, sir. From here in Brussels. I've checked, and the story has already been picked up by a blogging site in California. The link to the picture has been tweeted.'

The image was of poor quality, but it gave enough clues for me to place it. It was the entrance to a subway: the Schuman station near the Parliament building. I knew it because I had been there earlier that night. And my visit was what it showed. A tall figure in a black hood reached down to probe the wounds in a derelict's neck.

'Nobody has yet used 'vampire' in a headline but it won't be long I'm afraid, sir.'

'But it wasn't me.'

'I worry that your pleas of innocence would not stand up to too much forensic and medical scrutiny, sir. We've been feeding into police communications systems. A team of officers is focussing on the European Quarter. It seems you have been caught on several snatches of CCTV footage. They track your passage away from and back to here, while showing you in the vicinity of another suspicious death.'

'I was conducting my investigations. It's my job.'

'Do you see what happens, Fool-for-love, when you decide to become part of the story?' The Ancient slid his arms into the sleeves of his coat. 'You have your story. Write it up, and go back to sleep. That's my advice. You are not adapted for the twenty-first century.'

Sabaa left while we were still speaking. She wore no coat, just the checked shirt and jeans, and carried no bag. Viktor bowed his head to her as she passed.

The Ancient sniffed at the air. He was taking a pheromonal reading of her passage across the room. Something disturbed him.

'Tonight was precious,' he told me. 'You have upset us more than you know.'

Viktor bowed from the waist as the Ancient passed. We heard him descend the steps until his tread was muffled in the snow outdoors.

'Sir?' Viktor said, when I didn't move.

'They'll be followed?'

'There are those who are able to do that, sir, without bringing undue notice. If you would follow me to the car? It's snowing but the main roads from the city are still clear. I understand your research is to continue.'

East Yorkshire

22

'WE'LL BE LEAVING FROM Calais, sir, rather than Zeebrugge,' Viktor advised me. 'It's less convenient but there's a sailing in four hours and it seems best to get you to Britain before the media frenzy takes hold. I expect a tightening of border controls.'

'And why Britain?' It's not a question I had bothered with in my previous years of existence.

'You'll be going to find the baby.'

'Baby?'

'That ferry baby I've been doing the research on. That Chris. He's eighteen years-old now of course. Some would say that's grown up.'

'And what do you see me doing when I find him?'

'You'll be getting his story from him, sir. It's not often you get to interview a vampire baby.'

Viktor's enthusiasm is tiresome.

'Are you working on instructions, Viktor?'

'Yes sir. Yours sir.'

'I've issued no orders.'

'I'm sorry sir. I presumed. Since you were talking aloud and there's only me here to hear you, I thought you were talking to me. I'd best go find him, you said, sir. Now. Tonight.'

So that was me? I had heard somebody prattling. I was so used to lying as though dead, I had forgotten that my thoughts were reconnected to my mouth. It was true that I had decided to go and find the boy. I pulled my mind back to the moment I had given voice to the decision and then cast back further to see what had prompted it.

There it was. The call. I had written about it as experienced by others without ever experiencing it myself. The call was thin because it had to reach across the North Sea, but it was amplified by my spine. I would say that it called my name, but in the way a mother calls her baby's name before it distinguishes language. It resonated through me. Linked to the call was a magnetic pull, some intense attraction north north-west.

'Are you sure this is the fastest route?' Viktor was driving west. It was wrong.

'No route will get you to England quicker.' The wipers moved fast to keep the snow from the windscreen. 'The train line's blocked east of Lille but they're keeping the highways open and the ferries are running.'

Then it would have to do. I needed to be quick yet I also needed time. The call had faded the moment I voiced my intention but the magnetic pull remained. In place of the call was a sorrow so immense that it contained me. I say sorrow but perhaps it is compassion, for the one emotion is simply an inversion of the other and they are essentially the same. It was sorrow for the whole mess of the human condition. I don't usually let it affect me, but till then I had never recognised my option to mount a rescue. With just one bite I had the power to lift a being from that human realm, the way an Ancient once had lifted me.

This was Chris. It was his call from over the water. I knew this as keenly as I had known anything. Chris was there to be taken.

'Your passport, sir.'

Viktor had pulled up in a line of traffic waiting to drive past a concrete hut. I saw documents pass from the vehicles to the hut's open window, and then back again.

'Passport?' I could have raided Viktor's mind for the explanation, but frankly I find his mind a sordid place to visit. It is a far from clean environment, over-sullied by imagination. He had handed me a small booklet with a burgundy cover and an eagle stamped in gold as its illustration. *Reisepass,* it declared. *Europäischer Union. Bundesrepublik Deutschland.* I can see why the Ancient resisted the limitations of a name. The notion of a booklet that permitted one to travel is in itself ludicrous. These labels for a whole national identity were an invention since my last episode of consciousness.

'It's not a forgery. We have one of your kind positioned in government who is able to supply us with genuine documents. Usually you apply in person and then you supply your fingerprints. We took the liberty of taking impressions from your fingers while you were still in your bunk. The photo is from a wax model we had made up. It's impressively accurate, I would say. The biometric aspects of the passport are as good as can be but it's best we don't test them. Your kind don't do well in optical scans. I wouldn't trust you to an airport but these seaboard European controls are more basic. Give me back the passport if you would, sir. I'll draw just close enough so they can see you but just short of letting them enjoy full scrutiny. I may have to wind down your window but don't put your head out. They'll expect to see your cloud of breath. If they're alert, they might notice you don't emit one.'

He handed our two passports into the controller's cabin. We waited some minutes. A line of vehicles stacked up behind us. Viktor maintained an unblinking gaze up at the open hatch, his mouth distorted into a grin, his own steamed breath emerging. Ask a man to play-act suspicious, and none could do better.

The passports were returned. We moved forward to one more control point.

'That was the French letting you out, sir. Now we need the British to let you in.'

Viktor fixed his grin still wider. A woman's head peered out from the cabin. I couldn't make out her request but the interior light turned on without warning. I shut my eyes and then squinted to find the window lowered and the officer staring at me, back at the photo in her hand, and then at me again. It was true, her mouth steamed when she opened it. I find it an endearing human trait. I kept my own mouth closed.

'It was the photo booth,' Viktor explained. When we spoke it was in German but he switched with apparent ease to English to address her concerns. Apparently the waxen head in my photograph was glossy. 'It made him sweat so the photo came out sweaty. He is scared of closed spaces. That's what keeps him from flying.'

She spoke some more, presumably asking the purpose of travel.

'Business. For me, the business is driving. For him, it's trade.'

His grin grew wider still. It was astonishing that it could do so and yet remain on his face.

She held on to the passports some moments longer. I was preparing to invade her mind when she returned them. The barrier ahead of us lifted.

'No problem,' Viktor said, though his mind still thrummed with anxiety. 'You noticed my grinning just now, sir. A camera was fixed above that office window. I've noticed little kids screw their faces into silly grins when a camera's pointed at them, and I learned to do the same. I've a miserable face normally. A smile is my disguise. I'm hard to recognise without it.'

'You've done this before?'

'Guiding your kind across state borders? You're the first official trans-border passage since 9/11 I believe, sir. It hasn't seemed worth the risk till now.'

'The risk?'

'Security's become very tight. Officials tend to focus on those who look a little different.'

'So I was at risk just now?'

'Not exactly sir. But a principle concern of the Council is that you maintain a low profile. I feared you might be detained. If so, I feared the havoc and the damage you might cause. I wouldn't blame you, sir. You have rights that precede any bureaucracy's. The difficulty comes with the filming. You think a room is private, that a dark alleyway is secluded, then it turns out a camera has been focussing its lens on you all along. I wouldn't want cameras to focus on you, sir.'

Passport control let one car at a time hurtle out to cross the concrete expanse of the port. The snowfall had lessened and the snow on the ground had been pushed into steep banks. Viktor headed as directed toward Lane 125, following in the tracks of the preceding car. He parked near the rear of a single line of cars that were waiting to board the ship. The moment he switched off the engine, he turned on that tablet of his once more. It was seconds before he grunted and passed it back to me.

'Do you see what I mean about publicity?' he said.

The screen was filled with the picture of a young girl. She was eighteen perhaps, a little plump in a silver tube dress, dark hair pulled into a knot on top of her head with loop earrings and glitter in the make-up beneath her eyebrows. Her eyes were open and a smile was tucked into her cheeks. A smile was open on her neck too, the open gouge of a bite.

It's good she looked happy. She would have let herself be taken given the chance, I suppose. The sight of her made me hungry.

'The Ghent police released the picture twenty minutes ago. The media are over it already.'

'The Ancient has a new life to feed,' I noted. He had told me the pattern when they had spawned Chris; the need to feed his wife and the creature carried within her. They had fed just hours before, to fuel their act of sex. Ghent was just minutes on the train line from Brussels to the coast. It seems they had left our meeting in a hurry to feed again. That was confirmation for me. The wife was newly pregnant.

'And with the media looking for you he has no need for discretion,' Viktor suggested. 'It's good we have you out of the country. When he kills again, you'll have an alibi.'

'Unless he kills in England.'

'I don't think they're likely to do that, sir. Our informants tell us the couple have just moved into a vacant apartment by the shore in Zeebrugge.' As Viktor spoke, confidence sapped from his voice.

'They placed their son on the ferry from Zeebrugge to Hull,' I reminded him. 'That set a pattern. If they were to go in search of him, they would likely travel from there. Do they have two of your passports?'

'The Ancients don't ask our assistance, sir.'

'Nor, so far as I remember, did I.'

Passports were demeaning. The Ancient would never resort to one. I checked the magnetic pull in my head. It was still strong. It was me their son was calling, not the Ancient. His parents, it seemed, could never follow me to Britain without the right documentation. Yet I have been writing the true books long enough to know that my expectations were irrelevant. I had sensed fierce longing for her son in the woman's mind. Sabaa was newly pregnant. A mother such as she would not leave a child unprotected.

Traffic had been streaming off the incoming boat. Now the light turned green and Viktor was free to drive up the ramp and onto the car deck. I had mastered the seat controls. As Viktor drove, I manoeuvred my seat back into its vertical position. We came to a halt behind a large wagon that was already disgorging a family of six.

'You're not allowed to stay on the car deck during the journey, sir,' Viktor advised me.

'Then we shall go up to the salons and I shall eat.' The children from the wagon, all of them oversize and two of them already squealing, were squeezing their way between our vehicle and the steel wall. One of them gone would be no loss to the world. 'Let me follow this walking buffet.'

'You will feed from the children, sir?'

'Just one perhaps. The decks above will be brightly lit. With bright lights, close human contact, and nowhere to settle myself so I can grow still, I will feed. It is the best way to keep myself balanced.'

'I have a black cotton cover for the nights,' Viktor remembered. 'Perhaps you're right, sir. You know your own needs. If you lie flat, sir, and I cover you, I doubt anyone would notice.'

'I doubt it too, Viktor.'

I lay down. My mind blanked. I was the thrum of the ship's engines and then the blackness of sea and sky.

Viktor pulled back the sheet. He uncovered my face first of all and then concertinaed the sheet in folds down my body. 'Welcome to England, sir. We've docked at Dover.'

‘Already?’

‘It’s a short crossing, sir. Just a hundred minutes usually though we are somewhat late. Twenty-seven minutes late to be exact. The crossing was stormy. You’ll not have wanted to feast on the family in front, sir. I’m afraid most of them were loudly seasick.’

It is provoking to be woken back to the scramble of time, human frailty and blather about the weather.

‘If you could sit up, sir. We don’t want you looking like a stowaway should a customs officer inspect the car.’

I duly pressed the buttons and the couch turned back into a seat. The car moved from the gloom of the ship’s hold and into an early winter morning. Darkness was smudged by amber lamps and neon-lit signs. Strands of fairy lights were looped into the shape of holly and bells across a side street, Christmas already looked tired before it had arrived.

Brighter light was cast up the ruined walls of a castle above the town, and not far above those was thick low cloud. My head ached, and I realised the cause was the magnetic pull. The pull worked as a pulse in regions of my brain as the car wheeled around ramps and away from the docks. The pulse throbbed from new angles as Viktor steered the car around a sequence of roundabouts.

And then we entered a motorway and the ache settled in one particular lobe.

We were on course. I am a biographer. I am used to the chase. I chase down stories. Yet I confess that in pursuit of the Ancient’s child, I knew a story would not satisfy me.

This time, for my first time, I was there for the take.

23

THE CAR'S ENGINE was measured in horsepower. With slight pressure from Viktor's foot the equivalent of 220 horses surged into action. Viktor pulled into a service station to fetch himself some coffee.

The car was automatic, with one pedal serving as a brake and the other an accelerator. A wheel like a capstan steered it left and right. It was simple.

The automatic doors slid open and sucked Viktor in to a fluorescent hall. I slipped from the rear of the car to the front and settled myself in the driver's seat. The key was in the ignition. I turned it. The engine fired into life. I squeezed the button on the gearstick and shifted the mode to drive. All was so easy. The car moved forward on its own.

A man in a beard and a t-shirt jumped backward so I did not hit him. He raised his fist and shouted. I ignored him. Who but a fool would walk across a parking lot and not anticipate danger? Even of old I knew that any horse might bolt and that no driver was truly in control.

My wheels slapped the ice as liquid onto the underside of the car. Further out beyond the trucks the parking lot was clear. The car had a mixture of four basic functions: stop and go; forward and back. I drove patterns of geometric design through the sludge until I had mastered equal proficiency and speed both forwards and in reverse. Then I returned for Viktor.

He had run around the parked cars, spilling hot coffee over his hands, and had nowhere left to run to. I pulled up alongside him. My window opened at the press of a button.

'You can't drive,' he said.

The thought that I might simply choose to drive, that I might tire of being his passenger, had never occurred to him. Even the humans that know us best project their limitations onto us.

'I've been studying you since we left the port. It's not so hard.'

'But you haven't got a licence.'

I laughed. It failed to chill him.

'I'm the driver,' he persisted. 'That's my job.'

'We drifted between lanes when you were last driving, Viktor. I saw waves of sleep pass through your head. A lot has happened. A lot will happen. You are human and you are tired. If you turn the car into a wreck I can simply walk away. However I am in a hurry to reach my destination. You can get in and sleep or stand there. I am driving.'

I moved the car forward, just a few metres. It was enough. He opened a rear door while running and jumped in.

'That was nimble, Viktor.'

It was a genuine compliment. I checked in the rear-view mirror to see if it drew a smile. It did not. He reached across to the front passenger seat and took possession of his digital tablet. As soon as its power returned he started tapping his fingers across it.

'Just to inform you, sir, I am registering my official disapproval.'

I laughed. The thought that Viktor could claim a position as an official disapprover was genuinely funny.

'There's a speed limit, sir.' He looked up from his computer as car after car drew next to his window and then vanished behind us. 'Seventy miles an hour.'

'Then let's double it.' I pressed the accelerator to power us through an extra spurt.

Light flashed from behind us and glanced off the mirror and into my eyes. I squeezed them tight, just for a moment. It was fine. I insist we were fine. I had already registered the way ahead. There was no danger in driving it blind. Whatever the contents of Viktor's official complaint, it was better I was driving blind than he when asleep.

'You passed a speed camera sir. At great speed. It triggered that flash. We have been photographed.'

'They blind all fast drivers with flares of white light?'

'Was I blinded sir? I don't think so. Humans are perhaps better adapted to these driving conditions. Persist at this speed, sir, and such lights will flash again and again.'

'This is absurd, Viktor.' And truly it is. Humans develop capacities that outreach their limitations and then constrain them. There I was, in a human plaything I could begin to enjoy, and at once that pleasure was restricted. The tragedy of the human condition grows ever more pitiful.

I slowed down. Viktor's cheekbones as viewed in the mirror showed signs of relaxing. I believe it is what passes as his smile. It annoyed me so much I considered crashing the car and walking away. But I drove on.

For whoever has the sad task of recording Viktor's complaints, set beside it the numbing sense of duty I displayed on that drive to East Yorkshire while Viktor the driver snored on the back seat.

I should have closed my car door perhaps. Then the blare of horns from trucks might not have woken him.

'Sir,' he bleated. He scrambled from the car to stand on the asphalt and look out at me. A barrier edged the road, below which a slender iron railing bordered a walkway. 'You're not allowed to stop here sir. A police patrol will be along any moment.'

The bridge was hardly busy. It was easy for drivers to swerve around our car. This place was exhilarating.

'Come and join me, Viktor.'

I jumped to the top of the railing and stood there, my arms held high and wide. The whole bridge shook as vehicles passed, and the narrow iron rail quivered beneath my soles. A high wind blew and gusted behind my back, salted by a nearby sea. My body became one sinuous flow, adjusting to each shift in the environment. What humans find in sex I find in balance. I turned and walked beyond the range of Viktor's complaints and then faced the river below.

Its flow was wide, brown and fierce. I have walked the stone rim of aqueducts and bridges and the streams below intrigued me, but even the Seine and the Tiber were simply moving wetness. This was different. An ocean narrowed to pour itself in this wide brown surge across land. This river was something I could fly into. Its power was akin to my own.

What might we do together were I to leap? What might occur should our two powers merge?

'Sir!' Viktor had resumed his place in the driver's seat and driven forward. 'You are forgetting the boy!'

What boy? I confess the intent of my visit had slipped from me. There was still the pull of his call. It was thin beneath the call of the river and the wind singing through the cables above my head, but it was real. The boy was calling and he was close.

'The boy?' I said as the memory returned.

The river was timeless, and yet time retained its niggling presence.

Car doors opened and slammed shut. Voices other than Viktor's yelled on the bridge. 'Do you know him? Jeez, what's he doing up there? Come down man. That's crazy.'

I turned. The river was now behind me. A teenage couple had climbed out of a rusted blue car. A blonde girl squeezed herself tight inside her red padded jacket, while the boy slid down the sharp steel slope from the barrier to the walkway. He fell as he landed but kept on talking, rising into a crouch. 'Don't do it man. Come on, I'll help you.'

Black hair flopped over his forehead. He brushed it back so he could stare at me with pale blue eyes, and stretched out his hand for me to take. The girl on the bridge held her phone in front of her face where it flashed. It stunned me a moment. I closed my eyes and swayed. The girl shrieked and her camera flashed again. I had become an episode in a paltry human drama.

And so I leapt. Down from the railing and onto the walkway, up the slope and over the barrier. I climbed in through the car's rear door and Viktor drove off.

'Whoever thought a bridge could be like this?' I said. 'When did men build such a thing? And do they build them still? Might I join them?'

'I'll look it up for you, sir, when we're safely across and away. It's called the Humber Bridge. It's a suspension bridge. This held the world record for its length once, I understand, but it's been surpassed.'

'Oh never, Viktor. This bridge sways and groans and sings. It is the length and height it needs to be.'

'I aimed to bypass it sir. I'm sorry. I know how water can disturb your kind.' He pulled up alongside a booth and held coins out to pay the toll. The woman inside peered from her window to catch sight of me.

'We've called the emergency services,' she told Viktor. 'You'd better wait here.'

'Not here,' Viktor said. 'I coaxed him back into the car but I can't control him. He's excited. He could jump out and run back to that railing any minute. Let me through. I'll park as soon as I'm somewhere safe and phone the emergency services myself.'

She hesitated. I opened my door. The barrier lifted.

I had been set to do as he suggested, to leave the vehicle and run back to the railing. My excitement subsided as the car moved forward.

The call was louder now, and the pull was stronger.

'That way,' I said to Viktor. 'Take the highway along the river.'

'I think this route is best, sir.' He was following an automatic map he claimed was directed from satellites that orbited the planet. 'We head north toward Beverley this way and bypass Hull completely. We'll be in the boy's village in no time.'

'But he's not there,' I said. 'Turn around, Viktor. I sense him. I'll take you to him.'

We could hear the sirens behind us.

'It's not just about the boy, sir,' he suggested. 'There's his whole story to catch up on. We'll park up somewhere nice and quiet sir, and you can get to work. You're a biographer sir. It's your calling. I think the work will do you good.'

24

VIKTOR HAD NEVER assisted on a take before. His only knowledge came from the accounts I had researched and written. We were both amateurs.

Chris pulsed his location and it moved around the right side of my brain toward the rear. We were drawing further away from his call, not closer. An ache reached round my skull as though of loss. I groaned.

Viktor was driving slowly; perhaps for the snow, but he took extra care at sharp bends when the pulse seared from one point in my brain to another. 'We know where he lives, sir,' he offered. 'Isn't that part of the technique of the masters? They feel the call and then locate the home. That's the way I read it, sir. They don't lay in wait exactly, it's not a spider type of thing, but they insinuate themselves into a living space somehow. Those who call do not stop calling. They are not prey. It's not a chase. Theirs is a call to intimacy rather than attack. You feel the call from afar and they sense the presence when you are near. Draw close enough and you can wait for them to come to you. Forgive me if I'm wrong. It's just the way I see it.'

I was touched. I don't write my books for humans but Viktor had read them well. He had taken in my narratives and drawn from them a conclusion. Right or wrong, his interpretation showed a close engagement with the text. As a writer, I have found my own works hold surprises even for me. We write what we need to find out.

Viktor indicated left and turned the car through ninety degrees from the main road. Once again he turned cautiously. We were on a tree-lined lane. The pulse of Chris's call left the coating of my brain. I thought it had gone, but as we passed a sign that named the village ahead I recognised the shift. The sign read Cherry Burton. The call had moved to the centre of my brain.

We were in Chris's home territory. He had now located me.

This country lane appealed to me. I am an urban creature by circumstance rather than choice. Anonymity and feeding opportunities don't align with a rural existence. I had bypassed the twentieth century and landed in a tumult of mechanised speed. Now Viktor drove at a trotting pace and I could imagine myself to be in a landau drawn by a pair, their hoofs syncopating rhythm on the road. To my right was a high brick wall that was mottled by the weather of centuries. To my left a barred wooden fence edged an expanse of deer park, where trees were separate and regal and their branches laden with snow.

Where the road curved into the main village street, a grey stone church was raised on high ground. Its tower was typical of others I had noticed on the drive north through England; it was broad but lacked a steeple. Snow-capped gargoyles spread dragon wings from the tower's balustrade, which was crenellated with slits from where archers could shoot arrows. The place was built for a medieval battle of ancient myth, and garlanded with pagan fantasies.

When we consider what these Yorkshire villagers have done with their own Christian story, the wild fantasies that humans have constructed around our kind become more comprehensible.

They remain insane, but at least they are consistent.

It was a Saturday and early in the afternoon. Three children in a garden were lifting a head onto a snowman. A lady walked a scruffy brown dog on a leash that extended some twenty feet from her hand. The dog paused; its rump trembled and it eased its waste matter to the concrete paving. The woman set the leash to retract, walking carefully in her gumboots to be level with her dog.

Was she its servant, I thought? Had the hierarchy of this world gone into reverse? For she bowed to scrape the dog's waste from the concrete and into a bright orange plastic bag, which she tied and dangled from her gloved fingers as though it were a relic.

I heard the rumble. I watched the snow slide off the red tiles of the house that edged the paving. It found a lift from the guttering and slammed in force over the heads of woman and dog alike. The snow compressed the dog to the ground for a moment before the animal sprung high, shaking its body to spin snow from its fur.

I laughed.

The dog looked toward my passing car and a frenzy of sharp barks sent it juddering back into the woman's legs. She stared in turn toward my car. Snow had hit her. This was an insult from the natural world. She needed to lay the blame elsewhere and so fixed on me. She opened her mouth and yelled.

Four ducks had been squat within their feathers on the banks of a pond. The noises startled them into movement. They leapt toward the safety of the water. The pond was frozen. The ducks skidded across the ice, their bodies cannoned against each other and they paddled their feet for balance and stretched out their wings.

I laughed again.

So this was Chris's small and crazy world. It was time to set him free.

We turned from the main street into a road of recent housing. These buildings were large and square, of a honeyed brick with black tiles on their roofs. Pillared columns adding grandeur without purpose. Two stone lions mounted the gateposts of one such home. Viktor eased the car to a halt on the road just beyond this entrance.

The wrought-iron gate was unlocked. I walked the path to the front door and waited between the Doric columns of its porch as a bell rang in the interior. A wall of heat pumped out through the opening doorway and Susan appeared. Her blonde hair was marshalled into curls that tucked behind her ears. She wore blue jeans and a cream blouse, buttoned to its cuffs and up to the lace frill of its collar.

I do not know what my visit was interrupting in her life. The air was tense with chemical spray, as though the cleaning had recently been done. She stared at my feet but chose to let me across the threshold when I wiped my shoes on the doormat. She seemed eager for some company. Chris was away and her husband was in the study with the door closed. The only smells of food were stale, wrapped in chemical scents. Nothing was cooking.

We settled in the front room. No books were open, the television screen was blank, and the newspaper lay on a side table with its neat folds intact. Susan asked no questions to check my identity. She was more interested in talking. Susan was good at maintaining eye contact, but broke it occasionally so as to look sideways as though her memories were collected there.

When Richard came into the room to find her sitting with a stranger she offered him the line with which I had introduced myself. I was Konrad, an educational correspondent for an important journal who had come from Germany to talk about the ways in which Britain's educational system had let Chris down. Their boy achieved five A* grades at A2 level despite expulsion from a series of state and private schools. It seems his schooling did not have the rigour and breadth to contain him?

I stood up out of politeness but Susan waved me back into my armchair even as I reached out my hand to shake Richard's. She was keen to minimise the interruption. Richard sat down on the other end of the sofa. The middle cushion was left vacant as though for Chris.

'He was never a bad boy,' Susan reflected. Her husband's arrival prompted her story about her son to become defensive. She spoke fast and at length, with no need to pause for recollection.

I showed them printouts from different social media accounts in which Chris went by such names as vampiressuck, bloodfiend, bayforit and fangsforthememory. His adoptive parents smiled but their eyes showed fright when they looked at each other. 'Sometimes he seems old beyond his years,'

Richard explained, 'and sometimes so adolescent. All this blood stuff will find its place now he's got into medical school.'

'It's just that blood excites him,' Susan continued. 'It's a glandular thing. He has especially keen receptors in his nose apparently. He's alert to layers of smell we don't even recognise, but it seems these receptors are particularly responsive to heat.

'He went to a children's party once and a scarf was tied around his eyes for blind man's buff. They said he was cheating but he wasn't. They whirled him around and left him standing in the middle of the room, but he doesn't confuse that easily. Children were dancing around him like he was stupid, like they were so clever because he couldn't see them, but he knew where each of them was. He stood still, smiling, till the children got bored and started shouting at him to catch them if he could. Then he moved. It was horrible actually, though I did laugh later when we were safely home. He sensed the heat of their bodies as they jigged about and simply whirled between them. His feet kicked, his hands flashed out, nobody was bruised I think, no-one was really hurt, but every move he made was inch perfect. He went for their feet or their necks, tipping them from their points of balance. Children were standing and then they were all falling, it couldn't have taken more than forty seconds. Every child was on the floor but him. Blind man's bluff became this funny game of last man standing. All the children screamed. Chris went still and his little voice said, 'Can I take the blindfold off now?' He was always very polite.'

'You were telling about the blood,' Richard prompted. Blood was a particular interest of Richard's. 'That is of course what gives warmth to the body. People associate blood with death but blood is life. That's what Chris understands. He doesn't faint at the sight of blood like idiots do. It quickens him. It quickens me too. Of course it does. How do you think we dentists stay laser-sharp, one mouth after another, patient after patient? It's the sight and the smell of the blood that does it. We're not morticians. We're dealing with living breathing people. Blood sets us racing. We stay calm as it pulses out, but of course there's adrenaline too, blood can't just flow forever, you cut and release it then work to seal it again. Christians understand it. They drink the blood of Christ at the altar rail. They use wine of course so the whole tradition has become distorted. People sniff ancient Bordeaux and gasp with ecstasy, but Chris knows the real thing. He's a connoisseur of blood. It's just this tight taboo-bound culture of ours that sees the boy prosecuted rather than praised for his expertise.'

They knew me as a German educational correspondent but education is broad so they felt free to tell me anything. It was good to talk, they agreed. Not since he was an infant had anyone shown a compassionate interest in their boy. Others only saw him as a problem.

A grey cat mewled from the window ledge, asking to be let in. Susan smiled. 'Always trust an animal,' she said. 'Animals can always tell. They work from instinct rather than prejudice. Animals love Chris.'

'Well cats do.' Richard threw in the correction and let out a little laugh. 'Dogs can go crazy when they see him. They bark and bark.'

'How many cats do you have?'

'Oh none,' Susan said.

'But several ran to my feet when I walked in through the gate.'

'Well there you go. They do that to Chris whenever he comes home. Cats must like you too. That one on the window, she's just staring in to see if Chris is here. She's calling him out to go hunt with her. We never let them in.'

'We keep the doors and windows closed against them,' Richard added. 'Even the upstairs windows. It's not the cats so much, it's what they bring in, some little present for Chris hanging from their mouths. We were talking about blood, well here's a story. I got up in the night once and looked in on Chris. Cats had left their gifts all across his duvet while our little boy slept: mice, shrews, voles, a blackbird, even a young rat. Their necks were all sliced open. Susan had to throw the duvet away it was so filthy; not just the cover, the whole duvet. Chris was asleep, thank God; liking blood is one thing, but this was a trauma in the making. There was even a body on the boy's pillow, a dead mouse, its blood all over Chris's face from how he had turned over in his sleep. I don't know how many cats had been in with their offerings. There were only two there when Susan went in, sitting alert on the end of his bed with their ears up. We've done our best to keep them out of the house since then.'

'We did get him a toy cat,' Susan said. 'I'll fetch him for you.'

The couple had all the evidence of their son's true nature, and yet apparently no suspicions. Did love make them blind, or sheer ignorance? Or was their little boy able to enter their minds and structure the narrative that suited him?

Richard waited till she was out of the room and then leaned forward to speak in a half-voiced whisper. 'Chris came out ahead where parents are concerned, I can assure you. Others might not have been so understanding. For me though, I've had a professional interest in blood since my sister was hit by a swing when I was seven. It knocked out her teeth but I picked them up and did my best to stick them back in place. I knew even then where every tooth belonged. The blood didn't bother me at all. And Susan, well she's a woman so of course she knows a lot about blood. But having a menstrual cycle when you can't have children of your own, that's allowed her to develop a philosophical take on bloodletting.'

He gave me a nod and leaned back as Susan's steps hurried down the carpet on the stairs.

25

IT WASN'T THE STUFFED toy cat I expected. Susan carried a jar with a cat-shaped head. 'Here it is,' she said. 'It's Egyptian. We bought it from the shop in the British Museum. They had proper toy ones made for children but Chris looked at the hieroglyphs on the outside of those and said they were nonsense. I was surprised. They were made of shiny metal with bright images and the cats had big blue eyes, but this one's made of clay and dull brown as you can see. It's a refined taste, to say the least. I thought the cat's ears would soon get chipped off but you can see he takes good care of it. It's called Bastet. Richard thought he was calling it bastard and told him off, but Chris had made me read up on Egyptian history for him so we knew Bastet was just the Egyptian word for cat.'

She passed it over.

'It's heavier than it looks,' I said.

'Oh it's full. Bastet's just the name of the head on top. It's a canopic jar. The real cat's inside. Chris puts it in there to sleep during the day and takes it out at night.'

I took off the lid and reached inside. My hand closed around a small sphere wrapped in cloth. I pulled at it. A cat's head appeared followed by its swathed body, all bound tight in bandages.

'That's Niu,' Susan explained. 'He called him that even when he was alive. Richard thought he called him new because the cat was the latest thing in his life, but we put him right on that too. Niu is the God of Nothingness.'

'So Niu lived?'

'For a while. He was a grey cat who just turned up. When Chris went walking out in the fields the cat followed. They went everywhere together. We got so many funny reports from the villagers. They saw Chris and Niu in hedgerows, up trees, in the churchyard, on the roofs of sheds. It was just a boy and his cat out hunting, you know the games boys play, but it obviously bothered someone a lot. I woke up one day and found the cat on the ground outside Chris's window, its throat sliced open. There was no blood so it had obviously been killed elsewhere and thrown in. Now who would do that to a little boy's cat? I was set to dispose of it before Chris could see but then I felt his eyes on me and looked up to see him leaning out of his window. 'We can bury it,' I suggested, 'and mark the grave with a little cross of sticks.' He knew what he wanted to do though, so I read up some techniques in books and we mummified it. It's a bit rough and ready. We had maggots on day three before we pulled out the organs from a little slit on the side. I remember them now, the heart, the liver and the kidneys all dark and nestled in the palm of Chris's tiny hand. Chris felt the heart should be dried out and put back but there are limits. I made him take them to the bathroom and dispose of them. It took him a while, but when he came back he was smiling. He joked with me, the little rascal, and said he hadn't flushed the organs away at all, he had eaten them. Chris took such care, hooking out the brain through the cat's nostrils. A cat's a small thing really once the life is taken out of it, so it dehydrated on its own. We stuffed it with sand till I would swear it was fatter than when we started. It's done alright in the end. It's lasted.'

I fitted Niu back into his vase and replaced the cat-head lid.

'Did Chris have other friends?' I asked. 'Beside cats?'

'He's had lots of friends, hasn't he Richard? It's just he doesn't keep them long. His friends stay keen to know him but their parents forbid it.'

'They say he's too tough,' Richard added. 'Imagine that, a boy being too tough in this day and age. It's the parents who are soft if you ask me, and the children who need to toughen up.'

'Perhaps Chris wanted friends too much,' Susan suggested. 'He's a little old romantic at heart, really. He didn't just want friends. He wanted blood brothers. You know, cut your thumbs and press them against each other so the blood of true friends mingles. Parents got outraged. They said you can't do such a thing in the age of Aids, as though the children and teens of Cherry Burton are likely plague carriers.'

'It wasn't just thumbs, of course,' Richard reminded her. 'Children slit their arms and wrists and offered them to Chris. The cuts can't have been deep because when he sucked at them the bleeding stopped. The children swooned but they hardly entered a coma. It was nothing but a faint and they came out of it smiling. I have patients fainting in my surgery every week and no-one causes a fuss about it. Teachers got upset though. They said it was worse than glue-sniffing. What nonsense that is. My own adolescent experience of glue-sniffing—not abusing it myself I might add, simply experimenting on others—is that it makes you mindless. It prompts aggression. Chris's bloodsucking, it seems to me, triggers nothing but a natural high. Even hyperactive children grew calm for a while when Chris sucked at their wounds. They blissed out. Parents noticed the razor scars on their children and complained to the local authority about an outbreak of self-harm. If that was so, so it was. Self-harm. Why blame our Chris for that? It wasn't as though he was the one running round the playground flashing razor blades.'

Richard's voice rose as he spoke and his face blotched red.

'They weren't blaming him exactly, Richard.' Susan's tone suggested an attempt to calm him down but in fact she was contradicting him which stoked his anger.

'They expelled him!' He was shouting now. 'School after school expelled him. If that's not blame, what is? They couldn't even leave it there. Schools took out orders to keep him a certain distance from their playgrounds. First it was Cherry Burton, then Beverley, now vast patchworks of Hull are out of bounds to the lad. And why? Because kids are so screwed up by their upbringing they cut themselves and bring their wounds to Chris. He's not hurting them. He's not dealing drugs or anything. The boy's healing those kids. They come with their wounds and they see his smile and they press their flesh to his lips. What's wrong with that? Nothing's wrong with that. The boy's a saint and as with most saints everyone wants to make a martyr of him.'

Four cats now stood mewling on the window ledge, their cries like the wails of abandoned babies. Richard strode to the window and beat his hands against the glass to frighten them away. They didn't budge.

'Show the man,' Susan suggested.

Richard turned a blank expression on her.

'Roll up your sleeves and show him.'

Richard considered the request a moment and then walked towards me. He rolled up both white sleeves of his shirt and showed me his arms. They were marked with the scars of thin slashes.

'Richard has high blood pressure,' Susan explained. 'He used to self-medicate. Not any more though. When the danger signals are there, when the top of his chest starts to pain him and his breath is short and shallow, he just makes a slight incision. He hands the wound to Chris.'

Susan's words worked. Just the memory of the experience saw the red ease back from Richard's face. 'Would you call that self-harm, or self-knowledge?' he asked me. 'His lips touch the wound and the pressure releases. The world turns rosy with a texture of soft embrace.'

He grew silent. Susan nodded toward the sofa and he took her direction and settled himself down.

'We're both glad he's at medical school now,' she said. 'He's among healers. They'll see him for what he is.'

Two more cats had joined those on the window ledge. They all cried in chorus.

'Oh chase the damn things away will you, Richard,' Susan snapped. 'I'm sorry Konrad. They've never appeared before when Chris isn't here. And when he is here he quietens them. He leads them out to the scout hut and then the woods beyond for a little hunting. He's gone the whole night sometimes but that's OK. We know where he is. That's what's important. You can't just tuck growing lads in bed at night and think they're safe till morning. There's a wildness in them.'

Richard left the room to go out and deal with the cats and Susan stood too.

'I'll show you Chris's room, Konrad. It's his bedroom but also his school in many ways. Home schooling was never our preference, but as school after school excluded him it was either this or send him away. Chris isn't the sort of boy you can institutionalise. He's more elemental than that. I qualified as a teacher to satisfy local authority regulations, but most of the learning happened online. Chris and I learned together. You'll see.'

Richard had put on a scarf, a red puffa jacket and a grey woollen knitted cap he pulled over his ears. He pushed his hands into a pair of knitted gloves that hung on elastic bands from its sleeves. This was a careful man, keen to protect himself from the winter chill for the moments it might take him to chase the cats from the house. He opened the door a fraction, slid out, and closed it so the cats had no chance to slink indoors.

Chris's room was one of four bedrooms upstairs. 'We set up a separate study for him, like his father's,' Susan explained, 'but you know boys. Their bedroom is their lair. Here it is.'

The carpet on the landing was beige, the walls were magnolia, and all the other doors were white gloss. Chris's door was matt black. It swung open easily. The floor inside was of bare oak boards. I smelt the wood, but not the boy. Boys are easy to smell; the growth hormones, the pumped testosterone, the sweat, that sour incubation of a cooped-up life. That smell was absent.

'We call it the pit.' Light from the landing spread the shape of the door across the floorboards. Inside the walls were black, the window sealed, and a dim fluorescence shone from two wide screens fixed to a wall. 'We only call it that for the darkness. Not for the condition. Chris keeps the place spotless. He'll know we've been in here. I don't know how he knows but he always does. He even knows which of us has been in, and if we both go in together he knows that too.'

Richard had been clapping his hands and shouting 'shoo' outside the house. The front door now opened and he came back in.

'We get so little daylight in winter and yet still Chris keeps it out.' Susan crossed to the roller blind, which was black like the walls, and released it. It shot high. The grey light of outdoors washed in. And the cats opened wide their mouths and let out their wails. There were six of them lined up on the bedroom window ledge. Their cries were more like those of adolescents than babies.

'Damn things. Shoo!' Susan slapped her hands against the window. Two of the cats reared up, placing paws to slide down across the glass while Susan beat on the other side. Otherwise they ignored her. Susan stopped her banging and turned her head. She had noticed the cats were staring with a peculiar intentness. She looked to see where they were looking and so found herself staring at me.

Richard had taken off his boots but otherwise stayed in his winter gear to run upstairs and inspect the commotion. His appearance distracted Susan and she turned from me to him.

'Some job you did of that,' she declared.

'It's that ivy. It gives them the run of the whole side wall and up onto the roof. Well that's it. I've had enough. I'm chopping it down.'

'You can't. It's Chris's. You know how he feels about it. Remember what he was like when you cut it away from this window. I couldn't go through that again.'

'We'll have the boy take some responsibility. No surveyor would let ivy grow like this. It eats into the brickwork. This is Chris's house too. He can help me cut it down. What the hell's got into those cats now?'

As Richard and Susan talked I had taken the chance to walk into the room. The cats watched me. Their mouths stayed open mid-howl but no sounds came out. I was looking at the two monitors fixed to the wall. The images that appeared there were striking. The two humans picked up nothing of their impact, but the cats felt the power of my response and were stilled.

'Oh that.' Richard noticed where I was looking. 'That's Chris's latest pet project. We're linked in to the mainframe at work that ties in a number of dental practices in the region. It gives him the extra computing power he needs. He's not one for video games. His interest has always been more applied than that. I came downstairs one night and found him at the desk in my office looking through my patients' dental records. I kept them in a secure folder, but he had used the link from his bedroom to track my keyboard and capture my passwords. I had brought some patient X-rays home in my briefcase, and he had taken them out. He was working slowly, studying each X-ray and then examining the data to match it with the patient's name, age and gender. It was touching. Dentistry really is the most personal of the medical arts, but few see that. It had already dawned on young Chris. He was sitting there, probing the various personalities of a mouth. Then of course I grew concerned. I was in breach of patient confidentiality. I felt I should report myself to the General Dental Council.'

'Richard's very proper,' Susan explained. 'He came and woke me up. We both went down and stood there together, watching Chris explore the world of teeth. He's four years old, I said. They're just pretty pictures to him. You're hardly breaching patient confidentiality.'

'I took him with me to the surgery a few times. It comforted some of the more nervous patients, having a small boy sit on their laps. Susan made him his own tiny mask and cap. When the chair tilted back, he could raise his head and peer inside their mouths. The sight of him, peering at their teeth and down their throats with such intensity, eased the patients' nerves somehow. That lasted a few months. Then he had learned all he needed to know and never came to the surgery again. He's always moved on and found new interests to pursue. This is his latest.'

'It's his ancestry project.' Susan looked at the images on the two screens but did not understand the full import of what she was seeing. 'It seems it's slowing down. Maybe the program's run its course. When Chris got close to eighteen suddenly his birth parents became important to him.'

'He's not an easy person to buy for, as you can see.' Richard nodded at the room. Apart from the computer table, the equipment and monitors, the room was indeed bare. The computer and its keyboard sat on an otherwise empty table; there was no desk with drawers and not even a chair. Chris must stand when he's studying. The room did not even have a bed or a pillow, just a black sheet folded into a neat square and set on the floor in one corner. 'He's bought into his own austerity package. No bed, no duvet, and all his clothes are black so he makes do with very few. I was ready to buy him a car for his eighteenth and to reward him for getting into medical school but he's against cars on principle. He did want a DNA test though, so we bought him that. We sent off a sample of his hair to a place he found online. They set you against their international genetic database to locate ancestors in precise regions of the world. The results should be through shortly.'

'Meanwhile there's this project.' Susan's sentence rode the back of a long sigh.

'It's hard for Susan. She's his mother after all. She's done all the work. This project of Chris's is hardly parental rejection though. It's a fascinating piece of software development. Chris set the processors scanning photos of children and parents that he downloaded from Facebook and Instagram. Then he worked out an algorithm based on a broad range of facial features. I tested it out. Gave him a random sample of parent/child images and asked him to match them. He paired each of them successfully but for one. That one he said did not have an authentic match. He was right. That was the test I had set him and he passed it. I happened to know the backstory of the picture. The child's biological father was not who the child thought it was.'

'I think that was an unpleasant thing to do.'

'Pleasant or not, Susan, it proved a point. That's all our boy's doing. Proving his thesis. He's not getting emotional about it. Look at what he did for us. He ran off images, Konrad, of what our natural children might have looked like, a boy and girl aged eighteen.'

'It was horrible.' Susan shuddered. 'Quite unsettling. These two young adults, blue eyed and with mousy brown hair, their pale and needy faces looking out at us. Who would want children as insipid as that when we have Chris? That's nonsense, I told him. Brothers and sisters don't look alike just because they have the same parents. You can't say our children would look like this. Besides, you're our child. We don't want any others.'

'Then he put his own photo into the mix to work the program in reverse.

What would his birth parents look like? The image on these screens has been morphing for days. Now it looks as though it's settled.'

The light on the wall monitors was set to dim, but the images were clear. I recognised them both, the man on the left and the woman on the right. Neither smiled. Both stared into the room with dark-eyed intent.

The woman's hair hung straighter than I remembered it, but she had the same olive skin tones, the broad forehead and sharp arch of nose, the cheek-bones and the chin that I knew. On the left, the man's stare felt conscious. He was watching me, in the way some say the eyes of painted portraits can sometimes do. This was more than watching though. I felt myself read from the inside. For a moment I did not know where I was. All that I had learned of Chris, all the tales I had elicited from his parents, were drained from me. I was looking at an image of the Ancient. Living images of the boy's birth parents were lit upon his bedroom walls.

I shuddered.

'You're right, it's cold,' Susan agreed. 'Chris likes it this way. He keeps the heating in his room turned off. It's hardly healthy though. You've seen where Chris does his studies. That's all I wanted to show you, since you're writing about his education. Let's take you back to the warmth and make you a cup of tea before you go on your way.'

The three of us turned. A young male stood in the doorway, silhouetted against the light from the landing. We couldn't see the direction in which he was looking.

'Mum,' he said. 'Dad.'

26

'THIS IS KONRAD, Chris,' Susan explained. 'He's a German educational correspondent who's interested in misunderstood genius so we're showing him where you do your learning. We've finished now. We're just going downstairs.'

She spoke quickly but she didn't move. She was nervous.

'What the hell are you doing, Chris?' Richard looked down at his son's feet. Chris's black boots were crusted in snow and left wet imprints on the carpet behind him. He had clearly rushed in from outdoors and up the stairs though even I had not heard him. The cats had run in behind him. There were nine of them now. They looped a figure of eight between Chris and myself, rubbing against our legs. 'You've left that front door open again, haven't you? You know we won't have those cats in this house.'

Chris ignored his parents. He ignored me, which allowed me to study him. He walked around Richard, the snow from his boots now pooling onto the oak boards where he stood, and stared at both images. Though one was to the left and one to the right he did not move his head. It seems his peripheral vision is strong so that he sees clearly and equally in a wide field.

'This is absurd, Chris. Get them out, get them out!' Richard shuffled forward, as though ready to kick out at the stream of cats as four more ran in behind him, but a ginger one arched its back, bared its fangs and hissed till he retreated.

Susan somehow resisted the drama of swirling cats, looking between the pictures on the wall and her son's face. 'It's ridiculous, Chris,' she told him. 'Your birth parents can't look anything like that. These two are hardly any older than you. And they're wild things. They're not even proper people. Your computer's got confused between real photographs and all those fantasy games kids play. These are just cartoons.'

Chris moved closer to the wall, choosing between the images for his focus this time, veering right to stand before the picture of his birth mother. This was the woman who cursed me in unknown tongues, who spit blood into my face, and that was all I saw in the picture. I could trace no hint of a smile in the tight flesh of her cheeks. Chris and I were seeing differently. I entered his visual cortex and found no focus there. He wasn't seeing the woman but was staring at her eyes and his vision coursed through the tight-veined blackness he found there.

'We didn't expect you back so soon,' Susan said. 'Did they call off the game because of the snow? I wondered if that would happen. You didn't get sent off again did you?'

A mother's voice affects a child whatever it is she is saying. It is like the call of a ewe across a field of lambs. It asserts a bond and gives direction. Susan's words were making no impression on Chris at all.

'Chris plays rugby, Konrad.' Susan spoke to me so as to have someone listen to her, but stared at Chris. 'He's very good. Richard thinks he could turn professional. He got banned from all the local leagues but that's because he was playing against children. They say he used his head in the scrums but children's noses bleed, that's what they do, he was hardly headbutting and licking like they claimed. He's in different leagues now he's at university. He's playing against adults. They play rugby league in this part of the country of course. Richard thinks he may be better off with rugby union. Do you know the difference, Konrad? Scrums are bigger and tougher in rugby union. Perhaps that would suit Chris more.'

He didn't hear her. She was gone from him. What he heard, if anything, was the dull roar of winds circling within a vacuum.

Susan reached out to touch him. It was an instinctive move, reaching for her boy before he was lost to her. The touch was light, simply a placing of her fingers against the black cotton sleeve of his jacket. The contact served to jolt his whole body. Susan jumped back, kicking against one of the cats but the creatures didn't falter. They looped on, a linking path between Chris and myself.

The touch brought Chris back to his body. He turned from his mother to focus his gaze on the other image. He was looking into the eyes of the Ancient.

'Chris,' I said.

He didn't hear me. I was outside the slipstream as energy charged between the Ancient's eyes and his own. This was not what we needed. I had been woken for a mission and come to meet this boy. I wanted his story, not some story planted in him. I had not crossed the sea and driven through the snows of the north to be beaten by a pixelated photo. I spoke again, from inside Chris's mind.

'Hello Chris.'

He was confused. I sensed he did not recognise his name, but the voice within the dark sweep of mindspace broke his attention from the screen.

'Hello Chris,' I said once more, out loud. He turned his head and found my eyes. That's what I needed. He paused a moment, gathering his senses, and then he smiled. I smiled back.

Susan noticed the connection. 'We were just going down to have tea,' she reminded us. 'Let's all do that, shall we? Let's go down and have tea together.'

'You'll get those damn creatures out of the house before we do anything of the sort.' Richard was blustering out his authority even though he had edged himself back to a wall. The cats had indeed grown wilder. They had been walking in file before, as though mesmerised, but now broke into individual skirmishes, slashing and biting so as to be the ones closest to our feet. They were anxious for the hunt.

'I know you,' Chris said, 'don't I? Where are you from?'

'He's from Germany,' Susan said.

'Is that right?'

I scanned Chris's mind to see what Germany meant to him. The concept was some vast hollow waiting to be filled.

‘It’s a long story,’ I said.

‘Well not for here it’s not.’ Richard edged round the room to get behind us. ‘Go on, the pair of you. Get outside and take these creatures with you.’

‘They’re just cats,’ Susan tried. ‘Cats don’t matter.’

‘Everything matters. Go on, scat!’

Richard was shouting at the cats but he was doing more than that, of course. He was shouting at everything he didn’t understand. He was shouting at all the wildness he had let into his life.

I held contact with Chris’s eyes. ‘We’ll talk,’ I said. ‘You’ll understand.’

I reached for him then. Not the light touch of his mother but a firm hold. My hand closed against his upper arm and his muscles flexed in response. I turned him away from the images on the wall, away from the gaze of the Ancient, and toward the door.

The cats sprang ahead of us. They spurted across the landing, paused, and then leapt the first dozen stairs. They were fixed on the hunt but this hunt would not happen without Chris. As we trod the stairs they bunched in the hall, keeping to our side of the open front door.

The door had a wreath fixed to its outer side, made from a circle of dark holly that was studded with berries. A half-moon table in the hallway was layered in straw and set with clay figurines; a baby in its crib, golden-haired mother in a long blue gown beside a stout father with his trim black beard; three crowned kings, one black and two white, bearing gifts while a donkey, a goat and a sheep looked on. A mirror on the wall was garlanded in thick silver tinsel. Above it a selection of Christmas cards hung over a strand of green string. They rattled in the wind that blew in through the doorway and bunched them all together. A large branch of mistletoe had been taped between two recessed lights above the hallway. In the fanlight above the door the outline of a reindeer was marked by small white light bulbs while its nose flashed a bulbous red.

When I entered the house I had ignored this desperate trivia. This was Chris’s home yet I could not see how these ephemera were relevant to his life. I smelt the live resin in the front room, saw the scattering of green needles on the carpet beneath the tree, noticed the small teddy bear in silver frock with fixed-on wings that was tied to the topmost spur of the tree, and ascribed it all to some sentimental madness that flooded Susan's brain. My focus was on Chris.

I was wrong. It was like focussing on the beauty of a dragonfly, wondering how it could hover, while ignoring the spider's web that encased it.

I seldom reflect on Christmas. It is not my job to illuminate the human condition. Winter is a time of darkness and death yet people fear rather than welcome it. They bring a tree indoors to remind them of greenery. They hang it with baubles and lights to glimmer against the blackness. Of course at the heart of this nonsense lies the myth of an Ancient, a figure in human guise who is somehow still alive after millennia. Humans know something of the truth and then reduce it. The Ancient becomes a baby cloyed in human drama.

Chris descended the stairs and when he reached the floor below he stopped. It was the effect of artificial light. I was new to the era and electric glare was still painful. Chris was conditioned by an entire young life but now it hurt him. I entered his mind. It was still covered by the Ancient's darkness.

Richard had paused behind me while I stood still. Now he barrelled past. The sideswell of his guts pressed around my body and his elbow levered me against the hardness of the wall. The contact was offensive. The man had invited me into his house. This was gross disrespect.

'Look at the bloody things,' he shouted, shaking his arm at the cats. 'They're hanging around like they own the place. They'll be pissing on the carpets next. What are you playing at, Chris? Get them out, get them out!'

Chris simply stood and blocked the bottom of the stairs. His mind was still fixed in the stream of the Ancient's darkness. He needed to cross the hallway and be gone yet he could make no sense of where he was. He couldn't move.

Richard saw none of this. He pressed both his hands on Chris's right shoulder and he shoved. Chris is well-built. The shove did not move him. Richard kicked him. It was like the kick you give to a door that is jammed, the sole of his right foot slamming at the joint behind Chris's right kneecap.

The boy buckled. He knelt on the carpet, upright and with his eyes open, but I don't know how much he saw.

Richard was well-protected in his outdoor clothes. Tartan slippers guarded his socked feet as he began to kick out at the cats. He scooped one up from his toe to send it flying into the nativity scene on the half-moon table. It fell squalling to the ground inside a litter of clay figurines. Richard moved to kick at the cat again. The door stood wide as an open goal. He aimed to shoot the cat out across the threshold and into the garden.

He moved his arms wide for balance. Mittens hung from bands of elastic at the ends of his sleeves. His hands were naked. Perhaps the cats took direction from my mind. It's hard to tell with cats, they have such wildness in them. One sprang at the left hand and two slashed at the right, slashing claws against his skin. The attack and the pain threw Richard off his stride. He let loose his kick but the cat that squalled was now behind him and he connected with empty air.

The power of his futile kick span him around so he looked at me as he fell. He still wore a brown knitted hat but had neglected to put on a scarf. His neck was bare. It was white and puffed with fat but the presence of blood blushed beneath it. I glanced it with the nail of my index finger.

I was precise. My nail withdrew even as he fell toward it. The cut was precise and slight. The slice breathed open for a moment and then filled with blood. This was not a bloodbath as reports might suggest. I struck no jugular vein and blood never did more than seep.

I moved around him as he fell. My face stayed close to his falling head but as my eyes locked onto his eyes I saw their focus shift. I had opened my mouth. His eyes widened as he stared at my teeth. He took in air even as he fell and so smelt the power of my breath. For all his professional years of studying teeth and smelling breath he had known none like he saw and smelt then.

He stayed conscious but his mind fogged. It helped to relax him as he hit the ground. His puffed nylon jacket insulated the blow and his head had the carpet to bounce off. He was stunned and his mouth hung open. His breathing paused for a while but then he was gasping.

His fall landed him among cats. They spurted to escape but in their numbers ran against each other. The shadow of his falling body was cast in different directions by the various lights. It confused them. Three found their hindquarters trapped as he landed. They yowled and pulled themselves free. His body became a mound they had to cross to escape. Their bared claws streaked across the skin of his hands and face.

More blood flowed than was planned. These things happen.

27

BLOOD DOES NOT over-excite me. I weary at this need to defend myself from human reporting. Viktor has read too many tales of human fantasy. Whatever he saw and reported on was from an angle and from the garden. He was not even there. He reports a vampire crouched and salivating over a gash in a human's throat. This is a feeble projection of the man's own fantasies and longings and merits total disregard. I presume I need say no more.

Chris seemed unconcerned as the body of his father thumped down before his knees. His eyes were open but there was no focus in their blackness. He knelt with his body erect and his hands loose by his sides. His nose twitched though. It did so a fraction sooner than my own. He was responding to the pheromones in his father's blood. It was bringing him to his senses.

I pressed a finger along the slice in Richard's neck so that the blood oozed around it. Chris needed the colour as well as the smell. My finger shone a liquid, carmine red. I raised it and held it level with Chris's chin. The blood impinged the darkness in his vision. He saw the red. He was back in this world.

Humans make first contact with their fingers. They reach out to touch. Chris's hands stayed loose by his sides. Tension eased from his shoulders and the veins tightened in his neck. His head moved. The breath of his mouth warmed my skin as his tongue licked at the blood. He used the tip of his tongue, collecting the liquid with rapid dashes like a cat drinking milk.

The licks moved down from my nail, across my knuckle and to my finger's base. His head moved back. His throat contracted as he swallowed. His eyes stayed fixed on my finger, which was moist now with saliva but cleaned of blood.

I ducked my head. Chris was the boy who sucked wounds and here was a wound. I pressed my fingers to ease the skin a little wider and wider still and looked up. Chris was gone again, his dark eyes filled with the darkness of the Ancient's transmission.

Perhaps this is what Viktor saw, that I placed my lips around Richard's wound and drank. He was behind me though. He could not see that as I raised my head my lips were sealed. He would not know that my throat had not contracted. He would be ignorant of the fact that feeding is clean and that it does not rim the mouth with blood. He would know nothing of the control required to have blood pool in my mouth and yet not swallow.

I raised my head. The focus returned to Chris's eyes. He studied the garish bloom of red that was my mouth and his head arched forward. I watched his tongue emerge, its tip bridging the space between our mouths, then swiping one lick across my lower lip. It took the blood back to his mouth. He swallowed and the tongue came back to clean my upper lip. He swallowed again and I bared my gums, the pooled blood leaking between my teeth. And so he came to me. The move was his. His lips sealed against mine and his tongue pushed through. He drank from me, our two tongues clashing, his retreating with the blood to return for more, searching out every molecule till nothing was left to coat my mouth but his saliva.

Fingers curled into my hair and gripped. The hand was small and the grip was tight. My face pulled away from Chris's. His eyes were open and their focus had returned. He watched me go.

Susan had reached across Chris's head for my scalp. With her hold secured she walked past us on the stairs and dragged me backward, her arm locked to keep from me falling on the body of her husband.

'I don't know what you are,' she said, her voice turned shrill, 'but you can get out of my house.' She gave my head a shove as she let me go. 'You're sick. Get out. Go on, get out!'

She tried to stare me out, the pupils flaring in her eyes. I didn't touch her. I pulled my face closer, that's all, and stared back.

'Please go.'

That was better. At least she was civil.

She turned away. Some whimper from her husband distracted her. She crouched beside him. His face was a tired white but with splotches of red beneath the skin and his forehead ran with sweat. Susan cared enough to touch him and to even fake a smile as she looked into his eyes. 'You lost your breath when you fell, that's all,' she explained. 'You've got a few scratches but they'll mend. Don't worry. Chris is here.'

Her words had an effect. Richard's breathing had been sharp, his throat contracted, but it calmed at the sound of her voice.

'Chris,' she said, and looked up at the boy. 'Kiss him better.'

She stood up to make room and in moving back her foot crushed into the carpet the head of one of the nativity's three kings. She bent to pick up two of the scattered figures; Mary in a sky-blue dress and the swaddled, white-skinned baby. Their heads stuck out of her fist as she turned her attention back to the man on the floor.

The cats had quietened. Some sat and others had moved outdoors, returning to the threshold to look inside and then wheeling away again.

Richard turned his head so as to watch his son. His eyes were beseeching.

'Chris,' I said. 'Let's go.'

I don't, to be frank, recall if those were the words I used. Viktor reports that he heard a series of doglike barks that rumbled and then rose in pitch. The cats paused, he wrote, and then hissed and slashed and whirled as at shadows and fled the house. Two struck his legs, their brains scoured by sound, and then leapt on into the snow. The cats understood if Viktor could not. It was time to go.

Chris looked up.

'Now,' I said. Or something like. Viktor heard a roar. If their languages did more than skim the surface humans would not need to fight.

'Look,' I said, and Viktor heard a demonic laugh. He used that word, 'demonic'. Such is language for you. It trims its fears in words. I did not laugh. I demanded that the boy should see his world for what it was. A father gasping needs beside his feet. A mother with tamed hair clinging fast to figurines. A home of locked doors and sealed glazing, heat pumped into rooms that choked with recycled human breath, the drabness of beige, the gaudiness of lights, the fakery of the Christmas story. You hear the wild, Chris. Be the wild, or be this.

'Don't you dare shout in my house!' Susan had the elemental in her. Her voice turned lower yet exploded in volume. She had heard what I said. She almost understood. 'No-one shouts in this house! Look at my husband.'

She turned from me to the boy. 'His heart, Chris, his heart. The pressure's hurting his heart. He's wounded. Look at that cut. Look at him bleed. Kiss it better, Chris. Kiss it better.'

Her tone of voice was perfect. It spoke from eighteen years of practice. This was the voice that had pulsed meaning into the foundling's brain. It told Chris where to look and what to do. It was soft and called him by his name. Its language was composed of simple sentences strung in a pattern of repeating, a drip dripping response to the young man's needs. It is a way of speaking that perhaps I can learn.

Chris looked at Susan. Her eyes stayed open, holding his attention. And then his head moved. It swooped. His hands reached back to touch at their wrists behind his back. His fingers spread wide and trembled like a bird splaying its feathers. The tip of his tongue cleaned flecks of blood from the skin of his adoptive father and then swiped two lines along the run of the cut in the man's neck. The pupils of Richard's eyes rolled high in their sockets to leave just the whites. It was an eye-roll of ecstasy. Chris closed his lips around the wound. He sucked. His Adam's apple convulsed as he swallowed three, four, five times. And then all was still. His lips had tightened. He held it this way for perhaps fifteen seconds and then he released.

He pulled back his head. He did not bother to observe the results of his actions, but I was able to see clearly. The wound had sealed. It was puckered still, the torn skin rising to its join, but the bleeding had stopped.

Chris turned his attention to the man's hands and the scratches marked by the cats. With the cut on the neck Chris had been feeding; he sucked up mouthfuls of the blood before he cauterised the wound. With the hands it was not feeding. He simply licked them, wiping the broad sweep of his tongue across the skin. The blood was cleaned away and the hands left shiny with saliva.

'Good,' Susan said, leaning down to examine her husband's neck. She eased the eyelids down over his whitened eyes with her free hand. 'Good boy, Chris. He'll be fine now. Nobody soothes him like you do.'

A grey cat had slinked back in through the door to curl itself around my legs. I snatched it up. It was mid-air, held by the scruff of the neck to face away from me, before it fought. Susan backed away, the cat hissing and clawing at her face. Chris had risen to his feet. He moved no further away, but just watched.

The cat's claws were extended. They dug into Richard's right hand as the cat landed and then sliced back as it left. The cat fled the house.

'So your kisses can heal?' I said to Chris. 'Heal those.'

I nodded down at the four deep cuts that oozed blood on Richard's hand. The dentist was zoned out still, in the bliss of Chris's earlier wound kiss. His hand was like putty instead of flesh and stayed quite still.

Susan ran from the room. I thought she was frightened and her fright surprised me. Then I heard her speaking.

'Police,' she said. She gave her name and address, as though in response to prompts, and reappeared in the hallway so that the words she spoke into the phone were also addressed straight at me. 'There's a man in the house. An intruder, yes. A German intruder. He's attacked my husband. With a nail. A fingernail. He sliced open his throat. No I don't need an ambulance. My son's fixed the wound. But he's attacked again. He's thrown a cat. He made sure it was wild with its claws extended and he threw it. There's more blood. He's a madman. I'll stay on the phone so you'll hear if he attacks again. Tell the police to be quick. Who knows what he'll do next?'

She held the phone out to me, her arm rigid, like she was some great spirit of record.

'Show me,' I repeated to Chris. 'Heal him.'

He knelt. His wrists touched behind his back again as his head darted toward the wounds. He closed his mouth on each, the muscles in his cheeks tensing as he sucked. He was quick, applying himself to each of the wounds and only swallowing when all were tended to. He pulled his head back and stood. He looked at me.

The wounds were dry and white, the skin already knitted. For all of my years of close observation and enquiry, this was newly observed behaviour. Such healing is not part of the official record.

Viktor came forward and stood in the doorway. He had been out in the cold too long. His hair hung lank with the damp and his thin body was shaking.

'There he is,' Susan said, and pointed the Mary and Jesus figurines at my face. Confident that the police had arrived, she pressed the thumb of her other hand to cut off the phone call. 'That's the man. Arrest him.'

'We should go, sir,' Viktor said.

'Sir?' Susan repeated.

'The police will be on their way. We don't have long.'

'You're not the police?' she said.

'They are on their way,' I assured her, and turned to the young man. 'The police know this house well. Isn't that so, Chris? How many times have you been reported for sucking blood? And here you are, your father unconscious on the floor, and your mother with a tale of healed wounds. You will have a lot of explaining to do.'

He faced his mother.

'I'll do the explaining,' she said. 'You go to your room.'

'Your son fixed it. That's what you told the police. You say your son fixed his father's wounds. They'll know what that means. They'll know he's here.'

'It's you they want.'

I stared at her. This was a goodbye scene and she did not know it. She deserved better.

'Say goodbye to your adoptive mother, Chris,' I said.

'Goodbye?'

'And thank her.'

He stared at me.

'For all she's done.'

'Thanks, Mum,' he said.

She looked up at him. The figurines dropped from her hand to the floor. She tilted back her head to bare her throat. She would choose to be taken if given the chance, such is her love for her boy. I recognised that in her.

'This man's going,' she said. 'You're staying.'

'I've come for him,' I told her.

Her mind was open. I fed it the images of Chris's birth. It was an edited version. She saw the baby emerge from between its mother's legs and trail blood across her stomach. She saw the first transference of power between the mother's and baby's eyes. She heard the wail of anguish in the mother's voice as she shouted out among the passengers in the ferry, calling help to her baby on the ice of the deck outside. She looked out to sea as the ship that carried her baby grew small and entered the fog. She knew the fierceness of another mother's love for her boy.

We left her standing.

28

THE CATS HAD NOT FLED far from my shouts. The light from the doorway cast their darting shadows away from the path and across the snow.

Winter had closed the afternoon in darkness. Wood smoke charmed the air. Somewhere nearby a family had gathered around a log fire. The wood smoke took me back to a simpler age when there were trees to burn. The nostalgia shocked me. I had neither need nor yearning for the heat of a fire.

Chris had sent out the call. I had come but I had come too far. I had accessed the human condition. He had recalled me to a distant time when I was young like him and subject to future dreams, with some romantic view of a cottage and a garden and companionship.

That was no use. It was my job to take Chris to our side, not to stumble back toward his.

I held Chris by the crook of his arm and guided him forward as though he were blind. I cannot report accurately on his mindscape. It was still blackened by the Ancient's transmission but smeared through it was the tangerine pull of Susan's longing. My own entry as I investigated his condition set him on overload. His body stiffened, his walking stopped.

I withdrew.

The light the open front door cast across the garden pulled back. The door clicked closed behind us. Viktor had shut it. Whatever the power of Susan's gaze it could not penetrate a sealed door. I sensed Chris relax.

Enough light shone through the window above the door to colour the path that pulsed red with the flash of the reindeer's nose. It would have been good to move wide of the path and test Chris's adaptation to night-time vision. We could run with the cats and I could watch Chris coil and unfurl in the hunt. But Viktor sped past us on his little feet.

'Be quick sir, please,' he said.

I don't blame him. The police were coming. Even they could track footsteps across snow.

I know you, I spoke into the boy's ear. I come from your parents. I will tell you. I will show you.

His litheness returned and I adopted that loping walk of the young that he has, my arm now around his shoulder to link us. His warm breath gusted out as puffed white clouds in the cold.

I would chill his warm breath for him. I could do that.

I would bring him home.

Viktor is jealous of command.

'Chris will ride in front,' he announced as we walked through the gate. 'I've set up a monitor behind the driver's seat for you, sir. The headphones are hooked beneath it. Put them over your ears and press the green button to activate the system. The Direktor is waiting. She has an urgent communication for you.'

'The Direktor can wait,' I informed him. 'I have the boy. The police are on their way. Our situation is urgent enough without distractions.'

I opened the rear door and moved my hand to Chris's shoulder to usher him inside. I wanted him beside me. Viktor somehow imposed himself in the doorway—my eyes had been on Chris and so I did not spot the move—so that Chris had to halt. Viktor started speaking just inches from the boy's face.

'You will help me, Chris. You will guide me.' I said he was speaking but this wasn't his voice. He had been listening to Susan while waiting outdoors. He stared into the boy's eyes the way Susan had done. He spoke in the hypnotic rhythm of her pleading; the simple sentences, the repetition, the call of Chris's name. 'It is dark. It is snowing. The police are coming. We are lost here. You know the way, Chris. A quiet way. You can help us. Only you can help us. Show us the way, Chris. The quiet way. Guide us back to the city.'

His touch was gentle and barely brushed Chris's sleeve, and yet the boy responded. He settled himself into the passenger seat and Viktor closed the door behind him.

'You need your privacy, sir. Our car stands out I'm afraid. There is very little traffic and none of it bears a German licence plate as ours does. The lady alerted the police to your being German and so it is best for us not to be seen. We have the boy now. He can direct us to the city. This will keep him occupied. He can take us to a place where you and he can be together. Settle yourself in sir. Here are the headphones. We'd best be on our way.'

I did not need his persuasion. Chris was closed inside the car so that's where I needed to be. Viktor pressed the green button and the monitor sprang into a dazzle that stunned me a moment. The brightness dimmed and the image of the Direktor appeared. She was mouthing words. I fitted the headphones over my ears but turned from her as I did so. Blue light strobed the ceiling of our car. I turned. Viktor had driven forward but only by metres. A car pulled in to the space he had vacated, a beacon flashing on its roof.

'Stop, Viktor,' I said.

He continued, but slowly. I would haul the police from their vehicle before they had time to note down our licence plate. Then I would return to deal with Viktor. I pulled at the lever to open the door.

'It's not the police, sir,' he said, and dared to increase our speed. 'It's an ambulance. I watched as it pulled into the street. 'Ambulance' is written on its side. The lady mentioned an attack and a wound. This will be a paramedic they've called in as a precaution. It's a lone young woman. She must have been in the neighbourhood. Look, sir, no-one's getting out. She'll keep to the security of her vehicle till the police arrive. It's not her job to notice what we do, sir. We can leave her be. I'm turning left now, Chris, and you can direct us from here.'

We had followed a bend in the road to a junction where Viktor did not stop but skidded into the new straight road and eased his foot down on the accelerator.

'Konrad!' The call was a shout that hammered into my skull. We had driven beyond the tangerine reach of the village's street lamps. A face stared out at me from the light glow of the monitor. 'So I have your attention at last.'

She spoke in German. I did not care for that 'at last,' that *'endlich'*. Few use my name, and those who do would not dare to shout it. I reached toward the button on the monitor to turn off its power.

'The boy is in danger,' the Direktor said, snatching out the words as her image died. The screen went blank. I pressed the button again. She returned.

'I'll remind you,' she resumed, 'that I am invested with the powers of the Council. When I speak, I speak as their voice. You will do well to listen.'

'You spoke of the boy.' I did not need her threats. The Council was never a hierarchy and no one voice is stronger than another. 'Explain the danger.'

'You heard the call. The boy called to you.'

'So I am the danger?'

'You felt the call from across the sea. Such strength in a call is unprecedented.'

'Viktor reported this?'

'Viktor responds to our enquiries. You are important to us, Konrad. We monitor you as best we can. Viktor offers just one strand of information. Though he is indicating to turn right just now, that information does not come from him. Look, Konrad, his headlights show that the lane ahead is blocked. It is a minor road that has not been cleared of snow. He reverses . . . and resumes progress along the main road.'

She spoke as it happened.

'A camera relays this?'

'We watch your progress and see and hear what happens inside the car.

The boy and Viktor both turned their heads as the car reversed. Viktor did so in order to watch the road. The boy did not look at the road but at you.'

It was so. Chris met my gaze and held it. He did not smile but I noted the slight dilation of his eyes. He recognised me.

'When the boy looked at you, a line of pressure ran from your throat. It both tightened and expanded in your chest.'

'How do you know this? Cameras cannot show you this.'

'This is your first call, Konrad. Your first take. The boy looked you in the eyes. We know how that feels.'

'This is not typical.'

'This is your first time, Konrad. It is not typical for you.'

'You forget who I am. I am a keeper of record. You know what is typical because I have taught it to you. Chris sent out his call. Recognition should have been instant in the moment we met. It was not. I have seen little sign of it till now. The boy's senses were swamped. He has seen the face of the Ancient. A darkness swallowed him.'

The Direktor's mouth opened for speech but no words came out. She closed it. Our conversation had shifted from her script.

'How did he see the face of the Ancient?'

'The image was projected from his computer and onto his bedroom wall. He saw the birth mother also, in a separate projection.'

'How can this be? We have tried to access his computer and failed. The firewalls around it are too strong. This is more urgent than we knew. Watch this, Konrad.'

The Direktor disappeared from the monitor and in her place came footage which showed the rear of a truck. The left side of its rear doors was open. A man drove a forklift truck from just off-screen and lifted a ridged metal container to sit atop another one and so fill the truck's interior. A second man pushed the thick door closed and turned a large barred handle to seal it.

The image froze and the Direktor's voice returned.

'Did you see them?'

'See what? See who?'

'You are not used to film I suppose. Watch again.'

The film jumped back to where the truck's doors were open, and the fork-lift driver reappeared. The quality was grainy and the film monochrome, taken from a CCTV camera that was monitoring the loading, but that is an explanation rather than excuse. I should have seen. I wanted the film to be over, the Direktor to be gone, and my attention to swing back to Chris who was now talking to Viktor in the front of the car. He was asking questions about me.

'Watch one more time. And this time I will pause the film.'

She did so. Just before the film stopped I noticed the movement, no more than a shifting of black shadows. That is all they were; movement. Only as the image froze did they appear. Two figures had leapt up to the bed of the truck. Their feet had not yet landed but as the film continued they were already gone, their dark forms sliding into the blackness between the containers.

'The Ancient and his wife?' I asked, and as I spoke Chris broke from his conversation and turned to snatch a look at me. What made him turn? Was it my words, my tone, or did he pick up some mental picture from my shock of recognition?

'We tracked them to the depot. And there we lost them. We are lucky that a security camera was trained on the truck in the way it was.' The truck vanished from the screen and the Direktor reappeared. 'That truck is refrigerated, its interior chilled to minus six. No human could survive inside it. No official at immigration control would think to check it. There is no heat for a heat sensor to detect. The truck drove from the depot to the ferry terminal at Zeebrugge. It is now on board a ship that is crossing the North Sea, bound for Kingston on Hull. They are coming, Konrad. Coming for their boy.'

'When will they get here?'

'You are ahead of them, but not by long.'

'He is their boy.'

'Who heard his call? You did, Konrad. From afar. He is not their boy. He is yours.'

'He is the son of an Ancient.'

'Exactly!' The Direktor leaned forward to shout the word at me. 'You were taken by an Ancient. That is special. It is rare. That is why you heard the call. This Chris, as you call him, needs you. He is tired of the human condition. Break him free, Konrad.'

'Why do you care?'

'You joined us, Konrad. As the take of an Ancient you were under no compulsion to join us, yet you did so. That is important. It merits our honour. That is why we are there for you now.'

'Be clear. What interests of yours does the boy serve?'

'Ours, Konrad. These are our interests, not just yours. There is no you and us here, no yours and ours. You know we act as one.'

'Be explicit.'

'Why did you join us, Konrad?'

'It was not my choice. I am a biographer. I needed subjects. You granted me no access unless I joined. It was a condition made by the Council. I had no choice.'

'You are companionable. You were lonely. That is the truth. An Ancient took you and abandoned you.'

'And so I turned to you?' I let my disdain show in my voice.

'You have lain dormant for more than a century. No-one imagines that the loneliness ever left you, Konrad.'

Her remark left me silent. She waited a moment and then continued.

'Would you do to the boy what that Ancient did to you? Would you take him and then abandon him? I don't think so. You have a quality of care about you.'

I reached forward and pressed the button to turn off the screen. Her image blanked and then immediately returned.

'Why did you do that?' she asked. The power button was only for effect and she retained control of the system through some override. 'Why turn me off?'

'You speak as though I am a product of my emotional history. That is nonsense. I will not listen to it.'

I pressed the button to wipe her image from the screen once more. She returned immediately.

'Please excuse me Konrad. You have slept through an entire age of psychoanalysis. I have lived through that same age. It colours my discourse. You should perhaps read up on the subject. It offers possible insights to a biographer. But let's forget that now. Answer me one question. This boy, this young man, sits in the front of the car. Do you want to be with him, or do you want to be elsewhere, far away, on your own?'

It was a ridiculous question. 'He called me,' I answered.

'And you have come. Now turn him. Take him. It's what you both want.'

'What do you want?'

I spoke too harshly. Viktor checked me in his mirror and the boy briefly turned his head once again.

'We want what you want.' The Direktor leaned forward but her voice was now soft, a murmur of suggestion through the phones around my ears. 'What do we want? We want to know an Ancient. Intimately. And this young man, your Chris, is how we are going to do it. Is the son of an Ancient an Ancient too? It is as close as we are going to get. No Ancient will ever join us. Chris called you. You heard him and came from over the sea. Take him, Konrad. You must take him before the Ancient can reach him. Take him before the father claims the son.'

'You want us to claim him instead? So he too can choose to sleep on dusty attic boards for a century?'

'It is not so he will sleep. It is so we will wake. You are into your second day in this century. Tell me, do you like what you have seen?'

Like? I had no answer to give her.

'You haven't decided? Or you have no answer?'

'Do I want my nights illuminated, electricity pouring out light as though darkness were the enemy? Do I enjoy the press of crowds? Do toxins sweeten the air? Have I sensed any purpose in humans' extra velocity of travel? Is this remote conversation we are having preferable to silence?'

'Your answer in each case is no?'

'You have surprised me. I presumed I had no preferences. But you're right. No no no no no.'

'You have lived too long. Is this what you feel? For a while the new excited you, but it became repetitious. Nothing new was better than what you had.'

'What is our role, Direktor?' I confess I spoke her title as though it were a joke. 'Are we here to feed and cull? Is that the sum of us?'

'You don't know?'

'I once had a theory. Our kind outlived desire. We accumulated vast experience which amounted to wisdom. We could shepherd humans across the planet.'

'Let's be clear, Konrad. Humans have one basic desire—all other desires, including the desire to kill and the desire to procreate, are a subset of this—the desire to live. Disappointment, or the decrepitude of old age, can convert this into a desire to die.

'In my human life I was a psychoanalyst. In simple terms the psychoanalyst is one who restores the desire to live. One of our kind, who might otherwise have taken to the boards in our attic here and lain down for a century, came to me as a patient. You will not know about transference between patient and clinician, but the concept is familiar to you. Professionally one avoids transference. I acted unprofessionally. I wanted my patient's condition. I let myself be taken.

'I stayed conscious, even analytical, throughout the process. What I achieved was the fusion of both desires, to live and to die. That is our state. Death is achieved. It is no longer an option. So what do we do when our life disappoints? Do we live with disappointment forever?

'Essentially psychoanalysis is an exploration of the past in order to clear the future—so that the future is not a mindless repetition of unknown conditioning. Our kind cannot fathom the future because we are unconscious of our past; our deep past which stems from the Ancients. We don't know where we came from.

'You can find out for us. You have the son of an Ancient with you. He wants what you have. Take him. Take him and don't abandon him. He is our past and our future. Let him be ours.'

The Direktor stared out at me a moment and then disappeared.

Her place on the screen was taken by Chris. We were speeding along a highway cleared of snow. Viktor clearly did not need his directions but the boy stared out even so, reading the road signs, eager to be useful. 'Don't worry about the speed camera,' he said. 'It's not working.'

He leaned forward, as though bringing the next road sign that bit nearer could make a difference.

'Turn right at the roundabout and head for the city centre.'

There was a plastic clip to hold the sunshield in place. The screw that fixed it to the car's roof had a dark mirror at its centre. That must be the lens. A camera was angled on this boy. Who knew how many watched him? Tired old eyes fixed on a teenager as though he could give them hope.

We passed through a sequence of traffic lights. Houses of light brick were set back from the road and then they were closer. The housing stock aged, the bricks were darker, the gardens shrunk until the conjoined houses lined up directly alongside the traffic. And then the houses stopped and commerce started, blank-faced buildings of concrete and plate glass. Crowds massed on the paving behind each of the traffic lights and swarmed around us whenever we stopped. We were in the city.

'This will do,' I said.

'I can't stop here sir. There's nowhere to park.'

The lights turned from amber to green as I stepped out. I opened Chris's door as I closed my own. Car horns blared behind us.

'Out, Chris,' I said.

Out where no cameras are watching you. Out where Viktor can't follow. Out where I can have you to myself.

'I need you. Show me around.'

He stepped from the car to the pavement and was walking forward even as the car door slammed behind him. I stepped alongside.

'They're shopping for Christmas,' he said, like this was part of the human condition from which we were both apart. 'We'll find somewhere quiet.'

We moved like dark vapour through the crowds.

29

IT HAS ALWAYS SEEMED crude to name a creature after what it eats; carnivores and vegetarians are not separate species of humans. Yet as a human I adopted the terminology in which we are known as vampires. In my writings since then I have been mindful to avoid the term. I did not allow myself to be taken just so as to adjust my eating habits. I did it so as to discover all the layers of existence to our kind beyond our way of feeding.

I was naïve. Why did no-one tell me of that hunger of the take?

It has its own force, that hunger, like a parasite invasion. When did it enter? Looking back, when I walked through the black door into the boy's room what I found in its minimalist interior was both his presence and his absence. I stood in something of a hollow. The call had edged my brain till that point. It had tugged at me from over the sea and it still bit as I sat inside the boy's home for I was there and he was elsewhere.

Inside his bedroom the call let me go. It had been answered. That was the high point of a pendulum swing; a moment of inertia. The boy ran his footprints from the snow and up the stairs and entered his room and stared not at me but at the projections on his wall and that was it. The boy and I were together. The call switched. It became this hunger.

It nibbled at first. I never noticed it but surely that was its passage. Hunger does not announce its approach. It comes when you have been eaten, when it has gnawed at your bones. It has chewed you dry and needs more.

On the pedestrianised street I simply followed the boy. The street was wide and flanked by large, high stores. The crowd was wayward. Women walked the most direct path. Their hands were filled with bags and they marched. Men were fewer and they drifted. Teenagers were as random as infants, darting between windows, turning back on themselves, chasing each other. All of these people puffed clouds of breath.

Chris moved faster than all of them without showing any sign of hurry. He had an athlete's ease of movement, a fluid play of muscles from his shoulders to his feet. Breath steamed from his mouth too. I tasted it. The street was a stream of odours, of stench wrenched up from guts and the explosive spray of sneezes. Nothing is more redolent of the human condition, of their living dying organism, than the press of a winter crowd. I choose to avoid them but there I was, tracking a teenage human, tasting the particles of his particular breath within the human breath stream, wetting my mouth with its moisture, savouring its warmth and swallowing it down.

The street opened into a wide plaza and the crowd broke. A small girl in a red coat and white woollen hat stopped to stare up at a tall Christmas tree but her mother yanked her hand to keep her moving. A black statue of an aged Queen Victoria dominated the centre of the plaza. She was a giant compared to the midget queen I knew about when I shared her century, and old instead of young. A man emerged from the public urinals hidden beneath her pedestal and the shock of the winter air shook his lungs. He bent forward as he coughed. This was a man ripe for culling. Such men are loners. I could shadow that man to a doorway and take all the food I needed.

That was the instinct. Follow this sick man. Feed. The chain of need and response was too instant to be called hunger. But I was on a different mission.

Chris swerved to move around the man. I followed. Light blazed through the plate glass walls of a shopping centre but he spared me that. I thought he was heading toward a narrow street of older shops, a spangle of Christmas lights strung high between buildings and lampposts, but he spared me that too. He turned right, following the waters of a quay. Snow fizzed on a gas brazier above a couple who sat at an outdoor table and sipped coffee and drew on cigarettes. I smelt the gas, the nicotine breath, and then as I walked on I smelled just the living scent of Chris.

He turned left. This street was little wider than an alley. Lighting was dim. I lowered my hand and stepped closer to walk beside Chris. Cobbles beneath the snow pressed through the soles of my feet. This was a street from such centuries as I knew; a street from before my time of lying down. It was some comfort. It gave me the strength to speak.

'Take me somewhere quiet,' I said. 'We need to be alone. We need to talk.'

I needed Chris to listen, was the truth of it. With one sharp slice of my hand I could have this boy on the ground and feed as long as I needed. No-one would come this way. No-one would see us. And yet my brain said no. It said to go somewhere and talk. In this alley Chris would just be food. My brain needed more. It needed an offering.

Chris walked in place beside me and yet I could not have him. Not yet.

That was the hunger that wracked me.

I was in this world at the advent of twin-barrel shotguns. One morning I headed out into wild country with a party of men. We kept upwind of a herd of deer, our backs bent to keep us low, the tread of our feet muffled by heather, and yet still the stag detected us. He stood, his head erect, and looked our way. His deer kept munching at the ground around him. He knew this moorland and knew the distance that was safe. We were too remote to be of harm.

Our first gun blasted the air. The shot was not good but its explosion smashed the sense out of the stag's world. The deer raised their heads but none jumped. They just shook on their legs for the roar was all around them. There was nowhere to run to, just a dazed and shuddering dislocation. A second gun, the second ever heard on that stretch of land, burst a hole in the stag's throat.

That stag held the quiet spot in the centre of moorland. Such was the advent of guns.

Thin lines of black wires fed from the inside pocket of Chris's jacket to his ears. They ended in black studs that nestled in his lobes. I ignored the thin electronic beat that coated Chris's skull. It was like the click of the hammer of those first guns. I could not know that my sense of the world would be blasted to nothing.

Water dripped from the rusted iron of high guttering and splattered against a flagstone at the far end of our narrow lane. I heard it. It grew louder as our footsteps strode in pace toward it. My shoes gave the crisp sound of leather on wet stone and Chris's the duller sound of rubber soles. Such were natural sounds. For me, electronic music was an unnatural sound. I was severely out of date.

I slipped inside Chris's mind. Enter a mind and you find a quiet point at its centre from which to journey out. That quiet spot was always there and always vacant. Always.

There was no quiet spot in that young mind. How do I compare it? I was once trampled by a horse. Its hoof is still imprinted in my skull. The black mass of the creature, the whinny of its breath, its hooves striking stone, my body knocked from its feet, that whole roiling experience would have been death for any man. This is how I was inside Chris's mind. The blast of noise stripped senses from me. This was not music. It was battlefield. Men wailed and the rhythmic beat was cannon fire played at the speed of hailstones and the pitch of muskets.

The noise caught me. I could find no way through and no way out. My feet stopped walking. My legs buckled. Chris snapped his head round to face me. He had felt me in his head, I am sure of it, but his flash of anger dropped when he saw the pain in my face.

He stepped close. I reached out and brushed my fingers across the thin wires. The black buds sprang from his ears. The daze of noise within his mind went blank. It let me go. I pulled back.

'Are you OK?' he asked.

'Why?'

I let him take hold of my elbows and hold me steady.

'Why do you put that noise through your head?'

'You could hear it?'

I shook my head fast, trying to bring it back to some sense.

'I play it in town,' he explained. 'It helps me get through. It blanks out all the stuff in the minds of the crowd. Christmas is worst. It's not just the crowds, though their thoughts get over-excited. I hate Christmas songs. They come at you from everywhere. People sing them in their heads. I ramp up the volume at Christmas.'

'It's insane.'

'You were in there, weren't you? Inside my mind. What are you trying to do? Read me? Take control? Who are you?'

He was asking questions. That was good, but he gave me no time to respond. He jammed the black buds back in his ears and strode off.

There's a fluidity in human youth. Chris was at its peak. Every limb, every muscle, every sinew was in instant response. His hips swayed above the movement of his feet, his footsteps sprang, his shoulders floated the waves of his walk. He wasn't walking away and he was no longer leading me. I was forgotten.

I want to write about the self-absorption of the young, but I'll be honest. The young are no more self-absorbed than others. That quality simply grows less confident with age. It crumbles alongside the beauty of youth. I have kept much of the beauty that I had. It did not attract Chris as much as the beauty of his own image. He walked as though I were not there and I followed.

That, I believe, shows the extremity of my hunger.

He had to need me for the take to be effective. He had to want me. And yet he walked as though I did not exist. I was lonely for him.

I suspect loneliness is not the general condition of our kind as we approach the moment of take.

I confess it for the record.

Men stood with pints of ale outside a pub at the lane's end. Hoods and woollen caps obscured their heads and they sucked at cigarettes. The lane opened out into a square that was filled by a church even I knew to be old.

Fairy lights rimmed the old stone of its entrance. Would Chris lead me there?

I was born into a Christian world and chose to be taken from it when the chance arose. Such a world maintains no superstitious hold on me. If a church brought a sense of security to Chris, that was fine. I liked the age of its stones. The air inside would be chilled. It would likely be empty of people. Yes, this church could serve me well.

Solid iron railings blocked the approach from the front. A gate was open on the left-hand side. Chris veered right. He paid the church no regard. He walked instead to an old brick building on the corner of the square and entered through its dark oak doorway. I followed.

Beyond the doorway glazed doors opened into a small entrance hall. Chris had passed through. A plump young man stood behind a counter at the far end. He had short brown hair and round pink cheeks. 'Good afternoon,' he said. 'In out of the cold, are we?'

There was little indoor heat to speak of. Some came from a light bulb strung above him. More came from his body.

'The boiler's packed in, I'm afraid. I'd have shut the place early but the engineer's in, seeing what he can do. Take a look round if you want to. I'll give you a call if we decide to close up. Have you been here before?'

Despite the cold the man was sweating. I reached out a finger, wiped it across his neck, and brought it back to my nose.

The sweat smelled of spirits. I recognised the scent. 'Jaegermeister,' I said. 'It was just a swig.' His sweat changed. He was pumping out fear pheromones now that I had detected his drinking. 'Better to heat up from the inside than just give up and go home, that's how I saw it. We've got temperature-controlled exhibits here. I couldn't just abandon them to the freeze.'

I looked to my left. Chris hadn't gone that way.

'You're right, there's nothing temperature-controlled in there. That's the old schoolroom. Take a look. It had one tiny fireplace to heat the whole hall. Imagine being a kid in cold like that. We've set it up to show schoolkids what life used to be like. Of course no school group would set foot in the place at that temperature. Health and safety wouldn't allow it.'

'And the temperature-controlled exhibits?'

His mouth dropped open and he stared at me. His mouth gave off steam when he spoke. Had he noticed that mine didn't?

'You're German?' he asked.

I set my mind to recall my last sentence. He was right. I had resorted to German. Perhaps it was the sight of the recreated schoolroom, so familiar from my own schooldays. Perhaps it was that hint of Jaegermeister on his breath and in his sweat. Somehow I had slipped. It meant he was paying me a keener attention than was healthy.

I checked over my shoulder. The front door was furnished with an old-fashioned bolt. I could lock it, prevent any more visitors coming in to disturb us, and use this young man to deal with the baser levels of my hunger. When I am fed I am calmer. My work with Chris needed me calm.

'We get quite a few Germans,' he rattled on. 'Some have even heard of the famous pupils who came through when this place was a grammar school; the anti-slave guy William Wilberforce and the poet Andrew Marvell. That's not what they ask for though. They don't want the exhibits of city life either. They always want to know the way to the mummy. It makes me laugh, all these Germans travelling the world looking for their mummy.'

The world would not miss such a man as this.

A roar from further in the building made him look up.

'Feel that?' he said. Indeed, a stream of warm air came through a vent high on the wall behind him.

'Looks like the engineer's done it. I'd best make him his tea. I promised him a mug as soon as things were fixed.' He stepped from behind his counter to head down the corridor on the right, to beyond the neon-lit shelves of a gift store where he opened a door marked Private. He looked back before stepping inside. 'Go upstairs for that mummy of yours. The room should be back to its controlled temperature any minute now. We keep it cool. Keep the humidity low. Keep off the rot.'

I would follow the man. I could feed from him as his kettle boiled. The kettle's steam would add high humidity but to a low temperature. If I closed his office door no-one would smell him for a while.

Such was my state of mind. A door clicked open beyond the stairs and a man in blue overalls emerged. It was the engineer. The attendant called out to him. The two men engaged in some banter that excluded me. I caught Chris's scent, the trail of his body warmth up the stairs.

That's what my hunger needed. The rest was madness.

I followed my nose.

30

UPSTAIRS, THE CEILING of a high exhibition hall was striped with black oak beams. The floor was filled with large artworks from Ancient Egypt which I knew to be replicas but thought of as fakes. Tutankhamen still slept undisturbed by grave robbers when last I lay down to sleep. I ignored these artefacts. Chris was emitting some soft version of the call that had brought me over the seas from Belgium. He was all I wanted now. His presence stirred in the right side of my brain.

A doorway led into relative gloom. Chris's scent grew stronger as I approached. Inside this small inner room were two glass cases, oblong coffins raised to just so much height that children could stand and look down on the corpses inside. To the right, on the floor and sitting against the wall, was Chris.

'I was right. I thought this was a good place to talk,' he said. 'It's usually quiet. On the Saturday before Christmas I was sure it would be empty.'

'But for these two.' I nodded at the cases. 'Of all possible meeting places in this city, the mummy exhibit in the museum is a curious choice.'

'The one on the left is just the mummy case,' Chris said. It was brown, any brightness of inscription dulled away. 'This one's the mummy. A hundred years ago mummies were in vogue. This one was an exhibit on top of a rich man's grand piano. It's in relative peace here.'

I looked down at the creature. Its head was swaddled in grey bandages. Its feet had no toes, but the roundness and darkness of wooden clogs.

Remnant bones lay on the bottom of the case, disappearing into the bandaged remains at shin level.

'He was mistaken for a princess once, because of the size of his hips. Then x-rays revealed a tiny penis. He's a hermaphrodite. A priest who served the god Min. He's my friend.'

'You speak with him?'

'I tell him stuff. He listens. He doesn't get fazed. He helps me sort through my thoughts.'

'So he talks to you?'

'His mind is blank. I've searched him out but there's nothing there to read. He's just very old and very dead. That suits me. I've picked out what's useful from the minds of most people in the city. There's not much left to learn. Here I get to rest.'

'Do you visit often?'

'We hang out a few times a week. I sleep over now and again. I come in before the place closes, slink into the shadows, and then settle down on the floor before the alarms are set and the motion detectors kick in. There's a replica of Tutankhamen's bed in the next room. I've slept on that too but here's more restful. I go still and picture other worlds.'

'Other planets?'

'No. Just earlier times. Ancient times.'

I left the mummies and went to sit down beside him, both our backs to the wall.

'You read my mind, don't you?' he said. 'You're in there now. I can feel you.'

'I'm just visiting the edges. Now you've turned off that electronic noise.'

He still wore the buds wired to his ears, but pulled them clear as we spoke. 'You spooked me. I pick at people's brains and they never notice. No-one's ever picked at mine though. What are you looking for?'

'You,' I said. 'You called me. No-one's ever done that to me before. You did it though, from over the seas. Do you know you called me?'

'I never called. I don't even know you. I don't have your number.'

'Not like that. When you read people's minds, when you hook new knowledge from them, do you know how you do it?'

'That's like saying do you know how you think. I've read the minds of brain surgeons and even they don't know the answer to that. It's all neuro receptors and transmitters but none of it amounts to thinking. You just think. And I pick stuff from people's minds. It's natural.'

'You've exhausted the supply here, you say. You're at university now. Don't your professors have material you can learn from?'

'I sample lectures. I go to one session of each lecturer, scan them while they're telling us stuff and pick up all they have. By the second lecture, they're telling me what I already know. They each have little pockets of knowledge and they think their pockets are deep, but pick those pockets and they're empty. Nothing connects. One person collects one set of knowledge, another collects another, but it doesn't add up. There's no bigger picture.'

'So you reach out. You go looking for the bigger picture. You want to learn what other men and women don't know. Your mind goes searching. It sends out the call. That's why I'm here, Chris. You sent out the call and I've answered. I have what you need. I can give you what no man can.'

I felt his touch, that young mind of his reaching into mine. And then it withdrew. It snatched itself back.

'You just suck at me,' he said. 'There's light firing round the edges of your mind. It's bright and blinding. Then there's some dark hollow beyond that. Other people, I can step down gradually. It's like they contain ropes that spiral round each other and I can take hold and go down hand over hand. When I need to find my way out again it's easy. With you, there's just a black hole. I'm never scared but you scare me. I pull back. You're not normal.'

He didn't pull back though. He moved forward from the wall so he could turn his body a little toward me.

'You say you're scared because your heart's racing but that's not scared, Chris. That's excitement,' I told him. 'You've been bored. So very bored. You're tired of normal. Come on back. Enter my mind one more time. I won't suck you in, I promise. I'll bring up a story, a controlled story with just one image following another.'

'Like in a movie?'

Movies were new to me. I had picked up their existence but not their significance. Quickly, I read Chris's mind to learn what movies meant to him. He viewed them as the projection of a series of sharp, intense scenes, with a focus on the emotional states of fear that were responses to a sequence of violent actions. You will of course know more of cinema than this. For me, it was my first encounter with the medium. It is a suitable way of delivering alternative realities to the human brain.

'Yes, like a movie.'

'Who's in it?'

'Who does the movie feature? You know the characters already, Chris. You played the start of this movie in your bedroom this afternoon. A man is in it, and a woman.'

'Those two? The ones on my bedroom wall? Are they really my parents? Was I right?'

'You have to let me show you this movie to find out. Picture them, Chris. Imagine your way into the story. Call them to mind.'

He just stared at me.

'Go on. This is easy. Shut your eyes. Picture the images of those two people as they shone from your wall.'

He closed his eyes. His eyeballs shivered movement behind the eyelids and then they grew still.

'Now you see them, Chris. You see the man and the woman. Come into my mind. Find those people there. Lock on to them. And then the movie will begin.'

I waited.

The next move needed to be the boy's. He had to come to me. I have written about this factor of the take in my role as a biographer, but my information was second-hand. This first-hand experience of the hunger was so acute as to be almost insufferable. Chris sat beside me. One slice of my nail, one bite, and my hunger could be over. It would not be a take—Chris would be a victim and not a supplicant—but he would be dead. The immediate feed would do me. The hunger would be gone.

In truth though, the hunger would be lost. It was more than physical. It was not about sustenance and it was not about death; it was about transfiguration. Chris had to understand all that I could give him. He had to accept it.

I lowered my eyelids so as not to process images, and not to turn toward the play of soft light on Chris's cheekbones or to look into his eyes. I switched off my hearing so as not to strain after the speeding rhythm of the boy's heartbeats. I shut down all my receptors, so the warmth from his blood did not stroke across my skin and the scent of his sweat did not sweep into my nose. Though my body was folded into a seated posture, with my legs straight out in front of me, it absented itself from all pretence of living. That was my mode of the last decades as I lay on my attic boards. It was the physical absence I took in that earlier century.

In that distant year when I last entered this state I did so out of weariness. In this year the difference was extreme. I was not weary as I shut my system down. I was fired with intensity.

My brain stayed alert but as a receptor. It would not trigger action. I could not speak and could not move. That was the safest and only possible way. In that mode there was not a patience to snap. I could not slash a nail across Chris's throat and close my lips around his blood as it pulsed. The boy could stand and leave my side and I could not move to grab him.

As I cut off the physiological receptors the hunger did not fade. I switched off all physical needs and yet still the hunger flared.

In physical time, who knows how long it lasted. Perhaps it was no more than minutes. I was out of time, caught in some place between the instant and forever. My brain had only one focus. Its receptors were charged with only one intent. They keened toward the moment of his touch.

And then he was there. He came in the way of a cat who brushes the fur and sinews of its body around your legs. His mind furled around the edges of my own.

I noticed him. That was all I could do. My body was locked without motion while my brain flared at his presence. I had offered him a story because my mind contained the constituent parts of the story he wanted; the story we all want, the story of our origins. I would not give him a narrative—that is stale storytelling—but I could direct him toward the material. We each must assemble the narrative we need. His point of entry was the image of his parents. That would attract to it all that was necessary.

He furled in with that softness of cat. It was as a cat that he continued: he loped in bursts of movement and then grew still, a stillness that quivered with tension; he slashed out at what caught his attention; he settled in one direction and then shifted, as fluidly as water hitting stone, to proceed in another; and then he prowled, a steady gait as he circled up through the landscape of his hunt. And then he was gone.

My mind was clear.

I turned on my receptors. He was kneeling in front of me. His hand lay on top of mine, the four fingers and thumb pressed into my flesh like points of fire.

'You are cold,' he said. 'You are dead.'

I licked my tongue around my palate and opened my mouth. I restored my power of speech. 'Am I?' I said. 'Then who is talking?'

'You're dead. My parents are dead.'

'Dead or undead?'

'That was a sick story. You're sick in the head. You made up a sick story and planted it in your head for me to find.'

'So what am I, sick or dead?'

'You're both,' he said, and stood up. He moved to stand between the two glass coffins. He looked down at the mummy. The dim reflection of his face looked back at him from above the mummified face of the corpse.

'I'm alive,' he countered.

'It's true, Chris. You're alive and you are ageing.'

'How old are you?'

'I don't know. I lose count.'

'A hundred?'

'Oh not so young.'

'You look young,' he said, and he was regarding me now with full attention. 'Who was he?'

I shook my head to bring some sense to it. It didn't work. 'He?' I asked.

'My parents were there. I did like you said. I took their images into your mind and found my story. I saw the way they birthed me. I watched my mother cut herself and feed me blood. And then I stood on a quay as a ship sailed out into the night. It was winter. I was warm and everything else was cold. My father took hold of me from my mother's arms but he had shrunk. He was my father but in the size of a young teenage boy. The sea raced below us, scudded with low waves. I landed on deck, still in my small father's arms, and then my mother landed beside us. The deck was coated with ice. They laid me down. My mother passed through a door while we waited and then she was back. Someone else picked me up but it was not them. I watched them pass through the railings of the ship and dive into flight. I was in a stranger's arms and I was alone. That is my story. Am I right?'

I nodded.

'My story so far as you know it. You weren't there. This is a story as told to you. You are passing on a tale. Is that right?'

'Yes.'

'Who told it you? My parents?'

'It was around the time of your birthday. They were recalling the occasion of eighteen years before.'

'So did they just give you the details and you turned it into images for me to find, or did you go into their minds like I did just now? Did you pick out a story that played like a movie?'

I gave it some thought.

'It was a fusion,' I told him. 'I'm a biographer. I take what I find till it becomes my own.'

'It's not your own story though is it? It's mine. What was your birth like? Can you tell me?'

I couldn't. 'That's not relevant. That was another life. A human life.'

'So you think you have the truth about my birth when you can't even reclaim any memories of your own? You hawk bullshit. You're nothing.'

'I have learned when to trust. I question. I compare one set of stories against another. I can't assemble a story until I have its details. Those details merge into a version of the truth. Did it seem true to you, that tale of your birth?'

‘That I was some little thing that came squawking out of the womb of an undead woman? That I was given strength to live by the blood that victims donated to my vampire parents? Do you mean that story? Sure, that rings true.’

‘You’re being sarcastic.’

‘I’m eighteen. If now isn’t a time for sarcasm, when is?’

‘I know it’s hard to understand.’

‘Of course it is. It’s not true.’

‘Look into yourself Chris. Look into your own true nature. See how the story resonates with that.’

‘So what were you before you became a biographer? A teacher? You think you have the right to preach to me about the truth? I’ve been inside your mind, don’t forget. You’re no better than anyone else. You want to fit me to your story. You want me to live inside the constraints you’ve imposed on your own life so you can feel better about how fucked-up you really are. Well fuck you.’

‘I’m not doing this for me, Chris. I’m doing this for you. It’s for . . . ’

‘For my own good? Just listen to yourself. Didn’t you ever have a father?’

‘Once. He died.’

‘That’s it? He just died? And did he spawn you after he died, or before?’

‘Your story’s a special one, Chris. I’d given up on the world. I thought there was no story left that was worth telling. And then I was told about you.’

‘So if your father’s dead, who was he?

‘Who?’

‘That guy in your head. The one who’s at the forefront of everything you think. I found that man and woman OK, the ones you say are my parents, but I had to look hard. They were in the background. Right up front was this figure that towered as dark as a mountain. His face fused out of darkness and stared at me and drew me closer till I was looking just into the one shiny eye that shone like a cave’s opening into the world. I looked into this eye and watched a figure move through the dark red shadows of an Egyptian temple. It was this mummy here. That eye watched this mummy when it was alive. Snippets of movement were caught there. The figure was there in that distant time and place and yet he is there in your head right now.

'And then I looked through that eye and I saw you. You were as young as you are now and emitted the heat of blood. You looked up at this man's eye with longing. The scene played through for me to watch. You smiled as he leaned toward you. He placed a fingernail against your neck. The nail was sharp. It sliced through. He bent to the wound. You did not struggle.'

Chris walked out from between the glass cases and leaned toward me. His finger was so warm as he laid it on my neck.

'The scar is still there. The skin is pale and puckered. Could you not heal that wound?'

'I could. But I don't choose to,' I admitted. 'I keep the scar as a memento.'

'And this man,' the boy persisted. 'Who was he?'

'He was an Ancient.'

'An Ancient?'

'The one who took me. You don't need to know about him. You have your own story to learn.'

'Tell . . . ' Chris's mouth opened wide, like it was a puppet's. His lips were rigid. 'Tell him.' The voice rose deep and loud from his guts. 'Tell him my story!'

I stared. Chris's face melted a moment. Features of another man pressed into it. Chris's forehead expanded, his eyes withdrew into deeper sockets. And then this second face pulled back.

Chris shook his head. 'That wasn't me,' he said. 'That wasn't me talking. Did you do that?'

I stared at him, blinked, and shook my head.

'It was inside me. It worked my tongue. It found my voice and threw it at you.'

'The Ancient,' I explained. 'It was Istvan, the Ancient who took me. You found some seed of him inside me. Watch what you pay attention to, Chris. It can overpower you. Istvan spoke through you because you let him.'

‘He says to tell me your story. Does he often give you orders like that?’

‘Never before. He took me on the back of promises he made, and then he vanished. I have not seen him since.’

‘What do you mean, ‘he took me’? Is that some sex thing?’

‘Not sex, no. I was human once, like you.’

‘So what are you now?’

‘We don’t label ourselves. Languages are transient. We move between them and beyond them.’

‘You’re crap at straight answers, aren’t you?’

‘It’s not as simple as that. When you move beyond time . . . ’

‘See? Admit it. You’re crap. You talk in circles. You’re a vampire, aren’t you? Why not just say it? Go on. ‘I’m a vampire.’ Say it.’

‘That’s a human term.’

‘So? I’m human, aren’t I? You’re talking to me. Say something I can understand.’

I paused. I would have blushed, had the blood been there to suffuse my cheeks. ‘I’m a vampire,’ I said.

‘Good. We’re getting somewhere. And this ‘take’; is that the moment when a vampire takes a human life?’

‘It’s a moment of transfiguration, a shift beyond the duality of life and death, so that ‘take’ is also a misleading term, in that it exists in opposition to ‘give’ while the act of transfiguration requires both give and take.’

‘I’m human. Humour me. Cut the gloss. Vampire bites human and human becomes vampire. That’s what you mean by ‘take’, isn’t it? That’s the gist of it?’

I thought it through. Maybe I’d have said yes, given time, but really the issue is not so simple.

‘Hear that?’ I asked instead.

Chris wanted an answer, not a distraction.

‘The attendant,’ I said.

Chris listened. Yes, there was the young man’s tread, his cough.

‘He’s on his way upstairs. He’s seeking us out.’

‘So that’s it? Discussion over? Fine by me.’

'No Chris.' I stood up. 'You want vampire? Let me show you vampire. You make me so hungry. I'll feed, then we can talk some more.'

The attendant reached the Egyptian hall and heard our voices.

'Gentlemen,' he said, a silhouette with light behind him as he faced the darkened room of the mummy. 'We're closing up. Time to leave.'

'OK,' Chris told him, some fake youthful buoyancy in his voice. 'I've seen enough in any case. It's time to go.'

He edged past the attendant, hurried to the stairs, and ran down four at a time. My steps matched his, out along the corridor of cheap souvenirs and left to the exit. The glazed doors were open but the front door was locked. Chris turned a large brass key and pulled. I was through the door ahead of him, and waited outside as he slammed it closed.

'So you didn't want my demonstration. You prefer words after all?'

'You chill me.' Chris shuddered and walked away, across the open square to the front of the church. 'You were going to kill him, weren't you?'

'I'm hungry, Chris,' I said. 'I could have fed. I didn't. You owe me.'

A black cotton hood was attached to his jacket, which he flipped up to cover his head. It was a form of hiding. My feet sounded on the wet stone as I kept in pace with his flight. He jammed those buds back into his ears to flood his head with noise and block me out.

I kept clear of the electronic noise and instead read the thoughts that escaped his head. He looked ahead rather than at me. I was right by his side, keeping step. 'This guy's sick,' he was thinking. 'Should I run, or just walk, stay in the crowds, surround myself with people, will that be safe?'

I edited a thought so it still seemed like his and sent it back into his brain. 'Drown him out,' his new thought said. 'Turn my music to max. That got him last time. That will keep him clear.'

His hand obeyed. It tucked itself inside his jacket and span the volume control to full. The blast of noise inside his skull sent him staggering. I plucked the wires from him and leaned in close to breathe instruction into his ear.

'You can't run, Chris. Not now I've found you. Find us somewhere quiet. Somewhere we can talk.'

He started to think. I was inside his mind now the noise was gone, and looked around. He conjured the image of a wooden staircase that led up to a dark panelled room. Yes, Chris, that will do.

'I work at a pub some evenings,' he told me. '*Ye Olde Black Boy*. There's an upstairs bar that's hardly ever used. We could go there.'

'Let's,' I said, and looked up between the buildings.

The sky was dark. The street was old. I liked the winter chill. It felt like coming home.

Chris gave me a blank stare, both hostile and withdrawn, and then slipped his hands inside his pockets and walked on. His shoulders were caught in a shrug. It was cute. He was doing a teenage thing.

We took the route down the side of the church, crossed a road, and entered a tight lane between high old housing. The path was too narrow for two so I walked in the empty street. We were two young men out ghosting the town the way young men do. One exuded heat and the aroma of breath. The other didn't.

31

THE DYNAMIC, OF COURSE, was screwed. Chris was eager to be shot of me. That was normal for a victim, but so wrong for a volunteer. I wanted him. He was supposed to want me. That's how a take works.

'You don't know your own mind,' I said. 'It sent out a charge. I responded. I'm here because you called. You must know what you want.'

He started to walk faster.

'That's not what you want, Chris. You don't want to get away.'

He stopped and turned to face me. 'You're a creep. You know that? You're sick.'

I get insults. People shout abuse when they're afraid. They always turn away first though. They don't look me in the eyes. Unlike Chris. His vision met mine. He was looking for something.

'Not sick,' I said. 'Hungry.'

I snatched the hood back from his head and studied him. His face was moist, and his neck was strong and taut. His smell was human.

'You're a hunter,' I said. 'Find me something to eat.'

That would change the dynamic. He would hunt, and drop an offering into my hands.

'Here? You mean, like in a restaurant?'

'You stopped me feeding from the museum attendant. You owe me a meal. Find it for me.'

He tensed, and then relaxed. His nostrils flared. He was catching the scent.

An alleyway led beneath the brick arch of a building to the river not far from where we stood. I could smell the mud of the river's bed and the chill of passing water, but in truth no run of life around it. Chris leaned his body forward, walking and then running, his hands loose so the fingertips brushed the snow upon the ground.

He paused, his head tilted, and then he moved. He swung a hand into the shadows at the base of the building and brought out a rat. In the same movement as that with which he caught it, he turned and threw the rat toward me.

Its claws scratched at the air. I snatched it from the darkness and slashed my fingernail through its throat. The head tore free. I threw it to the ground. In my hand the rat's feet flailed while my lips curled around the stump of its neck and I sucked.

Chris laughed. It was a full-throated laugh that started high with a fine tenor ring about it. He moved nearer, leaning close enough to peer at the rat's stump that suckled in my mouth, and when I pulled the rat clear he laughed again.

The rat was sucked dry. I slung its body to the ground. 'What's so funny?'

For answer, he lowered himself into his hunting posture and ran off. I followed. He reached the river and turned left. The old wharf had been upgraded into a run of apartments but all their windows were dark. Chris shifted like a shadow under the amber street lighting, and reached low over the stone edging to the quay. He straightened and came back to me. Two rats now scrabbled as they hung from each hand, their necks pinned between his fingers.

'Again,' he said. 'Do that rat thing again. Tear its head off and suck its blood down and everything.'

He shoved one of the creatures toward me.

In truth I did not want it. The blood of the first rat had coursed through me, in some ways a lubricant. Another dose of rat blood and I would have to disgorge it. Still, the look on Chris's face was so open and eager. And a claw of the rat sliced at my wrist as Chris thrust it forward. That was enough to annoy me into action. I screwed its head off and sucked as Chris wished.

He laughed again, the laughter pulsing through his throat.

'That's so neat,' he said. 'You treat a rat like it's a bottle and its head's a screwtop. You just twist it off. And then you use its spinal column like a straw. Look at you, sucking and sucking. And your tongue too, the way it flashes out and licks the blood from your face. You want another?'

I shook my head.

'Just one twist, right?'

He pulled his hand forward to trap the remaining rat's muzzle shut over its teeth and he twisted, turning its body the opposite way from the head. It wasn't so simple. It takes technique. The spine broke, the body sagged, but strips of sinew and fur and bone kept the head in place.

Chris lifted it to his mouth and pulled the threads clear with his teeth. The rat's blood spurted against his cheeks before he could fit the stub of its neck in his mouth. Gulps of blood passed down his throat while his eyes stayed open, watching me. At first the rat's death throes were enough, shooting blood into his mouth that he simply had to swallow, but then his cheeks sucked in to pull up the last drops.

We pulled drained rats from our mouths, perfectly in synch, and tossed their bodies over the river. They arced above the mud, their tails hooked in the air like they were looped from the sky, and then down they plummeted, to land splash splash in the water.

'Ha,' Chris said and 'Ha', I said, the symmetry of our actions too perfect not to laugh at.

'I loved that,' he said. 'I've never eaten with anyone before. Not like that.'

'It's an acquired taste,' I said. 'You're an unusual boy.'

I churned my stomach to bring the excess blood back up through my throat and spat it out in a stream to land on the mud below. Some blood remained on my lips. I raised my hand to wipe my mouth clean.

'You're hurt,' Chris said.

I heard wonder in his voice. He looked at the scratch the rat had left in my wrist. Blood pooled from the wound.

'May I?' he asked.

The top of his tongue appeared through his teeth for a moment and then withdrew.

This was not how it should be, this boy feeding off my blood, but I needed to know. He could read a mind to drain it of knowledge. He sensed rat life before I knew it was there. He hunted with ease and drank blood as fun. How else was he different?

I held out my wrist. He looked me in the eyes. I saw his nose twitch and then his head ducked down. His lips curled around my flesh. They were moist and warm. The suction tightened. The muscle of his tongue licked the cut but not to clean it. It dug into the wound, pressing the top section back and then the bottom. He made the wound wider. And then he sucked.

I have only let someone suck blood from me once before, and that was when I was human.

I did not lose consciousness that first time. Istvan told me that for the take to work, I must remain conscious. His head ducked into my wound in the way Chris's did, but his left hand ground into my stomach and even pulled at my balls while the thumb and fingers of his right hand pressed into pressure points at the back of my scalp. His tongue was like a shard of cold steel. He orchestrated pain. Such pain is perhaps the ultimate human capacity and he racked me with it. I would not age and would not die but I was reborn as a creature of pain.

Even so that bite of an Ancient was ecstasy. What can match it? Chris's true mother once knew the bite of an Ancient. Such a transformation leaves its code in your psyche. I now knew why, as a mother, she sliced at her breast and fed its seeping blood to her baby. Her baby was the son of an Ancient. He was Chris.

He did not activate pain. The upwards and then downwards press of his tongue sent two spirals of light shooting high and deep in my inner vision. As he sucked in my blood an inner landscape that was blue became suffused with pink. The pink was blanched into a clear white light. A warmth washed through me, wave after pulsing wave.

Chris reached for the back of my head as Istvan once did, but not to dig into pressure points and sear me with pain. He took the weight of my head as it fell. He settled me gently onto stone while his mouth, flesh on my flesh, kept hold.

There is no doubt of it – swooning to that winter walkway beside the River Hull left me vulnerable. I did not lose consciousness. Rather, I focussed my entire consciousness on a sensation of pleasure.

As a kind we are driven by need. We bother with neither bliss nor despair. Humans instead are tossed between emotions. Their pulses tick away the seconds of mortality. Ours don't. We are steady.

That was what I thought.

Now I know I was wrong. Bliss is seeded in us. It is a relic of human memory. We were once bitten, we were once taken, and our system was flooded with the energy of transition. From that point, we were on our own. But some longing remained.

Are we lonely? Maybe so. Young Chris's mouth sucked tired blood from my wound and I was not alone. That is all I am prepared to say. I did not wish to draw the experience to a close.

I knew the underling was there, of course. Human stink has been deodorised since last I walked the world, but Viktor retains the history of sweat in his clothes. His bowels need purging. His breath heralds his words and makes it hard to concentrate. His voice came from just above me.

'I think you are done, don't you?'

His breath in my nostrils was an assault.

Chris pressed his tongue hard against the length of the rat's scratch, somehow curling to knit the flaps of my skin together. One final slick of saliva acted as a sealant. His lips broke contact. He withdrew.

Viktor crouched and took hold of my wrist even as Chris pulled back. He turned my arm around, the wet spot chilled by the passing wind. He found no trace of the blood he was looking for.

'I would advise moving, sir,' he said. 'That little display was more ostentatious than we need. Are you fit to walk?'

He was not going away. I opened my eyes.

'It was just a scratch,' I said.

I stood up with a speed that jerked him clear of me. It seemed I had not been leeched of power. Despite lying on wet ground with fresh snow falling on me, some unusual warmth now took the shape of my body from its insides. Chris had drawn my blood, but somehow left his body heat in its place.

'You were leading me to *Ye Olde Black Boy*,' I reminded Chris.

'The car's parked nearby, sir.' Viktor brushed some snow from my cape with his hand. 'Perhaps it's best that we move to a more trafficked road. The snow is forecast to worsen. I doubt these narrow streets get swept. Might I suggest we head for the Ferry Terminal? A ferry docked while you have both been strolling. A cabin on its imminent voyage might be as discrete a venue as any for a private conversation.'

He began to walk us away from the river, with his head turned to make sure we were following.

'This will be nothing new for you of course, young sir,' he said to Chris. 'You took the same ferry journey solo when you were just a baby.'

'You want me to take a ferry?' Chris asked. 'I haven't got a passport.'

'You have.' Viktor produced a passport from his inside jacket pocket. Chris reached out a hand and Viktor passed the document across. Chris opened it. The lighting was too dim to read by and Chris barely cast a glance at the page, but even so he picked out the details. Was he reading the document or picking information from Viktor's mind?

'Ezekiel Hart,' he said. 'That's not me.'

'It's an alias.'

'It says I'm German. I don't even speak German.'

'Don't worry. I'm driving. I'll do all the talking.'

Chris closed the passport, and with one flick of his wrist sent it twisting in flight, back the way we had walked. It skimmed the surface of the alley and came to a halt just short of the river. Viktor paused. He stared at the boy, looked at me, and then walked back to retrieve the document.

'That guy's human, right?' Chris said. We turned our backs on Viktor and moved on. 'Does he know about you?'

'He thinks he does.'

'He worries about schedules and traffic and all that shit. That's stupid, isn't it? You've got eternity on your hands. Why put up with him?'

'He has his orders.'

'Whose orders? Yours?'

'He's a servant. He does as he's told.'

32

WE EMERGED FROM THE ALLEY. The white walls of a public house were just to our left. A wooden sign hung over the street, *Ye Olde Black Boy* written in script. The painting above it showed a South-Sea Islander clad in a white loincloth and standing on a palm-fringed shore. The sign was lit from below, twin beams that highlighted the falling snow.

Chris pointed up to the window beside the sign.

'That's our room. You can sit in the window and look down on the street. When the snow looks to be getting too thick for you, you can leave. No bother.'

He drew a bunch of keys from his trouser pocket.

'You have your own key?'

'I don't like to bother people.' He pulled a long iron key clear of the bunch. 'I get my own keys cut. I come and I go and they never know. It's better that way.'

We entered a corridor and turned immediately right to where an inner door stood closed. Chris unlocked it. Viktor stepped up to join us, having measured his speed to show no signs of hurry.

'Please give Viktor the key,' I told Chris.

He looked at me and then worked it off his ring to hand it across. I leave on record that Viktor comported himself with surprising decorum in the passport-throwing episode.

‘Follow us inside,’ I told Viktor. ‘Lock the door and leave the key in the lock so as to block it. We must not be interrupted.’

He took his orders from the Council. My recruitment of Chris was their top priority. Viktor accepted this as part of the plan and closed the door. Chris’s footsteps did not falter on the wooden boards. He found his own way through darkness. He opened a door at the top of the stairs where some dim light filtered through from the street.

Viktor found a light switch below that illuminated the staircase to candle strength. He remained by the locked door as directed.

‘There are two bars up here,’ Chris explained, and pointed up a separate run of steps. ‘That one leads to an apartment one floor up. This one’s the most characterful.’ He led me to the right. ‘Dark wood panelling, beams in the ceiling, hand-pulled pints from the bar, it’s probably not changed all that much since the time you were human. It’s not heated I’m afraid. Should I light a fire?’

‘Are you cold?’

‘I don’t get cold. Well, hardly ever.’

‘Me neither.’ I settled onto a wooden seat with a curved spindle back, and nodded Chris toward the cushioned bench seat by the window. He could lie back there if needs be.

‘Are you nervous?’ I asked.

‘I was. Blood calms me though. Thanks for letting me suck from you. It was generous. You don’t have much blood to give.’

‘When humans invite you to suck at their wounds, do they know how much you take before you heal them?’

‘It’s bloodletting. There’s nothing wrong with it. Doctors used to recommend it.’

‘I’m not finding fault, Chris. I’m just asking.’

‘Nobody knows. They wouldn’t understand.’

‘They’d think you were sick.’

‘I’m blood type AB. I’m a universal receiver. It’s in my nature.’

‘So you feed off human blood. What does that make you, Chris?’

He stared at me.

'You have no words for it?' I challenged him.

'I'm just me.'

'You're on your own?' It was an adolescent bleat. I challenged him a little. 'There's no-one else like you?'

'We're all on our own.'

'Is that so, Chris? Then why am I here for you?'

'You're here for yourself.'

'You called. I heard the call. There is that. I was also sent. I represent the Council. It is a grouping of beings of our kind, yours and mine. I've visited your home. I've met your adoptive parents. I know how much you don't belong there. I'm here to take you home, Chris. I'm here to take you back.'

'To my birth parents? The ones you showed me?'

'They told me your story so I could tell it to you. So you would know who you truly are.'

'I'm a vampire just like you. Is that what you're saying?'

'You like to use that word. I don't care for it.'

'You're not like me then? You don't drink human blood?'

'I do. I admit to that.'

'And you want to drink mine.'

'That would be fair. I let you suck blood from me. Now I take blood from you.'

'And this will turn me into someone like you. Is that the story?'

'You'll no longer be alone, Chris. You will become at one with others of your kind. You'll be understood.'

'So what do I get out of it? You'll show me tricks?'

'Time. I offer you mastery over time. You are ageing. You are dying. I can arrest that.'

'What for?'

'You're young, Chris. You already think you know best. You know better than your parents, better than your teachers, better than your professors. Imagine if that were true? You stay as young as you are now, but add years and years of knowing to it. You can watch whole human cycles, challenge the most enquiring of minds, track the interweaving strands of Nature. This world is Eden, Chris. It's the best there is. Only death ejects you from it. It's a fractured paradise but you don't have to leave it. You stay, you learn, you help it mend.'

'And to do that, to live forever, I have to kill. That's the deal, right? I feed off the blood of others. They die so I can live.'

'We call it culling, not killing, but maybe that's wordplay. There are many agents of death. None but us, so far as I know, also have the power to grant eternal life. When we cull, we simply distort time a little. Each death is inevitable. A cull is a point of harvest. It saves a life going to waste.'

'The guy that took you, did he spin all these lines?'

'That was different. You're not naïve. I was.'

'What was his offer?'

'I was a writer. I wanted to tell his story. The story was beyond me. I couldn't tell it from the outside. I had to get inside his experience. I had to internalise his story, to know what it was like to be him. Then I could tell his story from the inside.'

'That persuaded you?'

'He was the most captivating being I had ever met. As I say, I was naïve. We want to become the thing we love. I could not let him walk away. I let him take me.'

'You got what you wanted?'

'I never saw him again.'

'So it was a lie. All he promised was a lie.'

'It's not so simple, Chris. I give myself to seeking the truth. If I ever found it, I would be rendered meaningless. I would have nothing to seek any more.'

'Maybe so. But here it is anyway. Here's the truth. Some vampire made you a promise and you fell for it. You were had. That's it.'

'You leave out all that I gained from the encounter.'

'He left you sad. Isn't that so?'

'Of course, but . . . '

'Bitter?'

'For a while.'

'He lied to you.'

'He did what he could for me. I had to do the rest on my own.'

'Is that it? Is that your truth?'

'There is no truth.'

'So how can I believe a word you're saying?'

Chris stood up. He did so casually.

'You're leaving?'

'You know the superhuman capacity I'd like for myself? The power to always know when I'm being lied to. It seems you've not got that to offer.'

I had a reply. I'm sure I did. The words choked inside my head though. Instead another sound gurgled from my stomach. It seemed I was going to vomit.

33

PAIN GRIPPED THE BACK of my head, like fingers stabbed into pressure points. I took hold of the rim of the table and tried to stand. My legs shot my chair backward as the force in my stomach swelled up through my throat.

'I.' What came out was that word, an 'I' drawn out as a long, loud wail of pain. It was not a cry though but the first word of a sentence. 'I never lie.'

The voice swelled from my lungs but it was not my voice. I was some dummy, charged to open my mouth in synch with words that passed through it. My brain was linked to the receptors in my eyes but what I saw no longer reflected an image I presented of myself. I had worked at being Chris's friend and mentor and spoke so as to win his trust. He was a kid who was enjoying the full challenge of conversation. Now that kid pressed against the window. Were the window open he'd have jumped. Such was his terror. He stared at what had been me, his mouth open, his lips curled to show his teeth, his eyes wide and fixed.

My mouth stopped speaking. It spread into the frame of a huge yawn, muscles cracking. Every bone and every sinew in my body heaved into a new position. My flesh stretched thin as my legs lengthened and my shoulders broadened.

'Forgive me, Chris.' The voice from my mouth was not my own. 'I should have shown myself sooner. But then you sensed me inside my shell, is that not right? My shell that goes by the name of Konrad.'

I scanned the window for a reflection but there was none. I tried next to enter Chris's mind and see what he was seeing. I could not. The skill had left me.

'You are the Ancient who took him,' Chris said.

'He knew me as Istvan.'

I wanted to see him. How could I see him? There was a mirrored panel behind the whisky bottles that backed the central bar. Turn to that. Look that way. I willed the move as hard as I could. It was my head that had shaped itself into Istvan's. All it had to do was turn and look.

I fixed all my attention on the move. Turn turn turn. There was no response at all. My eyes stayed fixed on Chris.

Perhaps if I drew closer I would catch Istvan's reflection in Chris's eyes?

'So you never left him.' The terror of watching my body morph into Istvan's had left Chris's face. His mind was sharp and taking control, working it all out. 'You've been inside of him all this time.'

That's a good question, Chris. It's what I needed to know.

'A part of me has.'

'You've been controlling him? Like a parasite that takes over a creature's brain?'

My head tilted back. My throat stretched. Istvan's laugh rose out of it. 'The comparison is not flattering, Chris, but if it helps you to understand then yes. I took Konrad's blood, and then in returning it to him I left a little of myself behind. That has controlled him till now.'

'So why show yourself? After centuries?'

'You.'

A hand shot forward. It reached out of my sleeve but it was Istvan's hand. I knew the bone at his wrist, the dark hairs layered around it, that slight backward curve of his thumb. The hand gripped Chris's neck, thumb to one side, fingers to the other with the index finger pressed into the boy's Adam's apple. I knew the hold. He had done it to me. It was dizzying to see that hand on someone else's neck and yet not feel it.

'You're worth it. Let me explain. Sit down.'

The hand pulled down at Chris's throat, the index finger hooked above the Adam's apple. Chris sat.

'Konrad and his kind follow a new code. They take no human without that person's consent. It saves overpopulation by vampires, or some such thing. People remain a sustainable food source. Not many, you can imagine, consent to a vampire's request. Tell me honestly, Chris, would you? Did Konrad offer anything to tempt you?'

Istvan felt the pressure of speech inside Chris's throat and withdrew his hold so as to release the words. Instead of speaking, Chris simply shook his head.

'Of course he didn't. You're the son of an Ancient, Chris. You are coded with powers Konrad can only dream about. What was I to do, shelter inside his body while you grew ever more disappointed with Konrad and his offering? Should I keep myself hidden while Konrad carries his hulk to the car and speeds away before the snow can thicken? I sensed your call from over the sea, Chris. I came for you. I get what I come for.'

'You think I'd want to be parasitised by you?'

It's not so bad, Chris. I could tell him it's not so bad. Let me speak, Istvan.

'I'm not Konrad, Chris. I don't wait for consent. But why would you give it? You see from Konrad how he retains his character. He observes a certain set of values. He's inside me now. I feel him squirming. When I take you, Chris, you'll not be extinguished. You'll be yourself, only more so. You'll be amplified.'

Chris gave that adolescent look of blank dismissal. You don't do that to Istvan. I wasn't squirming when he said I was, but I squirmed then.

Istvan's hand took a grip on Chris's neck once again. You can bite anywhere but why not the neck? It was a fine neck. Chris's feet slipped forward across the floor while his head became pinned to the cushion of the bench seat. Istvan's left hand shifted round. It gripped Chris's neck in place and inserted the pressure points of pain that would keep Chris conscious throughout the process. Istvan's right hand shaped into a fist that pressed into Chris's stomach.

I wanted to feel the touch of the boy through those hands. How could I see so much, these hands reaching out from what was once my body, and feel nothing?

'You have no fight in you, Chris.' Istvan spoke close to Chris's face. I looked for his reflection in the boy's eyes but found only darkness. 'Remember that. When I have taken you, you could fight me and win. That is the difference. We are both Ancients, Chris, but from different strains. We are light and dark, power and strength, justice and spite, fate and will. I won't obliterate you, Chris. I will add to you. Together we will be as one. One like this world has never known.'

He smiled. I know he did.

Chris did not smile back, as I once did when I was human for all the pain that seared me. Chris set his jaw and glared.

What smile was he seeing? Istvan's smile stuck in my memory. It was broad. It displayed teeth such as I once hoped would grow in me, almost luminous in their shine. His eyes glowed with what I was sure was compassion. And maybe I was right. He stayed with me after all. He never left me.

And now he was smiling down at Chris. He was close now, his mouth widening for the bite. Was that the reflection of Istvan in Chris's eyes? The image was smoky but I saw a face, I'm sure I saw snatches of a face looking out, and then smoke again. And then the smoke balled into a cloud and the cloud grew dense and hammered into my head.

My body reacted fast and turned with the blow so that my neck did not snap. The smoke cloud split into coils that curled like banded steel around my neck and thrust my body to the side.

I was a passenger inside my own body and did not even feel its pain. Its eyes were my window and all I could do was look out. Istvan was in command and as Istvan my body rose to its feet. The bar in this room was built into a curve in the corner. Above it were mirrored panels. Look that way, Istvan, I willed him. Stand and look that way. Let me see you again.

Istvan did not listen. He packed my body into a crouching form and watched the smoke cloud take physical form. Particles amassed into the shape of the Ancient, but one without colour.

'A projection,' Istvan sneered. 'So you've been hiding in your son?'

A projection must expend itself and fade to nothing. Much of its power was spent in its first attack. Istvan in contrast had allied with my physical form. He turned from the Ancient's projection and faced Chris.

The boy had moved to stand near the window. He watched the transparent cloud of his father, but it did not matter what he did or who he watched. Istvan moved and the view through the window of my eyes saw no transition. Chris stood before me, and then in the instant I saw the blackness of his hair pass close to my face. My hands held his head, my eyes moved to the skin of his cheek and my ear brushed against his ear. My mouth feathered a touch against the boy's neck. The eyes closed and at once I could feel again, the warmth of flesh against my cold lips.

My eyes opened. Bite, I willed. Drink. Taste. But my will was as nothing. The eyes opened. Istvan stared at the projection of the Ancient.

The pause was a challenge. Watch me take your son, it said. You can do nothing but watch.

The projection did not move but there was movement.

A second head appeared behind it, a second pair of shoulders, a second chest, all somewhat smaller but they swelled in size. It was the Ancient in duplicate; the same quiff of hair, the same low neckline against his chest, but in colour now.

Was the projection dividing? That was my first thought but then the second image grew in size. This was simply a matter of perspective; the second figure was approaching from a distance, from the second bar, and grew in size as it drew closer. It descended the steps that joined the two.

This was no projection. It was the Ancient himself. He stepped inside the perfect fit of his form. The Ancient and his projection were one.

And I heard him.

He took the command that bleated from my mind to my body's brain and he amplified it. Move, it said. Turn your head. Look into the mirror.

Istvan knew me well. He knew the power of my thought. He had been suppressing it entirely. But this? What was this sudden jolt of thought to his brain?

My body that was Istvan's started to spasm. My lips brushed Chris's neck and then broke away. My head cranked toward the mirror in the bar.

'This is what you want?'

I knew the voice. It was the Ancient's. He spoke the words into my brain. They were words for me, not Istvan.

'Then look.'

Istvan's head turned with a will that was not its own. There was a gap between the whisky bottles. Istvan found it. He stared into the panelled mirror. I looked through his eyes and saw him.

'This is what you've loved?' the Ancient asked.

The mirror was tinted and there was little light in the room. I write that, and find I'm looking for an explanation even now. This was not Istvan, I can tell myself. It was some warped memory of him wrought from the inappropriate fabric of my own body. It was the best model he could come up with from what my body could provide.

That is all hindsight. What I actually saw was this.

I saw a wreck. Somewhere on this planet a full-bodied version of Istvan has adapted himself to the twenty-first century. He walks with some strut, perhaps. In an era that caters for short attention spans maybe he has a quality of stillness. Where others are out to be seen, he simply watches.

Istvan in the mirror was a throwback. His hair was a tangle of lank curls. His chin, with its cleft I admired so much, was thrust forward like a petulant child's. His elbows jutted wide, and while he maintained his grip on Chris's head the small fingers of both hands were pointed high. Plucked eyebrows arched half-moons at his reflection.

The posture was theatrical. Faced with a mirror, he adjusted it. He judged his little fingers to be somewhat crooked and so straightened them. The face was white with no skin tone left as though caked with pomade. Istvan was some pantomime villain from a bygone age, hamming it up for an audience.

When I last saw Istvan, he was imposing his full attention on my eyes. Now his attention was on himself, and his hands were on Chris. Centuries had passed. I was removed from the picture. I had acquired some objectivity.

This was Istvan. That much was clear. Was this the being I had loved for all these years? Was this the creature I had longed for?

I shuddered.

In the mirror, Istvan's body shook.

Had I been breathing? I don't know. I took a breath now, a gasp, and then gasped again. Istvan's mouth opened. I felt the air rush between his teeth and down his throat and into his lungs.

Into my lungs.

Istvan turned his head from the mirror. I could see him no more. He looked at the Ancient. The look was pleading, perhaps. It held a question. He was losing his hold on this body of mine. What had happened? What trick had the Ancient played?

'When you took Fool-for-love, a part of him never died,' the Ancient explained. 'His love for you. You think he was in your control? It was never so. His love held you close to himself. That love was the strongest thing in this room, Istvan. Fool-for-love has yearned to see you through all the centuries you have been gone. That wish was intense. It was easy to grant. Now he has seen you. His love just died.'

I shuddered again, a tremor that branched out from my spine and spanned my entire body to tremble through my skin. I looked at the Ancient but he grew dim and all my vision turned to a pale wash. I closed my eyes and opened them. I moved my pupils, from left to right and back again. This I could do now. I had control of my eyes. Yet all they could give me was milky blindness.

My head was beside Chris's. And there he was, his face to my right, still held in my hand. To my left, moving my eyes, I saw the bar. Ahead was the same grey blur. And then I knew. I was standing behind Istvan. He had emerged from my body.

His shape shook. My body had constricted him. He gained height. He flexed his hands. They lost that empty theatricality and drew themselves into fists.

'This is impressive,' the Ancient said, and spoke to the projection as to a new being which had entered the room. 'So far as I know your body is overseas. You are the most remote projection I have ever encountered. Istvan, he calls himself? Does Istvan have any control over you at all? How long can you last without Fool-for-love? You seem, I'm afraid, to be fading.'

I could see the Ancient now, through the haze of Istvan's neck.

And then the haze cleared. Istvan had lowered himself, his head sinking into his shoulders, so I was looking above him. His arms drew back into his sides. A projection naturally dissipates at a distance, its energy scattering. Istvan had set some other pattern inside this form. When left on its own, it pulled its energy close to its core. The greyness became darker, grey at its edges but black at its centre, rounding its shape into a ball.

The ball hovered. And then flew.

'Ha!'

The Ancient's cry was half-laugh and half-surprise. The ball hit him on his breastbone and flattened against his chest. The blow of energy sent him backward and rammed his feet against the bottom step. His arms flailed as he fell. The ball moved. It shrank now and divided, just two dark balls that settled above the Ancient's eye sockets and bored in around his eyeballs.

'Now.'

Istvan was gone but a scrap of intent was left in my head. I heard his command in his own voice. It spoke what I wished for myself.

'Now.'

My body was my own. Sensation had returned. I felt the warmth of Chris's skin between my hands.

'Now.'

'You owe me,' I told Chris. 'I need you.'

The Ancient's hands pulled at the film of grey that banded his eyes. Istvan was almost gone. The Ancient would see once again.

'Now.'

My fingernail sliced a gash into Chris's neck. My mouth connected. The tang of Chris's blood against my tongue was the entire experience of taste compacted in a moment. My right hand curled a hold in the strands of his hair.

He didn't fight or pull. He knew.
I sucked and he knew.

34

SABAA HAD LAIN STILL in the frozen storage unit of a truck for the long hours of the crossing. The embryo inside her had no beating heart of its own and so simply ceased to grow. The truck rolled down the ramp from the Zeebrugge-Hull ferry and offloaded at a warehouse on the edge of the city. She and the Ancient peeled away into the city streets. They had separate missions. He sought their son. Sabaa paused first to feed for their unborn in some backstreet of Hull.

It was a messy feed and a functional one. She withdrew while blood still pumped from the veins to allow the victim to die and then returned for a few more gulps before the temperature of the corpse could plummet. Sabaa needed the heat. Her new baby needed the heat. Her breath blew thin clouds through the swirl of snow as she ran.

The Ancient had locked into the mind of their boy, and Sabaa in turn was fused with the mind of the Ancient. She knew where to go. Her fists banged on the wooden door inside the entrance to *Ye Olde Black Boy*. More of that and she would bring the landlord running from the bar.

I could not worry. My eyes stayed closed as I drew in the warmth of her son.

I believe Viktor held his ground. I doubt he even felt the wind of Sabaa's movement as her projection passed through the oak of the door and then through his body to stream up the stairs.

Her projection had little physical power. I felt its fingers grip my hair and the palms of its hands press against my forehead, but with such minimal force I barely moved. Its nails pressed into my eyelids. I felt their sharpness but they did not pierce the skin. The fingers took hold of my upper lip and pulled it back. The force of vision that pressed out through the projection's eyes belonged to the woman below. At the sight of my tongue inside the flesh of her son's neck she made the projection hold still for a moment, and then withdraw.

Chris was watching this apparition of a woman. I worked to keep our minds entwined but part of him escaped. His mother stood before him and he opened his eyes to see her. I opened mine too.

Her projection was naked. I confess it shocked me. I had seen her naked before of course, when she was copulating, but then she was on her back as though submissive. This was a mere projection but it stood so firm, legs wide, fingers splayed, that I could not mistake her. She was in elemental form.

Chris's body tensed. I checked his mind. It was confused. This was his mother. Her look sparked some memory of a baby's love. And yet she also had the appearance of a fierce and naked woman. She roused him.

This projection of Sabaa looked as she looked when she suckled him eighteen years before. She seemed as young as the girl who was once asleep with her sisters, naked on the bed of the Middle Eastern room when the Ancient first came through her window. Her skin was golden, the hair of her groin was thick and black, and her muscles flexed within a lithe body. Her breasts were firm above the ridges of her ribs. Her eyes softened as Chris looked at her. Blood from her recent feed coated her cheeks and also her mouth. Her grey lips were painted scarlet. She smiled.

I have watched soldiers massacre a town and yet I strolled through the ruins to sample blood from the dying. That scene sparked my compassion but not horror. I thought I was beyond horror. And yet that bloodied smile of that naked woman repulsed me. It came as a punch in my gut that spiralled up my spine to my brain. My sight of her went hazy for a while, waves of vision that stripped sense from my head as in a faint.

Chris kept staring at her.

Sabaa was not inside his mind. I checked. There was no trace of her. The full force of her projection was in its physical details. I checked her feet. They stood flat on the wooden boards, the knuckles high as the toes pressed into the wooden boards, each toenail varnished red. A trace of a bruise purpled her right thigh. She opened her arms as for an embrace and the bush of hair in her armpits spread individual strands.

Projections don't need such detail. The onlooker finds a focus and there the detail of a projection may be sharp; you give a projection eyes to stare at a hint of cheekbones, the curve of a smile below and a dash of style to the hair, but the rest is a suggestion. And yet here she was as a projection, every centimetre of her flesh and the muscles at play all absolutely clear and explicit.

Chris's eyes were flickering. The effect in his brain was like a spangling, a dazzle of tiny stars. He glanced across the sinews in her neck, the dark aureoles of her breasts, the tension in her thighs. His mind teemed with memories of sex, but they were not like this. Those memories were of a clash of desires; a girl's thin limbs curled round his body, holding him close, her fingers brushing his back, edging round to shape his penis, while every neuron in his body sensed the blood that ran just beneath her skin. Sex had been the flood of warmth from such flesh held close in the dark, the exquisite puncture of first bite, the tincture of iron as a girl's blood touched his tongue while his body rucked her to orgasm.

This was different. The naked woman before his eyes gave off no warmth of blood. She stood in the darkness of the winter room but somehow suffused herself with light. Her flesh was illuminated. The gap between her and Chris was electrified. It magnetised every teenage yearning in the boy. She opened her arms wider and moved her lips. He must come to her. Cross the room and be with her. Now.

His head moved forward. It pulled his neck from my mouth. I reached up my hand and covered his eyes. Her gaze switched back to glare now there was only me to watch her. She broke all hold on form and streamed from the room. I heard Viktor gasp below stairs, his body smashed against the wall, and the key turned in the lock of the door.

I placed my lips back against Chris's wound. We had been in perfect union. The flow of heat from his body to mine made us as one. His thoughts had eased away in a pink and silver cloud.

Now those thoughts were back. The chill of my hand against his forehead and his eyelids made him shudder. My lips were not the lips he wanted. They were chapped, and grated against his skin.

He strained to pull away. I held him back. I sucked. My hand clamped his head close to mine. Pain jolted his mind as he reached up to claw my hand free. My fingers parted.

He could see again. That was all he wanted. He wanted to see more of this naked woman.

She was gone. The weight of feet, real weight on fast feet, resounded from the oak boards as Sabaa raced up the stairs.

Chris turned to his father. The Ancient was pulling strands of grey from his eyes. The strands evaporated in the air, but Istvan had bored deep beneath his eyeballs so that the blindness would stick.

Chris looked to his right, to the doorway. His expectations were on fire but the woman who entered the room was not naked. That vision was over. Some snow still coated the shoulders of the black jacket Sabaa wore over her tartan shirt, for she had no heat enough to melt it. I wanted her to run to the boy, to take hold of him. Then he would learn how cold her touch really was. Colder than mine.

Instead she turned to the Ancient. She brought her hands to the sides of his face and moved her lips toward him. A kiss closed on the Ancient's right eye.

Chris took some steps toward the couple and I kept a check on his mind. Emotions shifted as he adjusted to what he saw.

This woman, one who had stood before him naked and inviting, was not for him. She was his mother. This man was his father. They belonged to each other. They were in love. He watched them kiss and decided it was good.

Though I had sucked from his blood I had changed nothing. Chris was the same feeble teenage human as before, locked in a pattern of family bonding. He was the son of this couple who stood partnered in a kiss in front of him. He felt an emotion press his heart and wondered if it was love.

What is this love he believed in? It is an ache of separation. That is the human condition. I could have cured it. I could have fed to the end and taken him. I could have given him separation without the ache. He watched a woman kiss a man's eyes and he read it wrong. So wrong. This was no man and no woman and it was no act of love. He had no part in it.

Sabaa turned her head from the Ancient's right eye and spat. I was slow to move. A jet of grey streaked across the room and hit the bridge of my nose. It parted. Some entered each of my eyes. It breached my mouth and shattered on my tongue. The taste was mixed, something sulphurous and fungal. It was Istvan; the last traces of the elemental form he had once packed inside me. I reached up my hand to wipe it away. The grey clung to my fingers and soaked in through their skin.

Sabaa spat again, this time to eject the load she had sucked out of the Ancient's left eye. The stream of grey shot toward the window and then arced toward me. Istvan knew where to go. It passed inside my open mouth and exploded down my throat.

'Now!'

The whisper was urgent. It came from inside my head and took command of it. I knew it was the voice of Istvan though it came with no sound, just a powerful thrust of command.

'Take him. Take the boy now. What can they do, kill you? He's yours. Nothing can stop the take.'

The whisper stopped. My senses switched off so all sound was dimmed to a low hum. The taste of sulphur and fungus was cleansed from my palate. My vision blurred. Smell was left, heightened and intense, but all I could smell was blood. Chris's blood. My body was a void of hunger. I had to fill it.

I moved.

Istvan was back inside me but he was depleted. The movement was mine, my feet creaking the boards as I stepped toward the smell. The warmth of it, its liquid iron, coated my brain. Chris stood still. I drew closer. Some sense of touch returned to my lips. They tingled as my head leaned forward to connect to Chris's wound.

Smell had driven me forward. It had its focus, that focus was blood, and the blood was spilling from Chris's neck. Suddenly that changed.

I stopped.

The smell of blood was everywhere. My head turned to locate it. My sense of hearing returned.

Sabaa was murmuring. It was low but constant, something of a lament but pleading too. My vision returned. I saw her, holding on to the Ancient's arm. She did not want him to do what he was doing.

He had bared his left arm. Blood shone from a line he had slashed across his wrist with a fingernail. He sliced again. A second gash twinned the track of fresh blood with another. He held the wrist out.

I reached for Chris even as he moved beyond me. His walk was steady. He took hold of the Ancient's arm and raised it. The Ancient looked at him. He knelt to the floor and Chris knelt with him. The Ancient nodded. Chris brought the wrist to his mouth.

His movement was not frenzied. He tasted with his lips first of all, just a sip. And then his tongue, just the tip of his tongue, catching drops of the blood and retreating into his mouth. His head went into spasms. And then it ducked forward and his mouth took hold, his hands stretching behind his back to link with each other. He started to gulp. The movements shuddered his spine.

'Now . . .'

The whisper inside my head returned.

'Now!'

Viktor stood in the doorway. I have no cares for his report, but even his dry witness must tell that I did what could be done. The force of my charge knocked both boy and Ancient to the ground. My mouth connected. Even as Chris's body rucked with the passion of his own feeding, my mouth fixed to the wound in his neck to draw the blood of my needs from him.

My mouth held on. Even as my head was gripped and raised, the clamp of my mouth stayed secure. Sabaa held me by the hair. My head lifted, as did the boy's neck beneath me, and the Ancient's arm beneath that.

She let go of my hair. We three males thudded to the floorboards, Chris's head pressed between the Ancient's wrist and my mouth. Sabaa's hands now closed around my throat. The squeeze was total. I sucked in the blood from Chris's wound, but could swallow nothing. My mouth filled. I could take in no more. The contact broke between my mouth and Chris's wound. I sealed my lips to keep the blood inside. Sabaa pulled my head away and threw me backwards.

My throat was clear. I swallowed.

The mouthful of Chris's blood swept inside of me. It was the best I could do.

Sabaa crouched behind them, taking the Ancient's head onto her knee and stroking at Chris's scalp while the boy continued to feed. His feeding was frenzied, and then Chris's body eased. His cheeks stopped pulling at the Ancient's wound.

Sabaa moved her hand to Chris's forehead and eased him back, breaking his hold. The Ancient's eyes were closed but she raised him, supporting his body against hers.

Chris was senseless. His head slid into the Ancient's lap. She directed the Ancient's head down toward the boy's neck, where the wound I had made still pulsed blood. The Ancient's nostrils flared as his mouth connected with the blood of his son, but his cheeks did not pull. His tongue licked the flaps of wound into place, and then his lips pressed a seal on the gash.

She pulled the Ancient back. He lay his head against her shoulder, and closed his eyes.

'He was mine,' I said.

The words just came. I only knew I had spoken when I saw the look in her eyes. It was not hatred this time. It was incomprehension. Her eyes were rimmed with tears.

'You had no right.' It was pointless speaking, but I am a man of words. They help me to understand. 'I heard the call. I came. He accepted. The take was mine.'

'Who are you?' Sabaa's voice was cracked.

I was not sure I understood her.

'I don't know you. Who are you?' she repeated.

I didn't know how to respond. It seemed too late for an introduction. I presumed she was looking for something deeper.

'I am like you,' I tried. 'We are the same kind. Chris was mine to take.'

'He's my boy,' she answered. 'Our boy. I could not keep him. Now we have him back.'

He lay unconscious before her, as she stroked her hand through his hair. I could smell him. I could sense the heat in his body.

'He's human,' I said.

Sabaa stared at me, blinking. I made no sense to her.

I tried again. 'You're not human. You're not a family.'

'He has a sister.' She moved her hand from Chris's head and lay it flat against her stomach. 'We can keep her. This time we will keep her. I will age and now her father will age too. He has given his power to his son. We will grow old and our boy will stay with us.'

This was my turn to hear words and not to understand them.

'He has given his power to his son?' I repeated.

'I do know you,' she said. 'You write books but know nothing. You!'

She turned her head to Viktor.

'Explain it to him.'

Viktor took a step inside the door.

'Others have written books while you slept, sir. I never gave them much credit. They seemed fanciful, but now I've seen what I have seen. One book told a story about the Ancients, sir. I thought it was myth.'

'What did this story speak of, Viktor?'

'A transmission, sir. An Ancient transmission, from father to son. Ancients are not like your kind, sir. They are more like me, perhaps. Nothing like me, of course, but there's something natural about them. They have powers. They have an inordinate time span. And they can breed.'

I felt sick. That sensation was novel. I can regurgitate at will but had not felt nausea since I held human form. I could not open my mouth to speak in response. I worked to quell my body, to keep Chris's blood inside me.

'Hence the Council's interest,' Viktor persisted. 'All of the Council, all of your kind, can trace a lineage back to an Ancient. That is a genealogy of the taken, sir. Some, like you, are first generation. You were taken by an Ancient. For most, that connection with the Ancients is much more remote.'

'And for Chris?'

I rushed out the words and clamped my mouth shut again. My stomach was heaving.

'He's one of them, sir, it seems.'

'But he's mine . . . '

I should not have spoken. I let go my control. My stomach surged. I had time to twist around and stand on my hands and knees like an animal, the blood from my stomach vomiting out to hit the floor.

Chris's blood.

It smelt so good. It was still warm.

'Lick it.'

That whisper of Istvan's sounded inside me again, with a new command.

'Lick it up!'

I turned my head. I still have some decorum. It seemed wrong to lick up my own vomit while others were watching me.

Sabaa spoke. Her voice was steady now. 'Who are you?' she asked again.

'I heard the call.'

'You? You heard nothing. You think you control what you hear? You can't even control your own stomach.'

She frowned and jabbed her head forward twice. My stomach heaved again. It felt like I was vomiting up its lining. The last remnants of Chris's blood sprayed from my mouth.

'You don't control your body. You don't know your mind. I know you now. You are Fool-for-love. You let an Ancient parasitise you. You invited him in. You think it was you who heard the call of our boy? He heard the call. He brought you here. You heard nothing. You are nothing.'

Somehow she was right. I work to separate emotions from facts and some facts were obvious. My head was clear of any aching residue of the call. My stomach was emptied and the hunger was gone.

I stood up.

'Help me, Viktor,' I said. 'We'll carry the boy to the car.'

Viktor hesitated, but I nodded him forward.

'You take the feet,' I said.

Me, I would take the head. Chris looked as though he were asleep. He had fed carefully. His lips were rouged but his cheeks were clean. Long eyelashes sealed closed his eyes. He seemed at peace.

Sabaa snarled. The bared teeth might as well have smiled. I didn't care.

'He has a mother,' I told her. 'She cared for him. She did a perfectly good job. He doesn't need you.'

The Ancient leaned against Sabaa's body and was supported within her arm. With her free hand she slashed out at my face. She drew blood.

What did it matter? When Chris came to, he could kiss the wounds clean. I pulled at his shoulders and dragged him clear of the Ancient's knees.

'I'm his mother.'

'You left your baby on a boat in midwinter eighteen years ago. That hardly counts as mothering.'

'This is his father.'

'You say the boy now has his father's power? Good. He has what he needs.'

'We are a family. He has a sister now.'

'He's eighteen. Do you expect him to stay at home with the baby? You should see his bedroom. You both light up his walls. He used a computer to fashion your images and there you are, twin projections. He didn't wait for you to come to him. He made you himself. And now he's ready to move on.'

'Do you think it's wise, sir?' Viktor bent down to curl his hands beneath Chris's thighs but did not take up their weight. 'Should we leave those images on the wall? The police were expected when we left. When Chris disappears they may ask questions. We have a new identity for Chris. We don't need questions. He was the miracle Christmas ferry boy, sir. His mother and a youngster were seen to jump overboard. He has no natural parents. Perhaps it's best it stays that way.'

'Now you let this human think for you,' Sabaa said.

'Just lift,' I told Viktor.

He did as told. We adjusted our joint hold on Chris's weight and started for the door. Sabaa was there ahead of us, the Ancient folded within her arms.

'You are right,' she said to Viktor. 'We must erase the parents. You drive as well as think, I presume? We'll await you in the car.'

By the time we had manoeuvred Chris through the door to the top of the winding stairs, Sabaa and the Ancient were gone.

35

THE SNOW WAS DEEPENING. The pattern of her footsteps, small feet with long strides, left the only tracks. We followed them to the yard where Viktor had parked the car.

I swept Chris's legs into my arms so that Viktor could open the car door. The boy was warm against my chest. His breath touched the skin of my neck. Held so close, his heartbeats felt like my own.

For him, the pulse was steady. For me, the effect was startling. My heart does not race, but it tried to. Beat for beat, it sought to match Chris's heartbeat.

It does not have the bloodflow to sustain such folly. My head went faint.

Viktor grabbed the boy before I could drop him. I sank to my knees. My heart stopped. The giddiness faded. I resumed consciousness. I knelt in snow and the car doors were closed.

Viktor stood in attendance. 'Do you need help into the car, sir?' he asked.

I had questions. Where was the boy? Where was the Ancient? I could not find the words. Viktor took that as general incapacity and took hold of my arm. I shook him off, maybe I slapped out at his chest, maybe my fingers were curled into a fist, and he staggered back. I recommend more training for human associates. They should know that uninvited touch can prove fatal.

The three of them were arranged in the back of the car. I saw them when I opened my passenger door. The Ancient and Chris lay on the flattened seats with their heads toward the front. Sabaa lay between them, her head at the rear. The eyes of all three were closed.

I chose not to enter their minds. I first needed to regain full control of my own.

Viktor scraped the snow from the windscreen. As his face appeared in view he looked away from me. He climbed into his seat, slammed the door closed, turned on the engine, the windscreen wipers and the rear window heater, and stayed still.

'Well?' I said.

He said nothing. I kept staring at him. He spoke, slowly, measuring each word. 'I . . . am . . . calming . . . myself.'

'Calming yourself?'

'The snow is bad. I need full concentration.'

'And?'

'My chest hurts. Where you hit me just now. It is bruised. Every breath hurts.'

'I hit you?'

'When I tried to help you to the car.'

'That was no hit.'

'You write books about your kind, for your kind. You don't know your effects on humans. I am in pain. I am upset. These are my emotions. They need not trouble you. I will be fine.'

He shifted the car into gear and pressed his foot on the accelerator. We lurched forward, skidding in the snow before the back wheels took hold and he steered us from the yard and spun a tight bend into the narrow street.

'Be careful,' I snapped.

'Is your life on the line, sir? I hardly think so. If I wrap this car around a tree at one hundred kilometres per hour, only four of the occupants will rise and walk away. I would ask you not to distract me any further.'

I have recorded that brief exchange and will not strike it out. Perhaps our interactions with humans should take some account of their frailties. Others might reflect on that. I left Viktor to drive in the same way that I would leave the driver of a locomotive to do his business.

What did I do myself?

I will tell you. Biographers can own no secrets.

For all the ages since Istvan took me, my body had registered his absence. Now I knew better. He had been present all that time. Was he inside me still? I looked for him.

I found nothing. Of course I found nothing. They call me Fool-for-Love but I am not empty-headed. I was once human. Then I was taken. Some vestigial part of the Ancient who took me has stayed with me ever since. I thought I was myself. It is not so simple. I was him and me. Can I review my entire history and say this was my doing, this was not my doing; this was me, this was him? I cannot.

The highways had been gritted. Traffic was sparse. Viktor dipped the headlights to avoid the dazzle of falling snow. He drove as fast as one might dare. An amber light pulsed on his side of the car and we turned right. The whereabouts of the road was now guesswork, for the space between hedges was all sheeted white. We moved at the speed of hounds maybe. A sign pointed left for Cherry Burton and we turned.

I looked up at the clock tower of the church as we slushed past. A few hours ago we left the village. Now we were back. The minute hand of the church clock judders through its process as though time is fixed. It is not.

Chris was not the same being who had left. I was yet to understand the nature of any changes in him.

Was I the same being? I examined myself.

I had lain still for more than a century. News of Chris had roused me. I heard his call and responded. I came to fetch him. Chris left the house with me. He was with me still. When we left the house again, that would not change. He would be with me. I am a creature of the moment and a creature of destiny. That is my nature.

I am who I am.

I sensed Sabaa come around. Her breaths when she resumed them smelt of her fecund state. In a human the smell would be of rot, but she was incubating a child. Something was feeding from her as though she were nutritious. She raised herself onto her elbows and looked through the window.

She sighed. It was so sudden and so loud that both Chris and the Ancient stirred, some slight movement in their shoulders. The sigh passed through Viktor as a jolt and he tightened his hold on the steering wheel.

I have sighed like that. Decades pass, life evolves, and the occasion comes when you look about you and consider what has been achieved. You look about you and wonder, 'Is that all there is?' She sighed such a sigh.

The car pulled up outside Chris's house. The red nose of Santa's reindeer flashed in the arc of glass above the front door. We should be far away and not here.

'Stay in the car,' I said to Viktor. 'We won't be long.'

Sabaa had already climbed over the Ancient, opened the door, and stepped out of the car. She marched through the snow and had set the door-bell chiming before I stepped on the path. Susan opened the door, just a little, but stayed set to slam it shut.

'Your boy's gone,' Sabaa announced.

Susan stared at her through the gap.

'I've got him. He is in the car. You have had him for eighteen years. For almost all of his life. I have come to pay you back.'

'He's in the car?' Susan said, and pulled the door wider so she could head out and find him.

It was not an invitation, but it was an opening. Sabaa walked past Susan and straight up the stairs.

'Your shoes,' Susan said, looking after her. 'Look at your footprints. You can't just walk dirty shoes on the carpet.'

I followed. My shoes trod their own wet tracks up the stairs. The staircase was scented with resin from the Christmas tree in the front room. The tree would have outlived Susan. Instead it was chopped from its roots and rammed in a pot. Susan had dressed it with baubles and lights, but she knew. The tree was dying. Her carpets would rot. You can keep up the pretence for so long. Only so long.

'Konrad!' Susan said. 'Your shoes!'

I wiped them clean on the carpet of one of the steps and carried on.

Three miniature toothbrushes stood on a glass shelf in the bathroom, banded red, yellow and blue. I sniffed at them. The red one was Chris's. I pocketed it for comfort, and left behind the electronic toothbrush it attached to. Chris would learn new ways of caring for his teeth.

Sabaa stood in Chris's bedroom, illuminated from behind by her and the Ancient's images projected onto the wall. A single black wardrobe stood in the corner. I opened its door and pulled a bundle of Chris's clothes off hangars and shelves. They were all black. I draped them over my arm. Sabaa stepped forward, bunched the clothes against her nose, and breathed in.

'I know,' I told her. 'There's no smell like it. It's human yet not human. And subtle. Have you entered his scent receptors?'

She shook her head.

'They're different. He has the usual nasal receptors, but a separate set seems to be coded into the skin beside his nose. My own senses are acute. When I entered his mind I met a sensory world that is beyond my reach. The smell of his own clothes might comfort him, as he adjusts.'

I could have sent Viktor to collect the clothes. It is not in my nature to be anyone's attendant. Still, something about the boy makes me want to care for him.

Sabaa went to the corner of the room, picked up his folded black bed-sheet, and held that to her nose.

'Good,' she said. 'This is mine.'

The computer was powered by a row of plugs on an extension lead. I turned the power from the socket. The images of the Ancient and his woman flashed to black on the walls.

From below I heard the understairs closet door open and a clothes hanger rattle on a steel bar.

'You hear that?' I said.

She heard nothing. Susan meant nothing to her. She blanked her out.

Now I heard the rush of a zip up a jacket. And the thump of a foot landing inside a boot.

'It's Chris's mother.' My choice of words made her eyes flare wide. 'You told her that you had her son. That he was in the car. She's getting dressed to go out and collect him.'

I spoke to Sabaa's back as she sped from the room.

Downstairs, Susan's other foot shifted inside her boot and she stamped both feet. The two women met in the hallway.

'Excuse me,' Susan said. 'I'm going to fetch my son.'

'You have no son.' The voice was deep. I could detect no emotion in it. I moved to the stairs so I could watch.

'You're his birth mother, I presume, though Lord know the birthing hardly aged you. You've had an easy life. And your visit is inappropriate. I'm not his foster mother. I'm his adoptive. His mother for life.'

'His while you live. I understand.'

'You can't just turn up here like this, you know. There are official channels for making contact. You fill in a report and submit it through the proper agencies. Chris can then choose whether he wishes to see you or not. From what I have seen, I will recommend against it. He is nothing like you. Nothing like you at all. Not in looks, outside of your skin colour maybe, and not in behaviour. I've brought him up to be well mannered. I know you're foreign but that's no excuse for bad behaviour. You have no right to simply waltz into my home and storm around. You have no right to my son.'

'My son.'

Again I heard no emotion in the words, but the power in their volume was immense. The words resounded as though echoing out of some great chamber. Susan was silenced a moment, and then she stepped back down the hall. It was no retreat. She returned bearing the phone.

'That's it,' she said. 'I've had enough. I've informed you about the official channels. I've tried to deal with you in a civilised manner. You don't seem to be listening. I'm calling the police.'

Susan was wearing gloves. They were to protect her against the cold outdoors. She went to punch in the numbers on the dial. The fingers on the gloves were too thick. She had to pause to pull them off. With her hands freshly exposed, she focussed her attention on the dial.

Maybe she dialled the first 9 of the emergency number. Maybe the second. But not the third.

I didn't see the move. There was just a whirl of speed, and Sabaa stood where Susan had been standing. Susan was in the hallway. Her head had crashed into the wall. She lay at the bottom of the stairs.

I had to step over her, while Sabaa moved to crouch by Susan's side.

'Is that it? Is that all there is?'

There was emotion in the depth of Sabaa's voice this time. It came from the same source as the sigh she had let loose in the car. She looked up at me.

'Scan her memory banks, will you? I've picked out everything she can remember about the boy. Can it be right? She has the boy for eighteen years and can recall so little?'

I slipped inside Susan's mind, and then went deeper and deeper.

'You have it all,' I confirmed. I don't know how to check for discrete banks of memory in that way, or even how to steal them, but I knew what Sabaa wanted to hear. I had my own business to achieve. I did not need her as an antagonist. 'The last eighteen years. It's as though they never happened. She doesn't know she was ever Chris's mother.'

'She never was. But look how she behaved. I have her memories. This is a very disturbed woman. She should never have been allowed control of a baby. Do you know what she did? I have accessed her memory of it. It is one of the early ones, but she keeps it vivid. She fixed the baby's mouth to her naked breast. My baby clamped to her dry breast.'

'She did her best,' I tried, but as a shudder passed down the birth mother's spine I could see it was useless.

I walked through to the kitchen and turned on all the rings on the gas hob, but left the oven closed so its pilot light could cause no harm.

Sabaa was feeding when I returned, her mouth clamped to Susan's neck. Blood was scattered across the carpet; Susan's blood on Susan's carpet.

I did not stay to watch. My suspicions that Sabaa is a messy feeder were confirmed, but I do not care about that one way or another. I continued to prepare.

36

THE CURTAINS WERE DRAWN in the front room. Lights spangled on the Christmas tree, and parcels wrapped in shiny paper had been stacked around its base since I was last there. A fire had been stacked in the fireplace, kindling on twists of newspaper with two fat logs on top. A large box of matches lay beside a brass poker. I took one out and lit it.

The mantelpiece was lined with sprigs of holly. A porcelain shepherdess stood at one end, looking toward a porcelain shepherd at the other, but their views were blocked by a seasonal detail that stood between them. This was a large candle in the shape of a fat wax snowman with a carrot for a nose and a red scarf.

I reached the match inside its black top hat and lit its wick. The light illuminated its brown twig of a smile.

I heard the constant feeding, Sabaa's slurping and gurgling and gulping. She fed fast. Her head rose for a moment as I returned to the room, but not to look at me. She studied Susan.

She must not feed to the point of death. Susan was ready to be taken, I am sure of it. An afterlife with her boy or death without him, it was no choice. Sabaa would not give her that choice. Instead, she watched Susan's legs judder through the point of death. That was it then. Susan was dead. Sabaa bent to resume her feeding before the remnant blood could cool.

Sabaa fed with her eyes closed. She did not see the figure come in through the front door. Chris closed it after him in the way that he was trained, and blinked in the brightness of the doorway. He seemed unsteady. His eyes blinked again for focus.

'Mother?' he said.

Sabaa looked up at him, her mouth scarlet bright from feeding once again, and she smiled.

'Come.' That low voice, rich with satisfaction now. 'Kiss her goodbye.'

Chris stepped forward and knelt by Susan's side.

'Is she dead?' he asked.

'A boy does not need two mothers. You can kiss her.'

'Kiss her better?'

His voice faltered. I spoke. He needed guidance.

'Not this time,' I told him. 'You've gone beyond that now. Feed. Feed a little. You need your strength. We've got a long journey.'

He looked up at me with his soft dark eyes. 'Feed off Mum?'

'It's what she would have wanted.'

He dipped his head. Held his hands behind his back. His lips closed onto the wound in her neck. His cheeks contracted as he sucked, highlighting his cheekbones. His Adam's apple pulsed as he swallowed.

The doorbell rang. I shifted around the boy and went to open it.

Richard stood on the doorstep in his red puffa jacket and his grey woollen hat. I wasn't what he expected.

'You're back,' he said.

I moved to close the door on him but he pushed out at it.

'No you don't. The hospital wanted to keep me overnight but I was having none of that. Why should I? I've never felt so well in my life. I got dressed and took a taxi. Promised the driver double because of the snow. My wallet's inside along with my keys. The driver's waiting. I'll pay the driver off and then come back and sort you out. What have you done with Chris by the way? Is he with you?'

Richard pushed past me.

'Chris,' he said.

Chris was busy. He did not look up.

'Susan,' Richard said.

Sabaa uncoiled herself from the side of his wife and sprang. Her fingernail sliced a line across the dentist's throat. She returned to her boy's side before the man's blood could spurt and hit her.

I caught Richard's puffa jacket against my chest, held him upright, and shuffle-walked him forward. When I settled him onto his back, the blood pumped down onto the red of his jacket. I moved back to the door so as to close it. I did not want the taxi driver coming in on the scene.

I was too late. I pushed at the door but it resisted. Someone was pushing from the other side. I presumed the force behind the door was a normal human force, a driver impatient for his money. I was wrong. I added extra force as I pushed at the door but it hammered back against me. I stepped aside to stop it pinning me to the wall.

It was the Ancient. He leaned into the open doorway, his hands out to the sides as he recovered his balance. There was strength in him still, but not the same infinite flow of movement he was used to. His nose quivered. I thought it was the smell of the gas, but he looked at the blood which spurted from the dentist's neck first of all, and then across to the feeding boy.

'Zeek,' he said.

He spoke softly. I did not recognise the word at first, but that he spoke to Chris helped me see it. This was their pet name for their son. They named him Ezekiel, and spoke of him as Zeek.

Chris paused. His mouth stayed fixed to Susan's neck but he was no longer feeding.

'We call you Zeek. Is that alright?'

Chris looked up. He wiped the back of his hand across his mouth.

'Here, Zeek.' The Ancient nodded down at the man by his feet. 'That one's for carrion. This one's for you. He's still alive.'

The Ancient looked down at Richard. He showed the same calm authority that a dentist might show for a patient, and Richard responded. His fingers stopped clutching at the pain in his chest. His limbs ceased some of their shaking. He almost smiled.

'You're doing fine,' the Ancient said. 'Hold on now. Hold for your boy. He needs you to stay alive for him. You can do that, can't you?'

Richard couldn't nod but he did stay still. I left the front door open. The inrush of cold air was welcome. If the taxi driver walked up now, I would deal with him.

Chris stood and walked across.

'Hello Dad,' he said. 'Shall I kiss it for you? Kiss the wound?'

Richard's eyes milked over but he blinked and they cleared. He looked up at his boy. Chris leaned forward and pulled the woollen hat from the man's head so as to stroke his brow.

'It will soon be better, Dad,' he said, and then bent his mouth to the wound. It was too long a cut for him to seal it with his lips so he slotted himself into the left side of it. More blood pulsed out to the edge of his mouth to coat his cheek.

The man was bleeding too quickly. The gash in his neck was too wide and too deep. It needed more mouths to regulate the flow. With a nod, the Ancient called his wife across and signalled that she should bend her head to Richard's neck too.

Sabaa knelt above his head and brought her mouth down past the dentist's nose and chin to fix her lips beside her boy's. The Ancient knelt to seal his mouth around the other edge of the wound. Each swallowed but none of them sucked. They were preserving the moment.

The Ancient broke first. 'Back Zeek, back,' he said. 'Let him die.'

Chris knelt upright. Father, mother and boy looked into each other's eyes for a while and smiled, while the man's legs spasmed beneath them.

The Ancient looked down.

'Now,' he said. 'He has died. Waste nothing. Drink what is there. He would want you to.'

Chris ducked his head back to the quiet wound. Sabaa joined him, and the Ancient too. The slurp of their feeding grew louder.

I edged around them. Susan was not cold. I felt the warmth in her forehead still. I stooped for my own taste. Just a short one. She had three swallows left in her perhaps. I sucked hard. Maybe four.

They continued to feed. Chris had pushed up the dentist's left sleeve to feed from his forearm. Sabaa was chewing into his right cheek, sucking up the juices and spitting out the flesh. The Ancient had pushed up the puffa jacket and buried his face in the man's stomach.

'Sir?' Viktor stood beyond the door and spoke above the carnage as though he did not see it. 'There was a taxi driver. I paid him off. We should leave now, sir, if we are to make the boat.'

He sniffed.

'Is that gas, sir?'

'I thought it best if we burn the evidence.' I walked back down the corridor and opened the door to the front room. The snowman's head was melting. I picked up Chris's clothes from where I had laid them on the stairs and walked past the family trio.

'Go,' I said to Viktor. You should train humans about group feastings, about the dimming of control, about the frenzy. More is never enough. I needed him gone before they raised their heads and smelt him.

'What about the boy, sir?'

'Don't you worry about the boy. I'll bring him.'

'It's no worry, sir. It's my duty. Chris!' he called.

The boy looked up.

'Can't you smell the gas? The house is about to explode. You'd better run.'

Chris lifted his head. He sniffed as instructed. He was not interested in gas. His focus was on blood.

He stood up. He smiled.

I think Viktor understood. Viktor ran.

Viktor slipped. Of course he did, running mindless through the snow. It is laughable to watch humans run. The speed they gain is negligible. They flounder and expend themselves. By the time Viktor reached the car he was in no condition to drive. His breath rasped. He clutched at the door handle and stared at the three passengers who looked back at him over the top of his vehicle.

Their presence steadied him somehow. Or perhaps it was the same as a child finding safety under the cover of his blanket; Viktor was steadied by his car. He climbed in and closed the door. There was no time to lock the rear. The passengers were already loaded. I climbed into my own seat.

'Viktor,' Sabaa said. She curled her fingers into his hair and leaned across the seat. Her tongue licked slashes against his neck.

I could drive. At least there was that. I could drive us all away once they pulled him into the back of the car.

The flash came first. The black of night became a negative of itself as trees stretched dead branches against whiteness.

And then the blast. It shook Sabaa's lips loose from Viktor's skin. The car was running. Viktor pressed hard on the accelerator. The speed threw us all backward, the family trio rolling together on the flattened back seat as the car skidded across the snow and then connected with a salted patch of asphalt and kicked up some speed. Fragments of brick from the exploded house dropped down onto the bonnet as we sped clear.

37

A SHEET OF THICK GLASS rose behind our heads and slotted into a groove in the car's roof.

'It's for privacy, Sir,' Viktor explained. 'Passenger privacy. See that switch? Flick it up to hear what they are saying in the back, and down for two-way communication. In the middle as it is, you have privacy.'

I flicked it up. They were not talking. I turned my head to check. Chris had turned to look out through the rear window. He watched the muted orange through the snow-packed sky, a sign of the blaze where his home had been.

A blue light flashed ahead of us and a siren wailed as a police car passed us by.

'Am I in danger, sir?' Viktor asked.

'Always.'

'I mean now. Specifically now. Having Ancients in the back is beyond my training. My blood's running cold, you might say.'

'You do what you can do, Viktor, that's all I can advise. Keep us on the road. Keep us moving.'

'What about heat, sir? I understand your kind prefer the chill. How does heat affect you? Does it sap your energy at all?'

'It brings discomfort. We don't have your capacity for sweat.'

'That sounds like a distraction. It can do no harm.' He turned the dial on the heating controls. 'I've set your seat at ten degrees, sir. And boosted the rear to thirty-two. Am I right with my theory of distraction?'

I checked the rear again. Chris still looked toward the blaze, while his parents were studying his face from the sides.

'It's a theory, Viktor. I've witnessed a feasting before. Two humans did not satisfy three feasters in that instance. Certainly an exploding house proved a temporary distraction.'

'Temporary?'

'We are observing a family dynamic. Perhaps feasting was one stage in their bonding. Perhaps the next stage has set in.'

'We might throw them together a little more, sir. That might help.'

He pushed another dial. The platform in the back reared and buckled into a seat. The family collapsed around each other before reassembling in a seated row. They looked normal: a young family on a Christmas outing.

Sabaa's hand hit the glass partition. It cracked. She hit again. The crack lengthened. 'When this breaks,' she said to Viktor, 'I slice off your head. Turn off the heater. Lower the windows before I smash them. Lower this partition.'

Her voice came through the speakers. Viktor looked down at the switch. It showed one-way communication.

'Do you think I need your speech?' she said. 'I know your thoughts before you do, long before you struggle to find the words. And do you think they are your thoughts? Do you think I prefer to roll around on a platform while you swing this car around? You have restored the seat to us. That is good. You can do better.'

Viktor took the hint. The partition sank behind our seats. The rear windows lowered so that snow swirled in along with a blast of cold air.

Chris turned to the window and breathed in deeply. He leaned across the Ancient and pushed his head outside, opening his mouth wide and exposing his tongue. When he pulled his head back his eyes were moist. He closed his mouth and swallowed.

'I can taste them,' he said. 'They are charred but I can taste them. I can taste Mum and Dad.'

'They are atoms, Zeek,' the Ancient said. 'Is it intelligent to call atoms Mum and Dad?'

'I fed from them. I drank their blood.'

The woman turned to him, touching her hand to his hair. 'You drank my blood once. I sliced my breast and fed you when you were born. It's natural. It's what you do.'

'But they're dead.'

'It's inevitable,' the Ancient said. 'They died. It's what humans do.'

'We killed them. We burned them.'

'*We* didn't burn them,' Sabaa said, and stared forward at me.

'We went back to remove the evidence,' I reminded them.

'To turn off the computer,' she said.

'The image was retained on the hard drive. It had to be destroyed. And then there was the further evidence. The media is obsessed with tales of a vampire killer on the loose. You gave them a Christmas feast in Cherry Burton. Bodies drained of blood from the necks and then gored. We could have left them those bodies to find. Now what have they got to go on? Dental records for identity. Cause of death: unknown. It will take days for them to work through the embers and get that far. We'll have Chris far away on the continent before they even think to look for him.'

'Zeek,' Chris said. His voice was confident and clear. 'I'm not Chris. I've never been Chris. I've never had a home. I'm new. I'm Zeek.'

Two fire engines stormed along the highway toward us, sirens blaring. They passed us by.

'You have a home,' the Ancient said.

'We are your home,' Sabaa added.

'Do you have an address?' Viktor dared to ask her. 'Somewhere I can drop you off?'

'Drop us in town. Half the buildings seem empty. We'll stay in this city a while.' She turned to Chris—I mean Zeek. 'You can show us around. We'll stay local till your sister is born. We'll be a proper family. You can show us where to feed.'

'You have a home,' the Ancient repeated.

And as he spoke we saw it. He placed us inside the vision.

Viktor kept his focus on the road ahead and the car's lights dipped against the streams of snow. The rest of us sat at a point of intense darkness, and then the darkness grew. It expanded across the dark plain of a solid rock floor, and swelled in height and width. We smelt the damp that sweated through its walls. The Ancient had set us inside a cave. We faced the interior of a mountain.

Gradually light from behind helped us discern its shape. The cavern was high, and disappeared to where the light could not follow. Some colours flashed from its interior, thin bands of gold, of lapis blue, of scarlet, but they were filaments that vanished the moment they were glimpsed. We turned and saw the bright blue of sky in the cave's opening, and a thick cluster of trees beyond.

And then the vision faded.

'You have seen this place. It is where I was born. The mother who birthed me lives there still. You must visit her.'

Viktor took a roundabout at speed. We were back in suburbia. A road sign welcomed us to the City of Hull.

'So your mother lives in a cave?' Zeek said. 'Is your father there too?'

'He passed his powers on to me, as I have to you. You have no need of him.'

'Where is this cave?'

'If what you saw is a cave, then what you saw is a cave. Don't stay fixed on what it looks like,' the Ancient answered.

'Is it in the mountains?'

'Yes, you will go into mountains. But if you arrive elsewhere, so be it. The journey is as important as the destination.'

'In what direction? Can you say that at least?'

'East. From here, keep going East. Hull is on a trans-European route that links Limerick in Ireland to Moscow and beyond. Ferries bridge the gaps where the way sinks below the sea. Keep some sense of the route, and be sure to walk into your shadow at every sunset, but stop thinking. You don't have to have a plan. You don't have to tell your body where to go. It will find its own stories.'

Zeek turned to his mother. 'Do you know of this cave? Have you been there?'

'She did not need to know of it,' the Ancient answered.

'Our family,' Sabaa reminded him. 'We were to be together.'

'We will. You, me and our daughter.' The Ancient turned to Zeek. 'You will come and find us. Meet your sister. Tell her some stories. Show us what you've found.'

'You'll be here?' Zeek asked. His confidence was gone.

'You'll find us. We'll be somewhat older. However old your sister is, those lines will be drawn on our faces. You can't tie yourself to a human life without ageing.'

'My sister will be human?'

'As human as we can manage. As human as you ever were. Till she is grown enough in strength.'

'You think I am strong enough?'

'What do I know?' the Ancient said.

The traffic light ahead of us was red. There was no traffic. Viktor ignored the light and turned left, following a sign toward the ferry.

'Stop!' the Ancient commanded.

Viktor hit the brakes. The car skidded toward a standstill.

'So, Fool-for-love, I presume you've heard enough to pique your interest? I expect you to follow the boy.'

'You showed me the cave. Does that mean I'll be allowed to reach it?'

'Does it matter? If you need an ending for your story, make one up.'

The Ancient opened his door, stepped out, and was gone.

'Mum?' Zeek said.

It was the word Sabaa wanted to hear. I saw her smile. She planted a kiss on his mouth to stop him saying more.

It was a brief kiss, just moist enough to leave a chill in the wind when her mouth moved away. She opened her door, and she too was gone. The doors clicked as Viktor triggered the central locking system, as though that could stop them returning.

'Drive,' I said to Viktor. In truth, we were already moving. By the side of the road a pictogram of a ferry showed we were on course for the port.

Zeek looked behind him. There was nothing to see but snow falling through lamplight.

38

'EZEKIEL HART,' VIKTOR SAID. Zeek came back to attention at the sound of his new name. 'What languages do you speak?'

'English. French.'

'No German?'

'A few words. Donner und Blitzen. Schwein. Hund.'

'Sieg Heil?' Viktor suggested.

'Yes. Those words too.'

'I think you'd best say nothing. Remember you are German. Close your eyes. Seem asleep. We are going through passport control.'

Viktor fanned out the three passports toward the woman in the kiosk. She noted the colour of their covers and nodded him through without further scrutiny. There was no line of cars to board the ferry. Its rear door had flapped back to form a ramp into what itself seemed liked a vast and empty cavern. We were waved forward by a sequence of men in yellow reflective jackets and directed close to the rear bumper of a green Range Rover, even though no traffic waited to fill the gap behind us. Machinery cranked and the ships' rear door rose to seal itself closed as Viktor applied the handbrake.

'Your passport,' Viktor said, handing the document back to Zeek. 'Don't throw it away this time. I've booked us a shared cabin. They'll give us the keys and then you're free to wander.'

Zeek did not wait. He bounced across the seat to the door and climbed out even before Viktor finished speaking. He closed the door and stood with his back against it as the family from the Range Rover in front filed past.

The parents went first, then a boy of about twelve. The daughter followed. She was around seventeen, her body stretched to its full height but still waiting to fill out. Her hair was black, cut to a fringe and hanging straight to her shoulders. Her eyebrows were plucked and coloured the same black as her hair. Her lips were shaded a grey edged with blue. A silver stud pierced her lower lip. The face that decorated the paperback book she carried looked something like her own. Its title, *Vampiress Diaries*, was designed in letters of red that seemed to drip blood.

She slouched a little. She did not want to be with her family. She noticed Zeek. Her eyes widened. She brightened. Her shoulders straightened. She brushed against Zeek as she passed him, and quivered a brief smile of apology while she glanced into his eyes.

He shadowed her through the exit to the gangway beyond.

Viktor lay on one of the cabin's beds and roared into sleep. I left his snores behind and went in search of Zeek.

He was on the deck. The boat had moved forward from its berth but was stationary, close to a broad concrete pontoon. Zeek was peering down over the railing. Far below, a crowd of seagulls flitted with the agility of bats. They were chasing whatever creatures were pulled to a pool of amber light.

'Can I fly?' Zeek asked.

'I doubt it.'

'If I jumped I'd find out.'

'You'd find out if you had learned to fly in those seconds before you hit the water. That's all you would find out.'

'My father flew. He carried me from the shore to a ship.'

'That was not your father but his projection. And frankly, I don't know how he did it. It took tremendous power. Practise, and then you will find out what you can do.'

'If I hit the water from here, would it kill me?'

'Can you be killed? Is that what you mean?'

He nodded.

'Your body can be destroyed. It's a fine body. It has to serve you a long time. It's worth taking care of.'

'I killed my parents today.'

'Not exactly.'

'I sucked my dead mother's blood. I drank from my father's living throat. My home exploded with their bodies inside it.'

'It's been a tough day,' I admitted.

He turned to lean his back against the rail. Snowflakes landed on his face and melted. He still had some warmth inside him. He looked through a window and inside the ship to a brightly lit lounge bar. The family from the Range Rover were gathered round a table. The father had a beer in front of him, the mother a glass of red wine, the boy a Coke, and the girl what seemed to be a Bloody Mary.

'Her name's Ana,' he said. 'She's from Denmark. She thinks I'm English. She wants to know where I'm travelling, both to and from. Who I'm with. What I do. She wants to put my number in her phone. I can't answer any of her questions. I don't have a home. I don't know where I'm going. I don't know who you are. I don't have a phone. I don't have a number.'

'Why do you need a phone? You have a mind.'

He looked at me, and gave a slight tilt to his head.

'She's thinking about you. She's open. You can place any information you want inside her head. You can pick up any messages she sends back.'

'But what shall I tell her?'

'Did you see what she was reading? *Vampiress Diaries*. Tell her whatever you want to tell her. Tell her you're the son of an Ancient, doomed to eternal youth and beauty. You're on a quest to visit your grandmother who lives in a cavern inside a high mountain in the East. Your travelling companion is a vampire and you're yet to understand the full extent of your own powers. What girl wouldn't fall for a story like that?'

'You think?' he said.

He stared through the window into the bar. Ana had just reached for her drink. Her hand jolted. The drink spilled a little onto the table but she did not care. She looked up, toward the window.

'She can't see me,' Zeek said. 'It's too dark. The window's just reflecting her back at herself.'

'Make her see you.'

He concentrated. Her face lost its frown of focus as she recognised him. She grinned. She waved her hand at the dark window to beckon him inside and got up to pull an extra chair to their table.

I followed him through two thick doors that sealed out the snows of winter, and back inside the glare and the warmth of the ship. We paused together on a stretch of red carpet before the entrance to the bar.

'This journey I'm on, you'll come with me, right? You won't do what Mum and Dad just did and walk away and leave me.'

'I'll stay with you. Until you tell me to leave you. And I know you mean it.'

I looked into the bar. Ana had pulled an empty chair beside her. 'Time to go and meet Ana.'

I stayed to watch his approach. He pulled the chair around so he could sit with his back to me and block Ana from view.

Back in the cabin, Viktor's snores remained unbroken. I looked through the porthole. England was behind. Mainland Europe was ahead. Everything was blackness. I picked up his electronic tablet and taught myself how to type into it. I began this book.

Dawn tinged the sky a metal grey. Viktor slept on. I went in search of Zeek, whose story had only just begun.